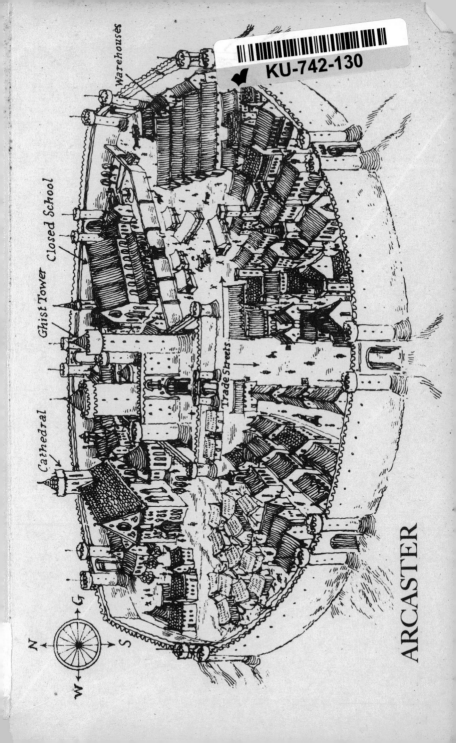

Warehouses

Closed School

Ghist Tower

Cathedral

Trade Streets

N
W — S
G

ARCASTER

Also by B. R. Collins

A Trick of the Dark

THE
TRAITOR
GAME

B.R. COLLINS

BLOOMSBURY

LONDON BERLIN NEW YORK

Bloomsbury Publishing, London, Berlin and New York

First published in Great Britain in 2008 by Bloomsbury Publishing Plc
36 Soho Square, London, W1D 3QY

This paperback edition published in 2009

Excerpt from *Pale Fire* by Vladimir Nabokov by arrangement with
Weidenfeld and Nicolson, a division of the Orion Publishing Group, London
and the Estate of Vladimir Nabokov.

A CIP catalogue record of this book is available from the British Library

ISBN 978 0 7475 9725 4

FSC

Mixed Sources
Product group from well-managed
forests and other controlled sources

Cert no. SGS - COC - 2061
www.fsc.org
© 1996 Forest Stewardship Council

Typeset by Dorchester Typesetting Group Ltd
Printed in Great Britain by Clays Ltd, St Ives Plc

1 3 5 7 9 10 8 6 4 2

www.bloomsbury.com

'I can forgive everything save treason.'

Charles

ONE

It made sense that it happened on that particular day. Michael could see there was a kind of sick logic to it. Like someone had developed a sense of humour. If it was going to happen, then, well, *obviously* it would be on that day. Not that there was anything special about the date – just, it was one of those mornings when you actually feel pleased to be alive and up and going somewhere. You know, one of those morning-has-broken mornings, a God's-in-his-heaven morning. Not that he believed any of that stuff, of course, but he could see what they were on about.

That morning as he walked to school in the October sunshine, leaves everywhere like yellow paper, he felt sort of better about everything – sort of *good*, actually. St Anselm's was always pretty – that's what you paid for, red-brick buildings and striped lawns – but that morning, with a blue sky overhead and no one around, it took his breath away. Michael was whistling as he went through the school gates. He looked at the drifts of leaves at the base of the wall and thought about kicking them up into the air, because it wasn't like there was anyone around to laugh at him, but in the end he didn't. You get hedge-hogs hibernating in piles of leaves, and it wouldn't be fair to disturb one.

He turned left, the way he always did, past the music block, on to the playing fields, and down towards the belt of trees. For a moment, looking into the glare of sunlight, he thought Francis hadn't got there yet. Then he saw him, leaning against a tree in his shirtsleeves, his jacket hung on a branch. Francis was the only person he knew who took off his jacket when he smoked. Michael grinned and jogged across the field, the bag over his shoulder bouncing.

'Hey.'

'Good morning.' Francis reached automatically into his pocket and offered the cigarette packet. Michael took one. It was a rule. You had to have a cigarette before school, just like you had to bunk off early on Friday afternoons. He used to feel queasy smoking first thing in the morning but now it was lux-urious, taking deep lungfuls of thin smoke and autumn air, standing in silence. He leant against a tree a little way off from Francis's and closed his eyes against the light.

'How was the wedding? On Saturday?'

Francis laughed. 'Really awful.' He took a last drag on his cigarette and stamped it into the mud. 'All those people. Having that many relations is just scary. And they all look the same.'

'Like you, you mean?'

'Exactly. It's horrible.'

Michael squinted at him sideways, smiling. 'I can see that.'

'Yeah, shut up. The whole experience is just purgatory. Seriously. Even getting there's like some kind of medieval torture. You wouldn't believe how long it takes just to get everyone in the car. And then when you get there it's all, haven't you grown and aren't your little brothers and sisters lovely and do *you* have a girlfriend, Francis?' He laughed again, but briefly. 'I mean, Jesus, they can *see* my little brothers and sisters and they're clearly *not* lovely. What's that about?'

'Compared to you, maybe.'

Casually Francis flicked two fingers up at him. 'And of course they all say, how nice that you still want to come to these family things, how nice that you don't have anything better to do. And I want to say, actually, Mum made me come, I *do* have better things to do. Frankly I'm seriously pissed off that I have to be here at all.' He shook the cigarette packet pensively, then got another cigarette out and lit it. 'But that should be it for a bit. I mean, Saturdays as normal from now on. Thank God.' He smiled and flicked ash at a pile of leaves.

Michael nodded and breathed out smoke. 'Good.'

'Which reminds me –' Francis crouched suddenly, his cigarette between his lips, and dug in his bag. After a few seconds he surfaced with an A4 envelope in his hand. 'Here.'

'What? Oh – thanks.' Michael held it for a moment, wanting to say, No, not here, give it to me later . . . But that was silly, paranoid. Francis would think he was crazy. It'd be fine. Just because they'd never given each other stuff at school before. What could happen? It wasn't like anyone was going to go through his bag. Anyway, Christ, it was just an envelope, just a plain brown envelope.

It was like Francis read his mind. 'It's not hardcore porn, you know. Unless my mother switched the envelopes.'

Michael forced himself to smile. 'Yeah, right.'

'I guess it could have waited till Saturday.'

'No, it's fine.' Michael started to kneel down and caught himself before he got mud all over his trousers. He crouched carefully and pushed the envelope into his bag, between two books to keep it flat. As he leant forward he felt the key round his neck swing coldly against his skin, like a talisman. 'What's in it?'

Francis winked. 'Wait and see.' He stamped on the butt of his cigarette and added, 'Nothing world-shattering. Don't get too excited.'

'No fear.' They grinned at each other.

They heard the sound of the five-minute warning bell carry across the playing field, clear and shrill. Francis sighed and picked up his bag. 'God, I hate Mondays.'

Michael shrugged, agreeing. They walked back towards the main building, away from the sun. There were more people around, now. Michael could hear shouts from somewhere, pre-pubescent shrieks that sounded like they were coming from the music-block roof, and the scuffle of a game of football from further away. Francis kicked genially at a pebble. It skittered forward and Michael chased it and kicked it back. When they turned the corner he wasn't even looking where he was going. He only knew something was wrong because Francis stopped dead and grabbed his arm. He turned round to look, stumbling. A little kid – a second-year, maybe, skinny and miserable –

stood unhappily on the grass, surrounded by a straggling circle of older boys.

Someone said, '*Bent dick?* Is that really your name?'

But the voice would have stopped Michael in his tracks, wherever he was. It was sly, malicious, *gentle*, so that you answered back, so you made things worse for yourself. He felt a sort of disbelief rise up in the back of his throat, outrage like nausea. *Not here, not now, it can't be.* He stared at the group in front of him, hardly noticing Francis's grip on his arm. The kid in the middle was small and thin and scruffy. You wouldn't have looked twice, except for the expression on his face. Michael stared and then wanted to turn and run. That expression. He felt the muscles on his own face tense, like he was trying to mimic it.

The voice said, 'Is that because your dick is bent? Or is it because you're a dick and you're bent? Was that why your parents called you *bent dick*?' He was leaning against the wall, smoking, like he wasn't paying much attention. Tall, dark, with hair that was just too long. Dominic Shitley. Shipley, really, but they called him Shitley because he was a shit.

Francis said quietly, 'Old Condom Shitley. He can talk.' Michael wanted to smile but he couldn't. He wanted to turn round and walk away but he couldn't. No one had seen them. They could just turn round and go the other way, round past the cricket pavilion. No one would know. But he didn't move.

Shitley said, 'So, Bent Dick, which do you think it is?'

The kid knew the drill. His eyes flick[ed] Shitley's face, then down. Answerin[g] would only make it worse. Michael knew he was thinking, *Just get it over with*. But he wished the kid would say something, anything, just to fill the pause.

Shitley stepped forward, peeling himself away from the wall like something reptilian. He moved in a semicircle so the kid had to turn to face him. He flicked his cigarette ash casually towards the kid's face. 'Personally, I'd guess you're bent.' He gestured, like a teacher giving a lesson. 'You know. A poofter. A faggot. A *pansy*, if you like . . .' And for a moment the imitation of Father Markham was so good Michael almost smiled, like it was all a big joke. They'd got it wrong, it was just a kind of game . . . But when the other fifth-formers laughed, the kid flinched. Shitley waited until they'd finished. He took a drag of his cigarette and leant towards the kid, blowing the smoke straight into his face. 'That's right, isn't it, bender-boy?'

Michael felt Francis step forward. He grabbed his arm, wrenching him back by the sleeve of his jacket. He felt the tension in the fabric as Francis tried to pull away, and then the material relaxed under his fingers. Francis turned to stare at him. 'For God's *sake*, Michael!'

'Leave it. Please. Just leave it.'

Francis frowned. '*Leave* it?'

Michael shrugged helplessly. He still had Francis's sleeve in his hand. He held on to it, like he was anchoring himself, like if he gripped hard enough this wouldn't be happening. He swallowed frantically. 'It won't help. Whatever you say. It won't help.' His voice sounded small and pathetic, and he hated himself.

Francis narrowed his eyes. Then he looked away, pointedly. He could do that, he could turn his head away so that you felt *dismissed*, shutting you out like you just weren't there any more. Michael had seen him do it to other people. It made him feel cold. He looked away himself, scared of what his face was doing.

Shitley said, 'Is that what you get off on? Working away at that little bent dick of yours?'

The kid raised his eyes and looked at Shitley. His face was rigid, blank. Michael felt the force of his hatred as though it was inside him: the hatred that ate you up, that froze your face into stone. It was dangerous, because it made you want to fight back. You had to brace yourself against it, like a wave.

Shitley shook his head slowly, smiling. 'Looks like I've touched a nerve.' He laughed. 'Oh, yeah, baby . . . Bet you're turned on now, just thinking about it.' He stood there, still, daring the kid to hit him, to retaliate, and Michael knew, with a spasm of shame that knotted his stomach, that the kid wouldn't do it. He wouldn't be able to. He couldn't even stare him out. Shitley said, 'Or would you like to . . . ?' His hand went to his flies. *No. No. Oh God, he can't.* Disgust hit the back of Michael's throat like a finger.

Francis hissed, 'Jesus *Christ*,' and stepped forward. He started to say something, loud and clear, 'Hey, Shitley,' but before he'd finished – maybe even before he'd started – Shitley had stepped towards the kid. Michael heard the kid's sob of revulsion, then saw him force himself to stay still, not to flinch, to keep his clenched fists at his sides. Shitley brought his cigarette up to his mouth and took a long drag. Then he

7

brought the glowing end of it down on the back of the kid's hand, grinding it down into the pale space above the wrist. The kid cried out and stumbled backwards.

'Stop it! Piss off, Shitley, leave him alone –' Francis ran towards them. But underneath his shout you could hear the noise the kid was making, the dry hoarse sobbing that you can't control, like your body's trying to shake the pain out of you, like it's trying to break it down into manageable bits. Almost like laughter. Sometimes they thought you really were laughing, and that made it worse; or if you were crying, properly, with tears, that made it worse as well. But now all Michael could think was, *Thank God, thank God it's over, thank God that's all.* He felt relief push up warm from his gut and despised himself.

Shitley swung round towards Francis, leaving the kid to drop to the ground. His henchmen followed his gaze. 'Mind your own business, Harris.'

'You sadistic bastard, Shitley, what the hell d'you think you're doing?'

Shitley blinked, twice. 'What did you call me, Harris?'

'A sadistic bastard.' Francis held his look, cold, challenging. Michael looked round at Shitley's mates and wondered if they'd fight another fifth-former. Surely not. It wouldn't be worth it.

Shitley shook his head slowly. 'Before that.'

'What?' For a second Francis looked genuinely confused. Then he said, 'Oh. Shitley. It suits you better than Shipley, don't you think?'

Shitley looked at him consideringly. Then he flicked his cigarette butt away. 'You'd better watch yourself, Harris. Don't mess with me.'

8

'What, is that a *threat*?'

Shitley shrugged. Like, it wasn't that he didn't know what to say, only that he couldn't be bothered to say it. He glanced down towards the kid, who was hunched over, knotted into himself, cradling his hand, still gasping. Then he started to walk towards the main building. He looked Michael briefly up and down as he passed. Michael met his gaze. It wasn't like Shitley could see inside his head. After he'd gone past, Michael was pleased he hadn't flinched, hadn't given anything away.

The henchmen followed, giving Francis dirty looks. He stared them out. Michael wished he could do that: keep his cool, gaze back at them flatly until they looked away. But it wasn't courage. Not really. It was only not knowing how things could be.

The kid pushed himself up with one hand. He was still breathing heavily, with a kind of catch in his throat on every in-breath. Francis said, 'You OK?' When the kid didn't answer he said, 'You should go to the medical room. Get that looked at.'

'I'm all right.' He wasn't.

'Want one of us to come with you?'

'No. Thank you.' The words came out tight with misery. He'd hunched his shoulders like he could curl completely into himself. Michael knew he didn't want them there.

'Look – I'll skip Prayers, make sure you're OK –'

Michael said, 'No.'

Francis looked up at him sharply, like he was surprised he had the gall to speak at all. 'I wasn't talking to you.'

'He doesn't want your help.'

'Like he wanted Shitley to stub a fag out on him, you mean? Like he wanted us to leave him to be tortured by those creeps? Like he wanted us to *leave him*?' Francis didn't expect him to answer.

'We can't *do* anything to help,' Michael said, trying to sound as though he was talking about something academic, something that really had nothing to do with him. 'He wants us to go away and leave him alone.'

The kid walked past him without looking up, as though he wasn't there. He disappeared round the corner, holding his hand up to his chest, across where his heart was.

Francis followed him for a few more seconds, but he stopped when he got to the corner. Then he turned on Michael. 'What the hell is *with* you? You selfish, arrogant, *cowardly* bastard. What the hell would you know about what he wants?'

Michael wanted to hit him. He wanted to smash his head against the wall. He wanted to tell him, for God's sake, he *did* know, better than anyone, how the kid felt. He wanted to hit Francis over and over again, until he gave up trying to fight and just took it. He wanted to knee him so hard he made the same sound as the kid had. He wanted to make Francis understand – wanted him to know himself how it felt, the shame of it, the way you wanted never to talk to anyone again. And the humiliation of knowing someone had *seen* – how that, sometimes, was the worst thing of all. He swallowed, turned away, and said nothing.

'You're not scared of Shitley?' A pause. Michael felt Francis look at him. 'Are you?'

'No.' And in a way it was true. Not Shitley, not

personally. Not of being beaten up, or burnt, or whatever else they did to people. Not that.

'What, then?' Francis's voice had changed. He wasn't having a go any more. He really wanted to know. That was worse.

'Nothing.' Michael thought, *Please let it go. Please*. He couldn't talk about it, he couldn't bear it. He looked down, away, anywhere but at Francis. A pause that stretched out like string, so taut it might break. Then Francis swung his bag back on to his shoulder and started to walk down the path. Michael followed him. His throat ached.

Francis said over his shoulder, 'His name's Benedick. Benedick Townsend. He's in the third year – Luke's class.'

'Benedick. His parents really should have known better.'

'Yes. Although if it wasn't his name, it'd be something else.'

'Yeah, I guess.' For Michael it had been being clever. Not that he was, especially, except that at the comp anyone who could spell their own name was clever. Or even pronounce it properly. That was him. Clever Boy. Even when he started to fail tests, stopped reading, couldn't think at all any more. Even then, they'd made him 'explain' Pythagoras' Theorem before they started on him, mimicking his accent. He remembered thinking, that day, *At least they didn't kick me in the hypotenuse* . . . laughing weakly all the way home, because if he cried someone might notice.

They walked past the hall. Prayers had started. Everyone was on their knees. They went round the long way, so as not to walk past the windows, and up the stairs to the fifth-form corridor. Michael tried to think of something to say, to explain, so Francis wouldn't think he was cowardly or cruel. But his mind stayed blank. Francis was first to the top of the stairs; he stopped right in front of Michael, and said, 'You should be in Prayers.' It took Michael a second to realise he wasn't talking to him.

Luke was standing at the lockers, his uniform already dishevelled, even though it was only ten to nine. He stepped aside for Francis to get past. He said, 'I was late.'

Francis had his head in his locker. 'Well, if you get reported and Mum goes ballistic and blames me, you're going to regret it.' His voice was muffled.

Michael went to his own locker and started to get out his books. Luke was still standing there, rolling his tie up and down his finger. He wore it short, like a flag, the way they all did. Trying to fit in, trying to be cool. Luke said, 'Will you take me paintballing on Saturday?'

Francis straightened up and cracked his head on the ceiling of his locker. He pulled his head out and stared at Luke, rubbing a hand over his hair. 'No, I will not.' He shoved a couple of textbooks into his bag. 'Why are you asking now, anyway?'

'Mum won't let me go unless you come with me.'

'Tough. I wouldn't touch a paintball with a barge-pole.' Francis caught Michael's eye and gave him a quick ironic grimace.

'Why not?'

'It's puerile. Anyway, I have better stuff to do on Saturdays.'

Luke put his head on one side and stared past

12

Francis at Michael. There was real hostility in his eyes; Michael felt it register somewhere inside him, like something cold. 'Going round to Michael's, like you *always* do. Are you two gay or what?'

Francis said, 'Get stuffed, Luke.'

'I just –' Luke changed tactic. Michael could have told him he'd blown it, but you had to give him marks for trying. 'Please, Francis. You'd like it. And I'll do your chores for two weeks.'

Francis finished putting his stuff back into his locker. There was a silence, and he looked up at Luke, like he was surprised to see him. 'Are you still here?'

'Michael wouldn't mind. It's only one Saturday.'

Michael said, 'How do you know Michael wouldn't mind?'

Luke looked at him – that expression again, like Michael was the scum of the earth – and didn't answer. He turned ostentatiously towards Francis. 'Francis, please. Please please please. All my mates are going.'

'In that case, *definitely* not. I told you, *no*. My Saturdays are mine. Ask Dad to take you.'

'He won't. You know what he's like.'

'Then you'll have to find someone else.' Francis slammed his locker shut and turned the key in the door. 'Piss off, squirt.'

'I hate you.'

'It's entirely mutual. Go on. I said fuck off.'

'I'll tell Mum you said that.'

'I look forward to it.' Francis raised his eyebrows at Michael. 'See you at break?'

'Yeah.' Michael watched Francis stride off. When he turned back to his locker Luke was still glaring at

13

him. *Stop looking at me like that. It's not my fault.*
Although possibly it was, possibly Francis knew how
much the Saturdays meant to him, how desperate he
got if they had to miss one. It was pathetic, really,
how dependent you could get. But Luke didn't know
that – did he? Michael said, 'What?'

Luke watched him in silence for a moment. Then
he turned and went down the stairs, without saying
anything.

Michael left it thirty seconds, then shouldered his
bag and trudged to double French. He sat down in the
sunlight next to the window, the desk where he
always sat, far enough back to piss around but not
too far back, not where Father Peters always looked
for troublemakers. Not that he felt much like pissing
around today. He looked at the trees outside.
Benedick. Bent dick. He was in Luke's class, Francis
said. That made it worse, somehow, although why
should it? After all, Luke was an annoying little
git . . .

And Shitley. What would he do? *If anything*,
Michael thought sternly to himself. *He might not do
anything*. Anyway, he'd been OK here so far. It was
just a one-off. It wasn't like the comp. It *wasn't*. It
couldn't be. He pushed away the dread, the voice that
said: *Feeling* safe, *Michael . . . how stupid can you
get?* He was being paranoid. No need to worry. He
settled back and tried to concentrate on the lesson.

When the bell went for break he felt better. He
fought his way back upstairs – *Get textbooks, then
coffee* – and made his way to his locker, pushing first-
years out of the way on the stairs. There was music
coming from the common room. He stooped to push

14

books into his locker, cramming them in precariously, but there were too many, and the bottom ones started to slide towards him. He grabbed them and tried to steady the pile.

There was a folded bit of A4 paper wedged into the bottom of the locker, as though someone had pushed it under the door. It said, *MICHAEL THOMPSON*. It wasn't handwriting he knew. Michael slid it out, bracing the books against his chest, and flipped it open.

It said, *I KNOW WHERE ARCASTER IS.*

That was when the bottom dropped out of everything.

TWO

Judas floors don't exist in the real world. At least, if they did, Michael had never heard of them, and he definitely hadn't seen anyone fall through one. But for a second he thought he knew how it would feel: the black, sick terror of falling, knowing that the best you could hope for at the bottom was cold stone, and the worst . . . well, if you were lucky you didn't have time to think about the worst. In his imagination he'd made people dance pavanes and galliards on the great Judas floor at Calston, but it was only now that he really understood the horror of it. One moment you were there, in the middle of your galliard, hopping around as gracefully as you could, and then –

He remembered, irrelevantly, that there was a net underneath the floor at Calston to break your fall, so for a second you'd almost think it was some twisted practical joke. Until you saw the vipers nesting in the ropes near your face . . .

He shut his eyes as tightly as he could and took a deep breath. When he opened his eyes the note would be gone. Or rather (that was too much to ask) it would be something else. Maybe he'd misread it. Maybe it said, *I KNOW WHERE ARCTURUS IS.* (Michael wasn't sure he did – was it in the Plough, somewhere?) Or, *I FANCY YOU*, although that was less likely. Or probably – and he felt warmer suddenly – it was just from Francis. His weird idea of a joke.

When he opened his eyes it must have taken him a second to reread the note, but it didn't feel like that. It felt as though the words went straight to his stomach, bypassing his brain. He knew instantly that nothing had changed. It still said, *I KNOW WHERE ARCASTER IS*. It still wasn't Francis's handwriting.

Automatically he raised his head and looked round, like he expected someone to be there at his shoulder, laughing at him. No one. Just people drifting down the corridor to the common room. It came to him with a shock that it was still break; it had only been a few seconds since he opened his locker. But no one was looking at him. And Michael had a knack for knowing when he was being watched; he could feel it in his bones, like old men being able to tell you when it was going to rain. There really wasn't anyone. He heard a kind of rattling noise and looked down: his hand was shaking, hard, so that the paper flapped like a moth. He scrunched it up into a ball and shoved it to the back of his locker. He slammed the door. *Please, please let it not be there when I come back.*

But once he'd shut the locker he didn't know where to go. He knew he should carry on as normal, get his coffee, go to the common room . . . but it was unimaginable. Like submerging someone's house and expecting them to live in it just the same. He couldn't breathe properly. He wanted to stay still, silent, just

17

leaning against the lockers, for ever, not letting himself think of anything.

''Scuse me, mate.'

Michael rocked back sharply on his heels and stepped away from the lockers. 'Sorry.' It was Dave Murray, one of Francis's friends. He didn't look round as he got a drink and a chocolate bar out of his locker, but Michael stared at his back and wondered if he'd come to see how he was reacting. What if Murray was here to watch him squirm? Or to report back to someone? Christ, what was he *thinking*? He was being totally paranoid. *Murray*, for God's sake! Amiable, uncomplicated Murray, whose only qualification was that he was one of Francis's mates. He must be mad.

And then it hit him. The full weight of what had happened punched into him, leaving him breathless and cold and weak at the knees. Francis had told someone. Francis had *told* someone. *Francis* had told someone . . . Francis, who only that morning had passed him an envelope as though it was something special. Like it mattered, like Michael mattered. He couldn't believe it. It was like learning something in Physics, about atoms, how everything was mostly empty space, even though it felt solid: he knew it had to be true, he *believed* it, but it didn't make any sense. He trusted Francis. Even now, even standing there with that note in his locker.

Slowly he opened the locker door again. He picked up the ragged ball of paper and, very deliberately, smoothed it out.

I KNOW WHERE ARCASTER IS.

The next thing he knew, he was crouching in a

toilet cubicle, retching and retching and retching.

Arcaster is a cathedral city about forty miles from the Evgard coast, south of Than's Lynn, west of Minnon, ghist of Sirrol and north of Longroad and Gatt's Farm. Although it's the capital of Ghist Marydd, it's much like other Evgard cities (the cathedral, for example, is within the city walls, not on the outskirts as churches are in most Mereish towns), fortified, and built on the slight incline that is the closest thing the flat Ghist Marydd landscape offers to a hill. It is renowned, in Ghist Marydd, at least, for urbanity and sophistication: its slave market is one of the largest in all of Evgard, as is its Closed School.

But that doesn't tell you anything worth knowing. If he shut his eyes Michael could see the long black-wood warehouses of the Ghist Quarter, and the patterned, formal gardens of the School behind high walls and great wooden gates with little sally-port doors set into them like cat flaps. He could hear the carts carrying bales of wool and silk, dyed the elusive blue-grey-lilac that was the colour of the marshes at dusk, the colour of the Mereish flag; he could smell the harsh rusty scent of the marsh-reeds they used for the dye, an odour like blood. He knew the weight of the Mereish accent, the heavier, softer sounds when the Mereish workers spoke Evgard, how it felt in their mouths. And outside Arcaster – he knew the roads, which ones were impassable in winter when the marshes flooded, how to get to Allhallows-gate for sanctuary if you were on the run, how to find your way to Skyph or Gandet or south to London, via Longroad and the Long Road. He knew it all so well he could close his eyes and *be* there, almost. When he couldn't sleep at night that was where he went, staring into the dark, walking down the Trade Streets or the shadowy back ways or the network of cellars under the School. Arcaster was as familiar as his own body – only safer, beyond the reach of the real world.

There was only one other person who knew where Arcaster was; who even knew it existed: Francis. It was as secret, *more* secret, than a love affair or a drug habit. Michael and Francis worked on it behind closed doors. Michael locked the papers and the Book in a big tin chest his mother had given him, with two padlocks, and Francis took one key home with him. Sometimes Francis worked on things on his own, and brought them round the next Saturday, but apart from that none of it, not the scrap paper or the roughs from a map or a drawing, ever left Michael's room. No one had ever seen it. No one else knew it was there. Evgard was private. It was the piece of Michael that he could hold to himself; the only bit of him that he could keep safe.

Sometimes, on a Saturday evening, when Francis stretched and stood up to go home, Michael would look up from whatever he was doing (a family tree, a poem, an account of the Mereish wars from the *Fabianus Letters*) and be shocked by the way the real world had carried on without him – as though, for a couple of hours, Michael had really been *somewhere else*, somewhere he wanted to be.

And sometimes Francis was there too, when they worked on something together, and that was almost better, because it felt so real. When both of them were talking about Evgard, arguing, joking, pushing at each other for ideas, Michael felt like he could stretch out his hand and nearly, *nearly* feel the world of Evgard beyond the real one, as though the shape of it would show through, like a face behind a curtain.

Some days it made Michael feel giddy, taken aback, that it had happened at all. He'd catch Francis's eye when he looked up from his drawing, or hear him say, 'No, but, *no*, you couldn't get from Than's Lynn to Arcaster in two days, it's *winter*, you'd have to go the long way round, via Gandet and Hyps,' and suddenly he'd want to grin like an idiot. It was crazy, they were fifteen, for God's sake, it wasn't like they were kids, but here they were *inventing a country*. He could imagine what people would say at school if they knew – it would be weeks of humiliation, endless horrible jokes that made you feel like shit – but they'd never find out. Francis knew as well as he did that telling anyone would be suicide.

These days, Evgard was as much Francis's as Michael's: almost all the pictures in the Book were his – botanical drawings, portraits, a verse from the *Ludus Umbrae* that he'd illuminated. He had a talent for cartography that Michael envied. The maps in the Book were detailed and delicate, with little drawings of sea monsters off the coasts and the Four Winds spitting out puffs of air like gargoyles. Beside them, Michael's originals looked clumsy and inconsistent. It made him wonder if it had been pity, originally, that had made Francis pick them up and admire them politely.

That had been the beginning of it. It had been the start of the summer holidays, after Michael had left the comp, and his mum had finally persuaded Gran to loan the money for the fees for St Anselm's. He still wasn't sleeping, still wasn't talking, still couldn't leave the house. He knew his mum didn't know what to do with him, but then he didn't know what to do with himself. She was trying desperately to cheer him up, make him pull himself together. He could have told her it didn't work like that, but she never asked, and anyway he didn't want to talk about it. He couldn't even fight with her properly. Michael thought sometimes that she *wanted* to have a row with him, but he couldn't even manage that. He remembered how she'd shouted at him – 'For heaven's sake, Michael, just *do* something! I don't care what, just anything!'

He'd said, 'I can't think of anything.' It was horrible, the way her face had gone when he said that. Like he'd hit her, only not angry, just small and sad. Her voice had gone soft, but giving-up soft, like she was too tired to care any more. She'd said, 'Why don't you dig out all the stuff under your bed and have a purge?' As if she thought he might not even be able to do that.

So when Francis came round, Michael had files and boxes of papers all over his room, his Year 9 notes on his bed, projects from primary school on the desk, loose papers in a pile on the floor. He wasn't planning to let Francis into his room anyway. He'd talk to him during tea if he had to, because Mum would be pissed off if he didn't, but that would be it. She'd asked around at church for anyone whose son went to St Anselm's, so Michael could get to know someone there before September.

How desperate was that? 'It'll be easier for you, darling, if you already know someone who goes there . . .' What she really meant was, *Then maybe you won't get picked on.* He knew she was trying to help, but it made him want to laugh. Asking Francis round for tea? So he and Michael could make friends? How old did she think they were, *six*?

It got worse. Michael was in the kitchen when Francis arrived; trying to look casual, but really jumpy as hell, dreading the whole thing. And when Mum ushered Francis into the room and started to bustle about getting him a glass of orange squash and a biscuit Michael wanted to die. For a start, Francis seemed completely at ease – that sort of private-school assurance that Michael knew he'd never have. And he was good-looking, easily four inches taller than Michael, with a sort of pale aristocratic face and dark reddish hair. Michael felt himself shrink down into the chair. He knew the type. You were either a victim or you weren't – and Francis wasn't.

Mum said, 'Why don't you show Francis your room, darling?'

Michael felt blood rush into his cheeks like boiling water being sucked up by a sponge. How did she not *realise . . .* ? For a moment he could have killed her. Adults – they thought they had all the answers – *Just tell a teacher, stand up to them, don't let them get away with it* – when they didn't have a clue. *Yeah, right, Mum, 'cause that's* really *gonna make him think I'm cool, and want to be friends with me.* He bit his lip and turned his face into stone.

Francis caught his eye. 'I'd like that.' And then, unexpectedly, he winked.

For a second Michael thought he'd imagined it. But there was a glint of mischief – or was it sympathy? – in Francis's eyes. He swallowed. 'Yeah, right.'

'No, really, I would.' It was weird how Francis could keep a perfectly straight face when you knew he wanted to laugh. That was the first thing Michael liked about him; only he didn't admit it to himself then. He stared at Francis until his mother said, 'Michael . . .' and he had to stand up, walking out of the kitchen without a word, not waiting to see if Francis followed.

But Francis did follow, although he didn't tag along at Michael's elbow; he left a decent distance between them, as though Michael had a bubble of space around him. That was the second thing Michael liked. He almost felt embarrassed that he hadn't bothered to move the boxes of stuff. Francis didn't really seem to notice, though. He looked round the room and said, 'Nice.'

'Not really.' It sounded graceless, but it wasn't meant to. It was just that Michael didn't know what to say. It was an ordinary room. There wasn't anything special about it.

Francis glanced back at him, and shrugged. 'I've got very low standards. I have to share with my brother. Belmarsh would be nice, if I was the only person in it.' He grinned.

'I thought you were –' Michael stopped himself. He turned aside, hoping Francis wouldn't notice he'd said anything. That was what happened when you let yourself talk: you started saying things you shouldn't.

'What?' When Michael didn't answer Francis put his head on one side and frowned at him amiably. 'Go on. What were you going to say?'

Michael shook his head. 'Nothing.' But Francis was still waiting, leaning loosely against Michael's desk. 'I

24

just thought – I mean, you go to St Anselm's . . .'

Francis frowned, then laughed. 'Oh, right, you thought we were *rich*.' He put his hands in his pockets and hunched his shoulders ruefully. ''Fraid not. Scholarship boys, all of us. Except my sisters, obviously.'

Michael stared at the carpet, wishing he hadn't said anything. It wasn't like it mattered. There was a silence. In the end he said, 'You can sit down if you want. I mean – just stick the box on the floor.'

'Thanks.' Was there a gleam of humour, again? Michael didn't know, and it made him uneasy. Francis lifted the box and looked round for an empty bit of carpet.

'Wherever. It doesn't matter.'

Francis nodded; but he put the box carefully down in the space between two toppling piles of papers. Michael followed his gaze to the nearest one and felt his face burn. Stuff from primary school – maybe even infant school. Stuff that Michael didn't even know his mum had kept. A face, with a sort of black crest, with three red legs. That was his self-portrait from Year 3. He started to bend down to pick it up and hide it under something else, but Francis got there before him. He looked at it appraisingly, then up at Michael. 'Is this you?'

Michael nodded, and reached for it. For a horrible moment he thought Francis was going to hold it out of reach, teasing him; but he passed it over quietly. Once Michael had it in his hand he felt safer.

'Why have you got three legs?'

'No reason.' He shoved it between a couple of books.

'Are you a tripod?'

Here it comes, Michael thought. *Michael the Tripod. Tripod Thompson. Or just Tripe, for short. There you go, Mum. At least it's a better class of insult*. He felt the dead weight in his stomach like tiredness. He turned round, slowly, as though his joints had gone rusty. He was going to say, 'Why don't you just piss off home?' but Francis had a grin on his face. It was fading now, in the silence, but a real *grin*. Like it was a joke. It was as if he thought Michael was a normal person. Michael shrugged awkwardly.

Francis picked up the papers that had been underneath the picture. 'Can I . . . ?' Michael wanted to say, *No, leave them, they're mine, get off*. But something about the way Francis had asked made that seem rude. Or not rude, exactly (Michael didn't have a problem with being rude, under the right circumstances) – sort of *unfair*. He watched as Francis leafed through, then leant back on his heels, holding one out to Michael. 'What's this?'

It was from ages ago. Back in Year 7 they'd had a Geography assignment to make up a country. The idea was that you'd have to think about how the landscape affected where the towns were, and the imports and exports, and things like that. It was the sort of thing that Michael liked, and he'd spent a long time on it. And then, after he'd handed it in, he'd carried on drawing maps, which were good because you didn't have to be any good at drawing. He had a whole pile of them, desert countries and green countries, post-apocalyptic cities and elaborate palaces. He'd stopped, of course, the way he'd stopped reading,

26

because that was part of the Clever Boy stuff, the stuff that made him a target. He stared at the piece of paper. 'Nothing. Just something for Year 7 Geography.'

It felt like Francis looked at him for a long time. 'It's good.'

'Yeah, right.' Michael held out his hand for it. But this time Francis didn't give it to him. He held it round to the side where Michael couldn't reach it. Michael took a deep breath. 'Give it here.'

'No, seriously, I like it.' He scrutinised it, turning his shoulder on Michael.

'Give it to me.' He didn't dare say *please*. *Please* was always when the game really got going. *Please* was when they started throwing whatever it was to one another like malicious piggy-in-the-middle. That was when the little pushes began, the nudges that got harder and harder until they hurt like punches; that was when they started whining to each other, *Please, pretty please, what's the magic word?*, in vicious mimicry of his accent. He took a deep breath.

Francis followed the line of the sea with his finger-nail. 'The names are great. What language is it? Cornish?'

'I said hand it over.'

'Not that I'd know Cornish if it came up and gave me a pasty.' He stared at the map, his forehead creased. 'Looks more like East Anglia, though. Are these marshes?'

'Give it here. Or –' He wanted to say, *Or I'll smash your face in*. But the voice in his head said, *Oh yeah, you and whose army?*

Francis glanced up. 'All right.' But he didn't. He

27

looked back down at the piece of paper, eyes narrowed. 'But why is –' he peered closer to read one of the names, 'why is Than's Lynn that shape? With the bit here like a peninsula?' He gazed up at Michael innocently, with that expression of benign enquiry that Michael knew better than any other look. *We were just wondering, Thompson – why are you such a loser?*

Something snapped. He lunged for the map and grabbed roughly, tearing it out of Francis's clenched hand. He fell forward, felt his other hand connect with something hard – Francis's face, maybe, his shoulder – and didn't care, felt his knee hit something with a sort of bony impact that meant a bruise at least and didn't care about that either. He dragged himself sideways, holding the piece of paper screwed up in his fist, breathing hard. He'd got it. He struggled to his feet.

Francis was staring at him. He wiped a hand across his mouth and his fingertips came away red. 'What the hell . . . ?'

The map was ripped across the middle. Michael screwed it into a ball, his hands shaking, and threw it at the wastepaper basket. It bounced off the side and dropped on to the carpet. He couldn't look at Francis. He knew now he'd got it wrong. He couldn't even talk to someone without mucking it up. He swallowed. 'Sorry.' His voice was almost steady.

Silence. Francis probed inside his lower lip with his middle finger and winced. He wiped the blood off on his jeans. 'What the . . . ?' Then he looked back up at Michael. 'Do you always hit people? Is that how you make friends?'

28

'I don't know. I don't have any.' He didn't mean to be honest; it just came out.

'Right.' Francis's voice didn't give anything away, but there was something odd in the way he was looking at Michael. Like he'd seen him before somewhere and was trying to work out when: speculative, interested, not unfriendly. Then his mouth twitched. 'Frankly, I'm not surprised.'

It should have sounded snide, but somehow it didn't. Francis was laughing at him, but with a kind of warmth, daring him to laugh back. Michael thought, *Like I've done something right*, and then told himself that was mad . . . Of course! It was *pity*. It had to be.

Francis was still looking at him, his eyes narrowed, like the beginning of a smile. 'You OK?'

'Yes.' *But* I *hit* you, Michael thought. *Don't ask* me *if* I'*m OK*.

Francis leant forward, picked up the little ball of paper and started uncreasing it gently. 'Sorry. I shouldn't have looked. I just . . . it looked, you know, I liked it, it looked interesting.' He slid his palm over the coastline, flattening it. 'Sorry. Mum said you – well, she said *shy*, so I guess that means just averagely discriminating about who you show your Year 7 Geography projects to . . .' He looked up and smiled properly, suddenly casual. 'You're planning to store your GCSE notes in a vault at the Bank of England, right?'

Michael nearly managed to smile back. He looked away from Francis, down at the papers on the desk. 'Than's Lynn – it's not a peninsula, it's the ruined bit of the city that got abandoned when the occupying forces left, only I can't draw.' It came out before he

29

had time to think, in a long incoherent squirt. *Oh, Michael, you* idiot, *what did you want to say that for . . . ? First you tell him you don't have any mates, and* then . . .

'Oh. Right.'

Now, Michael thought. *Now he'll take the piss.*

But Francis only nodded, as though Michael had said something interesting. 'Why was it abandoned?'

A deep breath. He meant to say, *Oh, I dunno, I can't remember, it was ages ago . . .* But he heard himself say, 'They had to rebuild the city walls and they built them in a different place. So the cathedral, and the old slums, and the bits that used to get flooded were all outside. And no one wanted to live there, so everything just went to rack and ruin.' God, *listen* to him! What was he thinking? He couldn't believe he even remembered that stuff – and now he was saying it aloud, to someone he didn't even know. He might as well hang a sign round his neck saying *I AM A WANKER.* He bent down suddenly and picked the map off the floor. 'Forget it.'

'I'm sorry you tore it.'

'Doesn't matter.' They stared at each other for a moment. Francis really did look sorry. Michael shrugged. 'It was from ages ago. I don't even remember doing it.' It might have been convincing, if it hadn't been far too late.

'Can I fix it?' Francis reached forward and started to tug the paper gently out of Michael's hand. Michael started to take his hand away and Francis held on to his wrist. That was strange. It should have been really weird, it should have made Michael flinch, as though Francis was coming on to him or something. But it was more like Michael was a kid and Francis was a grown-up.

Michael said, 'What?'

'I'll take it home, see if I can do anything with it.'

He stepped back and pulled his wrist out of Francis's grasp. 'It really doesn't matter.'

'I'd like to.' It was funny, the way Francis could get you to agree to things just by *expecting* you to say yes. It made you think you were being childish and unfair for wanting to say no. 'I promise I'll bring it back.'

That wasn't the point. But what *was* the point? Unless Francis was going to scan it on to his computer and email it to his mates from St Anselm's: *Guess what, I met this bloke who's coming to our school, he's such a prat, look what he does in his spare time* . . . The idea made Michael go cold. *Really* cold; he actually started to shiver. 'No.'

Francis sighed. 'Suit yourself.' He pushed the map deep into one of the piles of papers on the desk. Then he looked up, smiling. 'I'm just going for a slash, back in a minute.' He slid round Michael out on to the landing. As the door closed behind him, Michael felt himself relax; somehow he'd been expecting Francis to keep going until Michael agreed to let him have the map. He had the air of being someone who got his own way. But then, Michael thought, maybe he was really only being polite.

A week later Michael found out Francis hadn't put the map back into the pile at all. He'd only pretended to put it back; he'd hidden it in his back pocket as he went out of the room. It was only the next Saturday, when Francis, much to Michael's (and his mum's) surprise, came round again, that he found out; and then only because Francis, with a shamefaced grin, laid *two* maps on his desk – the torn original, and Francis's own beautiful, detailed copy. 'I wasn't quite sure about the contour lines,' he'd said. 'I guessed it was all pretty flat, because of the marshes – but maybe Arcaster should be built on a hill?'

That had been the beginning. And Michael still couldn't quite work out how it had happened. Once he'd tried to ask Francis about it – 'I don't get it, you must have thought I was a complete freak' – but all he'd said was, 'Well, I just thought, you know, us complete freaks should stick together.' And that didn't help much. Francis didn't even know about the stuff at the comp, so it wasn't like he was making allowances. When Michael said again, 'I don't *get* it. How could you possibly have wanted to come back, after that?', Francis looked up, irritated, and sighed.

'Give it a rest, will you, Thompson?' he'd said. 'It just happened, OK?'

'I *hit* you. For no reason.'

'Maybe I like the masterful approach.'

'But –'

Francis shook his head, like Michael was just being childish. 'What do you want me to say?' He leant back in his chair and looked at Michael reflectively. 'You were just sort of – interesting. And it gave me somewhere to go on a Saturday.'

That was as much as Michael could get out of him, and he didn't push it. It wasn't like it really mattered.

That was the beginning of it.

Now Michael stared at the wall of the toilet cubicle and wondered if this was the end. He could see *I*

KNOW WHERE ARCASTER IS as clearly as if it was written on the wall in front of him. He still felt sick, and empty, and his mouth tasted of bile. He wished his mind would go blank and white, like the wall. Somewhere a long way away the bell went for the end of break.

He closed his eyes.

TER

... yesterday my brothers went on a foray to a rebel village ... they set off on little Mereish ponies, sounding their horns and singing psalms ... they captured ten rebels, all men, except two boys and a baby, which will fetch eighty crowns all told, they say ... they [the rebels] are very thin: poor but vicious, as my eldest brother said ... (Flora to Valens, from the Fabianus Letters, *trans. MT)*

When I open my eyes I wish I hadn't. When they were shut, in the moment between sleep and waking, the world was bad enough: painful, tasting of blood and smelling of something worse, a world that you'd want to keep at bay for as long as you could. But now, staring into the silvery half-dark, I can see enough to remember where I am, and why, and I wish I'd had the sense to keep my eyes closed. It's difficult to tell if any of the others are awake; no one's moving, but then I know from pulling against my own bonds that the more we struggle the tighter the knots get. The only sensible thing to do is to stay still. My hands have gone dead, which should be a relief – one part of me,

34

at least, that doesn't hurt – but I know what it'll be like when they untie them. It's absurd to feel squeamish about that now, but all the same I'm dreading it.

It's either early morning or dusk. I've lost track of time. If I could remember which route we took up to the castle, which gate we went through, the turns and doors and staircases we went down to get to this room, then maybe I could work out which direction the light was coming from. But all I remember about that walk was the misery of it, how hard it was to keep going, and the biting cold that made my shirt, still wet from the marshes, chafe against my back. The Evgard men behind us were whistling and laughing. When they rode up to Skyph we'd heard them singing psalms, and knew to gather what we could and run; but as they dragged us through Arcaster the songs were jaunty, with comic words about hunting and bringing home the spoils and what they'd do with the virgins they'd captured. Thurat swore at them in Mereish, *varesh sbythagerdim, shudfargtts*, and they stopped chanting for a moment to slice off one of his ears. We were quiet after that.

It was a long way. I was so tired that I was almost sleeping as we walked. I found myself calculating how much they had reduced Thurat's selling price by, and wondering why they had. Surely they had more to lose than to gain by it? There was an idea that nearly came to me, the way you solve a riddle as you fall asleep and forget the answer before you wake up. But it slipped away when Geron took a false step and slid on a patch of ice, jerking the rope that linked us together, so that I caught my breath and nearly fell.

I think once we'd got here, after they tied our feet

again, they gave us food and water. I'm not sure. My mouth tastes of blood and dirt and salt, but I think I'd be hungrier if they hadn't. Or perhaps I'm feverish. It wouldn't be surprising. I hid in the reeds next to the Tharn for hours, so long that I thought I'd freeze to death if I stayed there much longer, so long that I was sure they'd have gone. My hair had frozen into spikes, like a hedgehog, and the sun had gone down. I was too cold to move smoothly, and I wasn't thinking straight. I should have known better than to stand up while the sky was still glowing blue; I must have been easy to spot, as clear as a raven on snow, clear as fire. They were only a few *hycht* away, crouched and waiting, fat and warm in their coloured coats. I ran, of course. But I was too tired, too cold, slipping on ice or falling through it, into water up to my knees, tearing my hands on the marsh-reeds. And I was lost. I didn't know where to aim for. There was nowhere to go to ground. In the end, when they surrounded me, I crouched down on the ice like an animal and waited for them.

I *waited* for them. And I knew what they'd do. I'd heard the stories, we all had. I'd heard what they did to boys like me, the worse things they did to girls. I should have fought to the death, or carried on running until I collapsed or stepped on a marsh-adder. There are some boys in our village who carry poison, who'd rather die than be sold for a slave. Ryn would have slashed her own throat with her knife. But I squatted on the ice with my hands clasped in front of me and *waited*.

Is that how you find out you're a coward? Can you go your whole life thinking you're brave – climbing the cliffs for a dare, catching venom-spiders to race, fighting imaginary battles where you conquer all of Evgard single-handed – and find out in one freezing moment that you don't have the courage to defend yourself? Is it only when you give in to cold and exhaustion and hunger that you begin to see how weak you've always been? Or when your father's oldest friend has his ear cut off, casually, so that it flicks away into the gutter, a lump of cartilage and bloody skin – if you stay silent, if you look away and try not to retch . . . does that mean you've always been contemptible? Does that mean you were always weak and dishonourable and pathetic?

I suppose it does. I suppose you're just finding out who you really are. You start to see how rotten you are, inside.

I only know I'm crying because my lips are stinging where they're cracked. I squeeze my eyes shut – my left cheekbone aches, along the edge of the eye socket, and I think the eye's swollen – and try to stop myself, but it's no good. Who am I trying to fool, anyway? I can't get much more spineless than I am already. Water runs down my neck into my shirt, and after a while I feel drips start to slide down my ribs. I open my mouth and take deep breaths. I'll stay quiet, at least; I won't bawl like a baby.

There are footsteps in the corridor outside, echoing, a long way away, but coming closer. More than one man. And voices, speaking Evgard, with the blurred quality that means they're drunk. Thurat raises his head, turns it this way and that, trying to work out if he can hear something or not. He must be trying to get used to having lost an ear. I know Geron has heard them too, from the way he stiffens, but he stays staring at the floor, not meeting anyone's eyes. We wait.

The door shakes and creaks as they unlock it and come in, moving in and out of the shaft of light from the window, unweaving the ropes that hold us in place. There are two of them, bulky men who smell of wool and aqua vitae, swapping jokes in Evgard, speaking so quickly – *quick as green*, my grandmother would say – that I can't keep up. I know most of the words, but from the way they're laughing I know I'm missing something. One of them catches my eye and says something too fast for me to catch. He bends down to untie my ankles, one hand holding my feet so I can't kick him. But as he bends to pull at the knot I jerk my knees up, and he recoils, grimacing and rubbing his forehead. He calls me *catelle*, whelp, and I wait for him to hit me, or jerk me roughly to standing. But all he does is call the other one to hold me still; and when he takes the rope off my wrists he doesn't tug any harder than he needs to. Their hands are firm but gentle, and that frightens me more, somehow. It's the way my father leads animals to the slaughter: matter-of-factly, calmly, without cruelty.

We're all so quiet. We must all be thinking the same thing: *Perhaps we'll be sold, perhaps we're going to die*. Either way we'll never see one another again. We should be saying *something*. The words of the old valedictory come into my head, but I don't have the courage to say them aloud. *May the sea run fresh for your asking, may the fire burn cool at your need; may the ice crack under your enemies' feet, may they spit teeth* . . . Ryn and I used to gabble it to each other, every time we had to spend a few hours apart, until her mother had enough and threatened to smack us; but I've never said it in earnest. And now, even if I dared to, it's too late. The men are barking at us to stand up and get into line. We get up, slowly, stiffly, like old men. The tingle in my hands rises suddenly to a rush of pain that makes me gasp and swallow hard in case I cry out.

Geron asks for water. His voice is creaky. One of the men laughs. '*Argwa*,' he says, mocking Geron's pronunciation. He reaches for the flask at his hip. '*Argwa?*' As though he'd even know the Mereish word for water. He uncorks the flask, holds it towards Geron. '*Visni?*' he says: *You want it?*

Geron nods warily. '*Si placet.*' He darts a glance at me, to check that's the right thing to say. I look away.

The man laughs. '*Zi blarged?*' He grins at his companion. 'Ahhh. Polite, aren't they? Sweet, good-mannered little traitors?' He turns back to Geron. '*Zi blarged?* What's that when it's at home?'

Geron blinks. He knows it's a question, but his Evgard isn't very good. And why should it be? He's lived in Skyph all his life, where we all speak Mereish. He turns to me. 'What's he saying?'

'He's taking the piss.' There's no point translating.

'Ask him for water.'

I take a deep breath. I start to say, 'Please – my friend is thirsty.' But they're not looking at me; one of the men catches my eye briefly and makes an unfamiliar gesture with his fist that could be obscene or threatening or both.

The other man leans close to Geron. 'You're thirsty, are you? Well then – open your mouth.'

Silence. I mutter, 'He says if you're thirsty open

39

your mouth.'

Slowly Geron opens his mouth. The Evgard man lifts his flask, as though he's going to pour a stream of water into it. Then he raises himself on his toes, and, with great deliberation and accuracy, spits into Geron's face. He tilts the flask and we all hear the water splash on the floor in a long stream. The saliva slides down the side of Geron's nose towards his open mouth. The Evgard man smiles at him. 'You want a drink?' he says. 'Just lick your lips.'

He looks at me and jerks his head towards Geron. 'Translate that for him, clever boy.'

I meet his eyes for a moment. They're so dark you can't see where the irises end and the pupils begin. I notice the creases under his eyelids, the coarseness of the skin. I stare until he's just about to say something else.

I turn to Geron. I keep my voice flat and expressionless. 'He says his mother was a fat whore who shagged donkeys.'

Geron's eyes flick to mine and away again. He nods soberly. Behind me someone gives a sort of barking cough. We all look at the ground, blank-faced, and the Evgard men watch, satisfied. They've asserted their authority.

They lead us out of the cell, down a dark passage that magnifies the noise of our stumbling unbearably, up an endless, slippery spiral staircase, and down another narrow corridor. The air smells of smoke and sweat, rancid and bitter. And as the smell gets stronger, so does the noise, and the walls start to glow golden round the edges. We turn a corner. I realise suddenly that they're taking us to the great hall of the castle. I have just enough time to wonder why, to feel an

40

abrupt weight of fear in my stomach, before we're marched past the guards with pikes and through a curtained archway, into the biggest room I've ever seen.

There's a long table facing us. The people sitting at it turn to look at us, breaking off their conversations. They must be the Duke's family. Seeing them, I understand why the Mereish hate Evgard so much: being ruled by people like that, people who look like foreign, poisonous reptiles or insects, fat and sweaty in shining robes. And the food on the table . . . the smell makes my mouth water, but it looks wrong. There's a swan sitting on a dish as though it's swimming in the sauce. Haven't they cooked it? Are they eating it raw, feathers and all? And a castle – made out of bread, perhaps, or sugar – that must have taken days to make. As I look, one of the boys reaches over and breaks off a turret, casually, and pops it into his mouth, still staring at us.

There are long tables at the sides of the room, too, although the people sitting there are dirtier and less garish. As I look round one of the men catches my eye and raises his cup to me. He shouts, 'Your health, little bastard – and your freedom!' and collapses, laughing helplessly. A woman leans across and presses her hand against his mouth, giggling, and he growls and pretends to bite her. There's an ironic cheer from someone on the other side of the hall.

But the space in front of us is empty. The centre of the floor is completely bare: white marble, I think, smooth and empty, the blocks cut into stars and triangles and diamonds, so the joins spread out from the middle like a spider's web, a tracery of lines, barely visible. It's beautiful, and strange. Why would they build something like that, these brash gaudy nobles? Why would they choose something so subtle, so delicate and unexpected? It reminds me of the marshes in midwinter, when the ice has frozen white and solid. It doesn't belong here, in this noisy smoky hall. The Evgard man who untied my feet sees me looking. 'Like it, do you?'

'Yes.'

He laughs, as though I've made a joke – a crude one, the kind of joke Evgard men make about raping virgins. But then he slaps a hand against my shoulder blade, almost sympathetically. I'm missing something here.

The man in the centre of the high table stands up. He must be the Duke; he wears a band of gold round his forehead, with a bright stone set into it. Suddenly it's quiet. He looks round, left to right, then at us, with a steady, arrogant gaze. He lets us wait until the silence deepens, until you could hear a candle drip. Almost everyone is watching him; only one boy at the high table is looking down at his hands, crossed on the table in front of him. He doesn't look up, even when the Duke starts to speak.

'My lords and ladies, gentlemen, servants, beggars . . . It is our custom, at the Sundark, to allow the rebels of Ghist Marydd to experience the clemency of the Arcastrian court. These men you see before you are traitors, to Evgard, to us, to themselves. As such, they have forfeited their freedom; tomorrow they will be taken to be sold, or to be put to death in the Winter Games. But tonight – we offer them a choice. Every rebel in this hall has a chance of regaining his liberty. If, tonight, any man among them simply has the courage –' There's a ripple of laughter, soft and malicious, and he waits for it to die away. Then he starts to speak again. 'If any man among the traitors has the courage to walk across this floor and look into my face, every single one of them will be sent home unharmed.' A few of the rowdier women clap. He quells them with a click of his fingers, and it's silent again. Then, unexpectedly, he repeats the last sentence in Mereish.

Someone to my left murmurs, 'What, you just have to go and look at him? He's not *that* ugly.'

Geron says, 'What's the catch?'

The Duke smiles. It's a nasty smile, I think, as though he takes genuine pleasure in the question. He says softly, 'No catch.'

There's something wrong. I know there is. No matter what he says – and they say Evgard nobles don't lie – there *is* a catch. But what is it? The men around me whisper and argue in low voices. 'If that's all you have to do – someone's got to – but he says – no catch, he says – yes, and when did you last believe an Evgard man? – but if we don't they'll kill us anyway – or sell us – come on, who'll do it? – they're just testing us . . .' I don't join in. Instead I stare at the Duke and the faces around him, trying to work out what's going on. They're sitting back in their chairs now, as though this is the prologue to a familiar and well-loved play. That boy is still looking down at the table, eyes hooded like a hawk's. I will him to meet my gaze, but he doesn't.

Someone shoves me aside and steps in front of me. 'I'm not afraid to look at the Duke.' Ermid, my aunt's name-son. He's tall, and wide, and wins every fight he has. He pushes me aside easily, as though I weigh nothing at all. There's muttered encouragement from behind me, then the hall erupts into applause, clapping, whistling, shouts of 'Bravo'. Even if they haven't understood the words, they know what he's saying. The Evgard men on either side of us swap grins.

The Duke nods. He jerks his chin up in a command. One of the Evgard men comes forward with a length of black material. A blindfold. They start to tie it round Ermid's eyes. He flinches and pulls back, pushing their hands aside, and one of them laughs and says, 'Afraid?'

Ermid starts to say, 'But I've got to – how'm I supposed to look him in the face if I'm –' but no one's listening. One of the Evgard men holds up the blindfold, stretching it taut between his fists. It's as clear as if he said it aloud: *You're playing by our rules now*. Slowly Ermid drops his arms and lets them wrap it round his head. His hands reach out. It frightens me, seeing the way he fumbles helplessly in the air, suddenly blind. Then they take him by the shoulders and start to spin him round, again and again, until he reels and staggers, until he must have lost his bearings. But I still don't understand. It looks like the beginning of a game: one-man's-night, the game we play at the Sundark in Skyph. The crowd has gone strangely quiet. The silence is so close and tense it itches.

The men turn Ermid round one last time and then push him forward. He stumbles drunkenly, a few steps towards the high table, then sideways. His feet are very loud on the stone floor. He gropes with his hands and walks slowly, more confidently, although he's going in the wrong direction. Five steps, six . . . and he walks into the corner of the long table. One of the men hisses at him and he flinches backwards; but now he knows where he is. He feels along the edge of the table, and then turns carefully, so that he's facing back into the middle of the room. I'm holding my breath. I let it out, as softly as I can, trying not to break the silence.

Now he walks back, retracing his steps, making each pace deliberate and determined. He's still on the very edge of the white space. It's odd, everyone's looking at his feet. He stops just short of the middle and makes a quarter-turn. He's facing the high table now; all he has to do is walk straight. But the hall is still tight with excitement. More and more people are leaning forward, putting their cups down, breathing faster. Ermid pulls himself up to his full height and puts his shoulders back. He lifts his chin. Then, straight-backed, he walks defiantly towards the high table, stepping out across the white floor as though it belongs to him.

And disappears.

The floor opens up beneath him so smoothly, so easily, that I don't believe my eyes. I blink. He's gone. I blink again, as though he'll re-materialise, condensing out of thin air as quickly as he went. He just isn't there any more. I screw up my eyes, praying that he'll come back. No one can just vanish like that. I stare and stare, trying to believe what I saw. But in the end it's the sound that makes it real. You can't hear that cry, that thud, that vicious little click of the marble tile settling back into place, without understanding. And the flash of dark we saw, for a split second, under his feet, just before he fell . . . The floor stares back at us, smug, unbroken. Which tile was it that Ermid stepped on? The five-pointed star? The arrowhead?

The audience are leaning back, relaxing. That was the punchline. That was what they were waiting for. Now they can go back to their greasy food and salted wine.

One of the Evgard men leers at us. 'Any more takers?' He says it on the edge of a laugh. We're traitors. We had it coming. He turns away, gesturing at someone to throw him a chicken leg, and starts to whinge about what a thirst he's got.

Thurat says, 'I will.'

This time the silence isn't immediate: it spreads out, slowly, like heat from a fire. The Evgard man breaks off his sentence and looks back at us, startled. Geron says, 'Don't be a fool!'

Thurat looks at him ponderously. 'What have we got to lose?' He turns to the Evgard man and says again, louder, 'I will.'

The men and women closest to us look up and go quiet. Their faces are avid; more excited, if possible, than before. They weren't expecting this. They catch the Duke's attention and he flicks a hand to quell the noise of conversation. He's smiling. He looks Thurat up and down, registering the broad shoulders, the grey hair, the missing ear. 'Ah. The fabled bravery of the Mereish.' He glances down at the white floor, then back at Thurat. 'If that's the word I'm after . . .' He lets the words hang in the air. It's hard to believe how easily he makes the whole hall listen to him, how he can make everyone in the room hold their breath for what he'll say next. We can't look away. He reaches casually for the dark cloak over the back of his chair. Then he holds it up, and with one smooth movement

46

rips it down the centre. He wads one strip into a bundle and throws it to the Evgard man at our side, who scurries forward to catch it. 'For the blindfold.'

The Evgard man bobs his head. 'Yes, my lord.'

I don't want to watch them blindfold Thurat. I don't want to see him die. I look down at the dirty bricks under my feet and try to forget that a few *hycht* away the floor is white and smooth and as treacherous as *yshgren*, ice in spring. I can hear the footsteps as they spin Thurat round, and the scuffle as they push him forward. I stare at the bricks until my eyes burn and the shapes blur. I hear him start to walk, slowly, gently. He's as sure-footed as a spider. I've never seen him stumble, never in my life. If anyone can cross that floor, Thurat can. And – if he does . . .

I can't help it. I look up. He's sliding his feet across tiles, feeling for the slightest movement. He's not facing in the right direction, though: he's walking diagonally. He staggers. My stomach drops as though I'm the one who's falling – but he gets his balance back. He must still be giddy, that's all. I hear someone murmur, *Please, please*. It's me. I bite my lip and force myself to take deep breaths.

His foot moves across a triangle, pressing down with his toe. His hands are spread out as though he's dowsing for water. I see him begin to shift his weight. My backbone goes cold. That's wrong. I don't know why, or how – but that tile won't hold him, I know it won't. *Not that one, don't step there, please, please* . . . I can't help myself. Desperately I start to shout, 'No – Thurat –'

His head whips round, as though he's not blindfolded. But it's too late. He's already transferred his

47

weight. Suddenly below his feet there's nothing but emptiness. His arms flail helplessly. He tries to throw himself backwards, away from the blackness that's opened underneath him, but there's nothing to push against. I try to run forward to help him but someone's got my arms; they're holding me back. He shouts as he falls, a brief guttural cry – but there's a dull sound as his arms smack down on to the marble – and somehow, somehow, he's clutching at the edge of the hole, his hands clench on the stone tile, and he's hanging there, blindfolded, suspended over black space. There's a roar from the spectators, laughter, mocking cheers. I throw myself forward, trying to wrench myself free of the men holding me, but my feet slide uselessly on the bricks and the men push me to my knees. I can't hear myself shout over the noise but I know I'm yelling, 'Thurat, Thurat,' as though I could reach him with my voice.

The Duke is standing now, leaning forward over the table. His face looks eager, thirsty. He watches Thurat hang there. He's waiting for his grip to loosen.

But it doesn't. I've seen Thurat harvest marsh-reeds, knotting them into bundles, and I know how strong his hands are. He could drag himself up by his fingers. He's going to climb back up. I watch, shaking, as the muscles in his shoulders start to bulge. There's more mocking applause from the watchers, but it doesn't matter. Nothing matters, except that Thurat can pull himself back up. *Please, please.* His hands clench harder on the stone, fingernails white as the marble. His arms bend; he's doing it, he's climbing back up . . . Slowly he eases one elbow over the edge of the tiles. I can't breathe. *Please . . .*

48

The Duke frowns. He looks away sharply and says something in a low voice to one of the women at his side. The woman smiles and tilts her head to gaze up at him, trailing dark enamelled fingernails across his sleeve. Then she stands up and walks to the edge of the floor, her dress swinging like a bell, peacock-blue. The noise grows louder. The men whistle and the other women clap grudgingly. Thurat has almost got his other arm up now. Just a few more seconds and he can stand up, safe, unhurt. But now everyone's watching the woman in blue.

At first I think she's dancing. The way she moves, gracefully, as though she's listening to music no one else can hear, counting the steps sideways and back. The way she walks with such precision, exactly, carefully, as though one false step would ruin the whole dance. She holds up her skirts and moves towards Thurat, along a line of tiles, then diagonally, like a knight's move in shek. Then I realise. Of course. She knows how to cross the floor without falling through it. She knows the design. I watch where her feet go, weaving an invisible pattern on the tiles. She gets closer and closer to Thurat; closer and closer, until she's there, right in front of him. But he doesn't know she's there until she puts one blue-slippered foot deliberately on the back of his hand. He freezes. The audience jeers loudly.

The woman in blue looks around, acknowledging the noise, licking her lips as she meets the Duke's gaze. She presses down on Thurat's hand with her foot, pensively, as though she's wondering what to do next; then she lifts it again, stands daintily on one leg for a moment, and kicks Thurat's blindfolded face as hard as she can.

He yelps and jerks back. His hands lose their grip and scrabble desperately on the stone. His palm slaps on the marble as he tries to grab for the edge, but it's no good. He cries out, and falls. There's a thud, like a sack of earth hitting a stone floor.

The marble tile clicks back into place. The woman curtsies.

The noise in the hall swells painfully, and then subsides. People pick up their bits of food and carry on with their conversations. A couple of children spit bits of stale bread at us, sniggering. The woman dances back to the high table, light-footed. The Evgard men start to herd us out of the hall. No one meets my eyes.

Behind us, the Duke says, 'One moment.'

We turn around and shuffle back into place. The Duke is grinning fiercely. He's looking straight at me. My throat tightens and I look away. But when he speaks, I know he's speaking to me, as clearly as if we were the only people in the hall. 'You. You tried to warn him. Didn't you?'

I can't help glancing up. And when I meet his gaze I know I don't need to say anything. My stomach fills with ice.

He nods, watching me. 'I'm afraid that's against the rules.'

No. *No*. The panic rises up like flood water, battering at me, sweeping me off my feet. I feel sick. Because I know what he's going to say before he says it.

'So now it's your turn.' He's grinning as though he's going to go for someone's throat. 'After all, now you know how it works.' He picks up the other half of his torn cloak and holds it out for one of the men, look-

50

ing at me all the time. I want to turn and run, but there's nowhere to go. My legs are going to give way. Someone pushes me forward and starts to wrap the cloth round my eyes. It's happening so fast. I need to keep my sense of direction. But now they're spinning me, roughly, so that everything whirls round me and I don't know where I am. I'm going to die. I'm going to *die*. I'm so dizzy I can hardly stay upright.

They let me go. The floor tilts sideways, levels, tilts the other way. I'm going to be sick. I take a deep breath, open my eyes and stare at black cloth. Maybe I should run, to get it over quicker. I take a step forward.

Someone giggles, to my right. One of the kids, the one who was spitting bread at us. The little dark oily one. Which means –

Which means I'm facing forward. I know where I am. Relief hits me, irrationally, like a warm wave. Why am I relieved? I'm still going to die. Knowing which direction I'm looking in isn't much consolation.

Except that . . . don't be stupid. But there's a voice in my head, now. It's telling me I could do this, if I wanted. I could cross this floor without falling through it. I might be able to stay alive – to keep us all alive . . . I can't help myself. I crouch, quickly, and run my hands over the floor in front of me before any-one has time to realise what I'm doing. Someone barks, 'Oi!' and the audience shouts derisively; but as I stand up I can feel hope prickling somewhere in the back of my head. Maybe I can . . . A diamond. So the line of arrowheads is about a *hycht* to my left. I stand still, breathing, making myself think. How did she get from the edge of the floor to the middle? It must be

51

symmetrical. It must be built over a framework. It *must* be. So . . .

The noise is building again. They're impatient. But I have to get this right. If I can only remember . . . It was like a dance, like a strategy in shek, like a spider weaving. She stepped on the arrowhead, the star, two triangles, over the diamond on to the rhomboid on the other side. I squeeze my eyes shut and try to see it. Like a spiral, only not quite. Like a web, only not quite. Come on, *think* . . . The shouts are raucous now, aggressive, and I have to move soon or they'll send her on to the floor to push me. All right. I take one step sideways, to where the central axis should begin. If I'm thinking straight. I feel my heart push against my ribcage. I walk forward. The floor holds.

The star must be two foot-lengths to my right. I don't give myself time to think about it. I take a long step: and I'm still standing, still alive. *Be careful, don't lose your sense of direction. Stay facing the high table.*

And the triangles must be – that way. For a moment my memory flickers, like the floor trembling under my feet. *Was* it that way? Or was it then that she stepped over the diamond? If I get it in the wrong order . . . I try to concentrate. The noise hasn't lessened, if anything it's getting louder, but I have to block it out. There's a little cold flame of fear burning under my diaphragm. I ignore that too and focus on the shapes in my head. The arrowheads, the star, the triangles . . . And suddenly I can see it: as though it's been drawn out for me on the inside of my skull, silver on white, gleaming, symmetrical. I can see it stretching away into the distance, repeating itself over and over. Once you see how it works it's easy. It's like a melody. It fits together.

So it must be the triangles next. I turn carefully, letting myself judge the angle by instinct. One step on each. One. Two. And the world stays solid beneath my feet. Not far now. I can smell my own sweat; my cheeks are wet where it's run down my temples. I can't let myself think about that. I keep the pattern of the floor-tiles in front of my eyes, like a map. I know where I'm going. I have to trust my body to take me in the right direction. Now it's step over the diamond, on to the rhomboid. A big step – but not too big, because I have to land on the right tile. Step. My ankle shakes as I put my weight on it. I feel the tile begin to give way. It's too late to go back. I've got it wrong. That's it. I brace myself for the fall.

The floor stays steady. The breath rushes out of me. I'm imagining things. I breathe in and make myself count to five, *yn, duuzh, ter, kyth, mearn*, before I think about the next move. A couple more steps, and I've done it. I can pull off the blindfold, look the Duke in the face, and be granted my freedom. But those steps. Forward – is it? I concentrate on the pattern so far. Yes. Forward.

Before I lose my nerve I stumble the last few steps. I almost trip, and I launch myself forward. My knees hit the ground and I find myself kneeling, my hands scratching at the floor, trying to find the edge of the marble. It's there. I feel the place where it joins the brickwork. I'm safe. I've crossed the floor. We can go home – all of us . . . I hear myself breathing in great sobs, as though I've been underwater all this time. I pull off the blindfold, tugging at it until the knots yield. My eyes sting in the light and the smoke. My face is wet.

The hall is weirdly quiet. Everyone's staring at me; but no one's cheering, or applauding, or even scoffing. I want to say, 'Now let us go,' but my mouth's too dry.

The Duke looks down at me, his face unreadable. Then he stands up. He beckons to me and walks out of the hall. One of the men-at-arms stands up too and follows at my shoulder. I don't look behind me, but I feel him there as I go out of the hall. I go down a little corridor and through the open wooden door at the end of it. I don't know what I'm expecting: my mind's gone blank. When I go in the Duke is seated at a table, leaning back on a cushion, waiting for me. This must be his privy chamber. The man-at-arms waits outside the door and lets me go in alone.

The Duke looks up at me and nods, as though I'd said something. 'Clever boy.' When I don't reply he raises one eyebrow. 'Do you understand Evgard?'

'Yes.'

'Good.' He pours a cup of wine and runs his finger smoothly round the rim. 'How did you do that? Walk the floor blindfolded? Have you been here before?'

'No.' He waits until I have to say something else to fill the pause. 'I just saw the pattern.'

'Clever boy,' he says again. He sips his wine, gazing into the middle distance.

'I want you to let us all go.'

The corner of his mouth tautens. There's a glint in his eye. 'No doubt.'

I try to keep my voice flat. 'You promised us our freedom. If one of us crossed the floor and looked you in the face.' He throws his head back and laughs. 'You gave your word.'

'As if I cared for that . . .' he says lightly. The look in his eyes is predatory, as though he enjoys watching me struggle to stay calm.

'You *promised* us –' I have to swallow. I can still see Thurat's hands, clawing desperately at the floor as he fell. 'So my friends – they died for nothing. And you'll still . . . you won't give us our freedom. You won't send us home.'

'Of course not. After all, we need slaves for the Winter Games.' He has a gaze like a hook, that you can't get away from. He stands up, and walks round the table to me. 'But I think I'll keep you alive, for a while. You're rather interesting. *Saw the pattern*, did you?' I try to step backwards, but he catches hold of my shoulder and holds me where I am. 'Did they teach you that in Marydd, Clever Boy?'

'My name's Argent.'

'Because of your eyes, no doubt? How apt.' He strokes my cheek with a cold fingertip. His hand smells of attar of roses. It makes me want to retch. He must see the look in my eyes because he leans closer. 'I wonder what else they taught you in – Skyph, wasn't it?' The ball of his thumb drags at my lower lip, pulling at the scab. I flinch, and he smiles that vicious, feral grin. 'I think perhaps I should like to find out.'

I shake my head. I can't speak. I'm scared I'll cry. I wish I still had my sheath-knife. I'd happily die if I could kill him first.

He tilts my face towards his until there's a finger-breadth between us. 'Well, then, Argent,' he says. 'Show me what you've learnt.'

Then he locks the door.

55

FOUR

Michael knew he should get up and unlock the door. He should pick up his bag and go to History, down the corridor and across the court where the flower beds were. It was Thompson's Third Law: don't bunk lessons, because someone will notice. Do everything you're told. Don't draw attention to yourself. The worse things got, the more you had to hold it together. But he just couldn't make himself move. He was late already anyway. Father Sewell would be looking at his empty desk, shaking his head vaguely, murmuring about autumn colds and the influenza epidemic in 1918. He'd just assume that clever, inconspicuous Thompson was ill. Bunking off? Thompson? Surely not. A boy like him? And what do you mean, a *personal crisis*? A fight with a friend? But Thompson's not the sort to have friends . . .

And how right he was. Michael grinned to himself, fiercely, pushing the misery away. *Stupid, Michael, stupid. Letting yourself think Francis was actually a mate. Letting yourself like him, letting him into Evgard. I mean, Christ, Thompson, what were you*

56

thinking? Why didn't you take a few pornographic photos of yourself and hand him the negatives, while you were about it? Or handcuff yourself naked to a lamp-post and give him the keys? He actually laughed aloud, but it made his stomach hurt. And when he closed his eyes again he felt a kind of despair swelling up into his throat. He'd rather he *was* chained naked to a lamp-post. He'd rather there *were* pornographic photos of him on the Internet. He raked his fingertips down over his forehead, hard, pressing against his skull. *You* dare *cry, Michael Thompson . . .* He said to himself, *If I let myself cry I swear I'll go to the science labs and turn on the gas taps and sit there and wait for the whole bloody thing to blow.*

He swallowed, and the lump in his throat eased. Better. Suddenly he desperately wanted to smoke. And he couldn't sit in a toilet cubicle all day. For one thing, someone might see his feet under the partition and call a teacher in case he'd OD'd or slit his wrists, like the kid at the comp. He'd thought about that, but he'd never been brave enough. And that wasn't how he'd do it, anyway. Imagine dying in the stink of other people's shit, looking at their graffiti. Imagine your last sight on earth being *FITCH-MARTIN TAKES IT UP THE ARSE.* Although that might make it easier, in the end, especially if you happened to be Fitch-Martin.

He picked up his bag, unlocked the door, and made his way out into a deserted corridor. It was so quiet at St Anselm's. At the comp it was always noisy. You never knew if there were people waiting for you just round the corner, or coming up behind you, ready to jab their elbow into your kidneys as they passed, disappearing round the corner before you even felt the impact. But here – you could stand still and listen, and if there was someone there you'd know. You'd hear them *breathing*.

Sometimes he'd play a game with himself, listening, choosing alternative routes, trying to avoid seeing anyone at all on his way to the classroom. But now he took the most direct route to the front gates, not caring who saw him. He walked past the classroom where Francis was doing Geography. He didn't mean to look through the window in the door, but he did, and with a shock he met Francis's gaze as he looked up idly from his work. Michael's feet carried him past before he had time to pause or wonder whether to nod or smile. But it shook him. Francis had looked – well, normal, ordinary, the way he always did, raising his eyebrows briefly in a greeting. Michael wondered what his own face looked like. Surely he looked different. Surely Francis couldn't look at him and not know something had changed? Jesus, how could Francis look so cool, so unruffled, so – Michael searched for the word – so *mild*? But then, he must have been doing that for weeks. He must be pretty good at it by now.

Michael stopped on the stairs and gripped the banister, tightly, as though he needed to hold himself steady. He stared at the A-level Art project on the landing and made himself feel nothing. He was tired. Not upset, not furious, not desolate. Just really, really *tired*. Francis had been lying to him for weeks. Everything they'd done together, the work they'd done on Evgard, everything, was a sham. Just something for Francis to amuse himself with and show to

58

his mates, laughing. *Yeah, he's a real loser. Look, he makes all these maps, and family trees, and he writes poetry, how sad is that? Yeah, well, I go along with it, I think it's hilarious. The poetry? Sure, if you're interested I'll nick some to show you.*

He'd kill him. He'd *kill* him. For a moment, involuntarily, Michael saw himself taking a drag on a cigarette so that the end glowed red, and then deliberately grinding it down on the back of Francis's hand. He pushed himself away from the banister and stumbled down the stairs in a kind of panic, as though he was running away from something. God, he just needed to get home, that was all. He made himself sign out, smile carefully at the receptionist and saunter out of the school gates, like he was perfectly happy, like he was in control.

When he got home he went up to his room. He sat on the floor against the bed, staring at the double-locked box that held the Book and everything else to do with Evgard. But Francis had managed to show it to someone – sneaking it out of the room, probably, the way he'd stolen that map, the first time . . . He wondered what they'd seen, Francis's mates. Everything? Or just the odd little titbit, a particularly inept drawing or a map, maybe, one of his mock-scholarly articles about the Mereish language or the way they counted in base twelve? He felt his cheeks burn. All right, so it was sad, so he was a loser. Worse than that. He saw himself, suddenly, the way Francis's mates – no, the way *Francis* must see him. Not just a victim, the way he'd been at the comp. He was a freak, he was *laughable*. He thought: *I'll never be able to look him in the face ever again. I want to die.*

He closed his eyes and brought his hands up to his face, clasped, like his wrists were tied together. That last term at the comp he used to come home and sit like this for hours, not moving. You pretended you were made of stone. You just sat. And sometimes you went into a sort of trance and the pain receded. It wasn't like Evgard, it didn't make you feel *better*; it just made you feel *less*. Sitting there now, Michael felt like he'd never moved. He'd been there, sitting like that, since he got home from the comp that last evening. He thought, *I will never,* never *let this happen to me again*.

In the end he made himself move. He got up, knelt by the box, and reached for the key to his padlock, tugging at the chain round his neck so hard it bit into his skin. Normally he liked knowing it was there, feeling the small weight of it under his shirt, knowing it meant Evgard was there, safe, in a box in his room. Now it made him wince. God, how childish . . . At least Francis didn't know about that. Francis just kept his key in his pocket, with the loose change and paper clips and cigarette lighter.

He unlocked his padlock, and stared at the other one. It looked pretty sturdy. He pulled at it, not expecting it to give. He didn't think he could pick the lock, either. He went downstairs and got a hammer out of the cupboard under the kitchen sink. Then he went back to his room, turned the box on its side, so the padlock was facing up, and he bashed it and bashed it with the hammer until he was out of breath and the box was dented and the padlock was lying open on the carpet. He didn't give himself time to assess the damage. He pulled out the Book and the piles of papers, heaping them recklessly on the floor, not caring if they got creased or trodden on. They looked pathetic, like old school notes that he hadn't got round to throwing away. Even the Book looked tatty and amateurish in its green binding. He'd been proud of that cover. He'd thought it made the Book look more official, somehow. And Francis had spent hours on the endpapers. Or at least he'd said he had. He probably knocked them up in a few minutes on the Friday night, just so he could play Michael along. Michael remembered how he'd bent over them, saying, 'Wow, Francis, these are fantastic. Seriously, they're brilliant . . .'

At the time he thought Francis looked sort of evasive, like he was really pleased but trying to be casual about it. But really he must just have been looking shifty. There must have been moments, Michael thought, when Francis actually felt sorry for him, the way you'd feel a kind of pity for a slug you were about to drop salt on. Especially if the slug was so dim, so completely dense and useless that it looked up at you enthusiastically and told you how wonderful you were. Michael could still hear how Francis had said, 'For you, Thompson, anything . . .' in that kind of flippant way he had. Michael had grinned and flicked two fingers up at him amiably. Now he felt a pulse of anger so pure and cold it was almost enjoyable.

He kicked the papers into a rough stack. He opened his bag and got out the envelope Francis had given him, only that morning. Was it really only that morning? He slid out a few sheets of paper and spread them out on the floor. A star-map, with names for the constellations in Evgard. The front elevation of Arcaster Cathedral. A battle-map for the Glacies campaign – which, Michael thought automatically, was conducted by the White Company in the Long Winter, the only time in Evgard's history that the Mereish occupied Arcaster. He stared at the detail, the tiny notes in Francis's cramped block capitals, the careful colours. All that effort. A treacherous tentacle of disbelief and hope uncurled in his stomach. Maybe – somehow – he'd got it wrong. Maybe Francis had just mentioned it to someone, without meaning to take the piss. Maybe if Michael just *asked* him . . .

No. If he asked, of course Francis would deny it. And repeat the conversation to his mates, afterwards. *He just asked point blank – and then when I said no, he actually* believed *me. I mean, how thick can he be?*

But he could find out some other way. If Francis had just told someone without thinking, then he wouldn't bother to hide it from Michael. He'd say, 'Oh yeah, by the way, I met this girl at the wedding, and I said something facetious to her about Arcaster . . . what, someone actually wrote you an *anonymous note*? Oh bollocks, sorry, she must have told someone else . . . Don't worry about it, though, I didn't say anything incriminating.' He'd laugh at Michael, for letting it get to him. He'd reach across and ruffle his hair or something, teasing him. 'What, you thought I'd completely set you up? Jesus, Thompson, what kind of person do you think I am?' Michael found himself smiling into empty air, reassured, like Francis was actually there in front of him. But he wasn't.

He thought, *I have to be careful about this*. He couldn't be obvious. He'd plan it, so Francis wouldn't know what he was doing. He'd be cool and calm and calculating. He'd give Francis a chance to prove his innocence. He just had to think of it as a game, that was all. He'd play Francis's game. And he'd *win*. *After all*, he said to himself, *now I have the advantage, because he doesn't know I know. Now I know what to look for, I can watch him betray himself. He won't fool me any longer.*

He picked up the pieces of paper on the floor. He made himself put them on top of the others, with the Book, back in the box. He'd have to think of a way to explain having broken Francis's padlock. An accident? Yeah, right . . . But then, why would Francis be suspicious? He wasn't exactly going to think, *Ah, of course, Michael must have found out I'd been taking the piss all along, he must have attacked my padlock frenziedly with a hammer.*

Although if that does occur to him . . . Shut up, Thompson, you'll think of something.

Michael closed the box carefully, making sure he didn't crush the papers on top. He thought vaguely, *I must look at that star-map properly before Saturday, or Francis might get suspicious.* He sat down at his desk and started to doodle on a bit of paper. He had to think out his strategy. The game plan. He was on his own now. He found himself drawing squares of black and white, like a draughtboard. He thought, *It's just like a chess problem. It's just a game.*

All the time he could feel the hurt, the misery, just waiting to kick in. He tried to fight it off, but it kept pushing at him. Francis wasn't really his mate – Francis was screwing him over . . . He gritted his teeth and bent over his bit of paper: writing as if it could make him feel better. As if it could change something.

Michael had never been a good liar. His mum was: she made up elaborate, meticulous stories, just for the hell of it, it seemed to Michael. A few weeks after he left the comp he'd heard her on the phone, turning down a dinner invitation. 'And then we had to have the builders in . . .' she'd said, and he stopped at the top of the stairs, intrigued. 'No – the underpinning had gone completely – the outside wall, of course . . .' *Builders? Outside wall?* Michael thought to himself, *Christ, can we have had builders here and I didn't notice?* He turned to go upstairs again. His mum said, 'Yes, I know, they say they can burrow through any-thing, given time. No no, not English moles, some kind of African species, they import them for fur, but then those awful animal rights people . . .' She was winding the phone wire round and round her hand. Michael watched it coil and uncoil endlessly, like she was trying to break it. 'Yes, much larger. Carnivorous, of course . . . yes, well, next door's cat went missing, and I can't help worrying that . . . thank you, that's sweet of you, but you can't help feeling . . .' She nod-ded, like she was talking to someone face to face. Then she glanced up and saw Michael. Her face didn't change. She said, 'Michael's having the time of his life, of course. Trying to catch one . . . yes, the adolescent male instincts . . . Oh well, hopefully by that time they'll have . . . yes. Well, have a lovely evening, so sorry I couldn't . . .' She laughed, with a sort of brittle note in her voice. 'Circumstances beyond our control, yes. Well. Hope to see you soon.'

She put the phone down and looked up at Michael. He wanted to laugh. No. He wanted to *want* to laugh. But he couldn't. She stared at him for a long time. She said flatly, 'I have to do *something* I enjoy.' Then she turned away.

And Francis. Francis came out with all sorts of excuses at school. 'Sorry, one of my little sisters put it in the washing machine.' 'Sorry, my little brother threw a tantrum and trashed our room, and it got ripped.' 'Sorry, my father went on a bit of a crusade and threw any books by non-Catholic authors out of the window.' He judged it perfectly, the combination of embarrassment and simplicity, the glint of humour, like he knew what he was saying was funny but what could he do? And even afterwards, when Michael teased him, asking why didn't he just say the dog ate it, he'd look at Michael straight-faced. 'What am I supposed to say? It's true.' And only the eyes – slightly too wide, slightly too innocent – gave it away. Michael admired that. It took a kind of bravery to choose a lie and stick to it. It was like you were standing up to the world, saying, *Hey, you know what, I've got a version I like better.* Michael was a rubbish liar, normally. He mumbled and blushed and contradicted himself. Even the simplest things. He could *conceal* things, that was easy; he could hide cuts and bruises and blood on his clothes, he knew how to keep secrets. He could keep secrets for the Olympics. But actual sorry-I've-left-my-locker-key-at-home stuff – that was different. He didn't know why. It just was.

But the next day, when he went back to school, it felt like someone else had taken over. It was like Michael's whole body was just a mask that someone else had put on, and the real Michael was actually lurking, disembodied, at arm's length, wondering what had happened. Because he was *good*, this new guy, whoever he was. He could offer Francis a cigarette and say casually, 'Oh yeah, I bought them yesterday on the way home. I just couldn't face History, so I skived off.' He could lean back – what was the word? *insouciantly* – against a tree, playing idly with his cigarette lighter.

'I thought you were ill,' Francis said.

The real Michael would have said, 'No, no, we had a timed essay in History and I didn't fancy it, and I thought, you know, why not just bunk it, and, yeah, I hope you weren't worried or anything when I wasn't around in the afternoon . . .' And by that time his face would be scarlet and Francis would know he was up to something. But this new character shrugged. 'No. Just couldn't be bothered to come back.'

'Right.' Francis glanced at him sideways. But there was nothing to see on Michael's face. His expression was artless and innocent. Michael flicked his ash on to the mud and ground it into a grey smear with his toe, not meeting Francis's eyes.

'Oh, by the way,' Michael said, judging it perfectly, as though he'd really only just thought of it, 'my mum's having people round on Saturday, so I thought we could go into Canterbury for the day. I want to go to the cathedral anyway, and otherwise she might get me to have lunch with them.'

'Yeah, sure.'

It wasn't unheard of for Michael to suggest going somewhere else. Mostly it was London – to the Science Museum (although that was Francis's idea),

66

the National Portrait Gallery, where they spent hours picking out faces and matching them to people from Evgard, the Tower (of course), and once to the London Dungeon, where they chased each other round the exhibits like kids and argued about the torture chamber in the castle at Arcaster. That had been the day Michael came up with the idea for the Judas floor, and Francis borrowed a bit of paper from someone on the train home and sketched a design for the great floor at Calston, shading in the tiles you could tread on safely. That day when Michael got home he'd found blood on his arm and couldn't work out where it had come from. It had taken him ten minutes to realise it must be fake blood from one of the exhibits, that somehow he'd got on himself by mistake. He'd looked at the smear of red on his skin and thought, *I'm not sure I want to wash this off*.

Even now he knew the pattern of the Calston floor, knew it by heart, and the simpler versions of it they had at Than's Lynn and Arcaster. He could walk them blindfolded. Except that they didn't exist.

'Great. We'll go to the cathedral, then.' He threw his cigarette away. It was only half smoked but he didn't feel like finishing it. He thought, *Good. That's the first move*.

They walked back up to the school buildings. A day ago the silence would have been companionable. Now Michael felt like he was behind glass, watching Francis through a one-way mirror. He was in control. He thought, *If we see Shitley I won't wait for Francis, I'll just keep on walking*. But they didn't.

Francis turned his head to watch some kids trying to swarm up a tree. One boy was already in the branches, swinging his legs idly at the others' faces. He said, still looking away, 'Why Canterbury?'

Michael shrugged. *Because that's where they murdered Thomas à Becket. Because it's the nearest thing I've got to somewhere that looks like Evgard. Because in the cathedral in Than's Lynn they still have trial by ordeal.* He said, 'Why not?'

'Fair enough.'

They didn't say anything else. They went up the stairs to the fifth-form corridor in silence. Francis had his head lowered and his hands in his pockets; when he passed Luke coming the other way he didn't say anything, just nodded curtly. Michael wondered vaguely why Luke seemed to follow Francis around. Philip didn't. Philip ignored Francis when they went past each other in the corridors, so that it had taken a while for Michael to click that the skinny little boy with the red hair was actually another one of Francis's brothers. He ignored Michael, too, which was fine. Anything was better than the way Luke glowered at him, like Michael was personally responsible for – well, for something unpleasant. As he caught Luke's eye he felt a sudden flash of unease. Of course. Bent Dick. The kid Shitley had . . . In Luke's class. But now that seemed a long way away.

He opened his locker, noticing the weird new precision in his movements. It was a strange feeling, like he was playing chess or something, bringing each piece into play. He looked at his timetable the way he thought an actor would look at something on stage, without actually seeing it. He knew Francis wasn't watching – he could feel it in the back of his neck – but all the same he grimaced, as though Chemistry

68

first thing was all he had on his mind. He got out his books. He put his lunch on top of his exercise books. He pulled out the bit of folded paper wedged under the locker door. When he unfolded it his hand was completely steady, like something dead. His name wasn't on it this time, he saw.

I'VE SEEN EVGARD.

He felt the impact of it in his bones, the way you'd feel sound if you were deaf. Distant, not painful, but inside you somewhere. He folded it again; looked up; saw that Francis was going through the files in his bag, muttering, 'Double Chemistry, French, double English, lunch . . .' He hadn't seen anything.

Without thinking – as though some instinct had taken over – Michael reached over and slid the note underneath the door of Francis's locker. Then he drew his hand back, surprised at himself. Suddenly he was breathless, excited, like a chess master who's made a risky move. He packed his books into his bag swiftly and said, 'Just gonna get a coffee . . .'

Francis glanced up and nodded. 'RS, Latin . . .'

Michael stopped halfway down the stairs, his hands fumbling at his shoelaces. He saw Francis open his locker and take the note out, frowning. Michael felt his throat tighten. Francis's expression made him go cold. Not surprised. Not panicked, like Michael had been. Not knocked backwards by the unexpectedness, the *betrayal* of it. Not confused or worried. Just – annoyed. Pissed off. Like someone had trodden on his toe. Or like someone had got the wrong locker.

Francis screwed up the note. He threw it, with a flick of his wrist, and it fell in a little parabola into the exact centre of the bin. He glanced around briefly. But by then Michael was running down the stairs, trying to cling to the behind-glass untouchable sensation, feeling anger batter against him like a huge moth.

All that day he kept seeing it in his mind's eye. Francis's face. *I'VE SEEN EVGARD.* That look of, *Jesus, can't they do better than this? For God's sake, guys, it's the locker* next *to this one* . . . And his hand taking aim, and the curve of the ball of paper falling into the bin. The way it dropped expertly into the middle, precisely on target.

FIVE

He should have known then. He should have believed what his eyes were telling him. He should have thought, *OK, Thompson, now you know. Stop mucking around.* He should have confronted Francis with *I KNOW WHERE ARCASTER IS*, looked into his eyes, watched it all fall into place. It was stupid to keep wondering, to keep scrutinising Francis as though he still wasn't sure. But he couldn't help it. The uncertainty sat in his stomach like a hollow ball; he couldn't get rid of it. It was like there was a treacherous little voice that kept on and on at him, insidiously, saying, *Maybe, maybe not, maybe . . .* And he had to be *certain*.

So he didn't do anything. He let the other Michael keep going. He let the adrenalin of it carry him through the day like a skateboard, because it was exciting, in a weird, sick, black way, like standing at the top of a tower, wondering if you were going to fall. And the other Michael was loving it; he was getting high on hatred like a drug, *enjoying* it. The other Michael had it all worked out in his head, like a battle, with Canterbury Cathedral in the middle of it like a fortress. He could see it all as a tactical exercise, a sort of logical problem, that you could win or lose. Michael was grateful for that; he knew if he let himself feel it he'd go to pieces. He imagined himself inside the walls of the cathedral: safe, powerful, ready to trap Francis, to get the truth out of him. Come Saturday, he'd be sure. Then he'd decide what to do – but not till then. All that week he held himself apart, steady, untouchable. Cold. He stuck to the routine, because that was all he had. He didn't dare to wonder, what if, what if Francis *was*, if he *had* . . . because what would he do? He could live like this, in limbo, for a week – but after that? He found himself looking round at the other kids in his class. Dave Murray, Dan Holdstock, James Kenner. They were OK. But they were Francis's friends. They might have been the ones he showed Evgard to. They might have been laughing at Michael for months. He could survive on his own, he knew that, and in a strange sort of way he was thankful for it. He wouldn't *die*. But he was scared, shit-scared, of the loneliness. Jesus, if only he'd never been friends with Francis. If he'd had any sense at all he would never have let Francis get close to him. The voice in his head said, *Stupid, stupid, stupid* . . .

He wasn't sleeping, either. Not that the nightmares had come back, thank God, but he just couldn't fall asleep. After the second night it really started to get to him, because didn't you go mad, eventually, from sleep deprivation? And in the daytime the other Michael was finding it harder and harder to take control. He had to fight to keep the mask from slipping. Francis was sharp: Michael couldn't afford to let him notice anything. But it was like he was trying to hide something in his hand – like a magic trick, like he was cheating at cards – and it was getting heavier and heavier, and all the time he was trying to pretend he was fine when really he was nearly dead from tiredness. By Saturday morning, when they were on the train to Canterbury, he wished he could just stay on the train for ever, letting it carry him all the way to Ramsgate and back again to London, over and over again until they found him years later slumped in his seat with long hair and a beard like a prisoner from the Bastille. He leant against the window, staring out, without talking. That was OK because he was always a bit spaced on train journeys, and Francis was never the kind of person who talked for the sake of it, just to fill the silence. Michael let the landscape slide through his head. He thought dreamily, *Maybe I should just tell him now, tell him everything, and whatever he says I'll believe it*. But he kept his mouth shut.

It was better once they got off the train and started to walk. Francis was smoking and Michael could almost taste the bitterness of the cigarette smoke; it made him feel a bit sick, for some reason, but at least he felt like he was really *there*. It was good, because everything else was still a bit blurry. He felt weird – like every time he passed a doorway there was someone there, watching him, disappearing as soon as he looked at them straight on. And Evgard was there too, nearly close enough to touch, not letting him forget. Nudging at him, infecting the real world. They walked past a section of the old city wall and for a moment Argent was there, inside his head, staring at the wall of Arcaster Castle, sick with misery and shame. It felt more real than the real world, somehow: dragging Michael in, like a current. He could feel the momentum of it, the clarity, so that it was hard to resist the voice inside his head. And he wasn't sure he wanted to. Anything was better than this, here, now. But he had to concentrate, so he pushed Evgard away, struggled against it, like sleep. God, he was so *tired*; and every time he blinked he could sense Evgard surfacing. He dug his hands into his pockets and said aloud, 'Not now, not now.'

Francis looked at him sharply sideways and Michael felt himself flushing. He thought, *For God's sake, Thompson, pull yourself together. Think about real life for a change.* But he didn't want to. Real life hurt too much. Francis had betrayed him; Francis had been laughing at him, all along . . .

They passed a chip shop and bought two bags of chips. *Come on, chips, Michael, you don't get more real than that . . .* He forced himself to smile at the girl behind the counter while Francis ordered. Then they found a bench and sat down. Michael could see the outline of the cathedral roof. He started to eat his chips mechanically. Francis ate his quickly, smearing ketchup over the paper. Michael thought, distantly, *It's like he wants to keep his mouth full, so he doesn't have to say anything.* He ate his own without tasting them. He hadn't been hungry for days.

Francis screwed up the paper and threw it at the bin opposite them. It was one of those covered ones, with just a slit in the side to stick your hand through. Michael thought, *I wonder if he actually* practises *throwing things into bins. Maybe it's his party trick.*

Francis said, 'OK, Thompson, spit it out, what's wrong?'

Michael would have loved to frown convincingly and say, 'What?' But the other Michael, the one who could have done it, had obviously given up in disgust. He looked down at the mound of drab yellow chips and felt his face go stiff and hot. His fingertips shone with grease. 'Nothing. I didn't sleep very well.'

He was expecting Francis to raise one eyebrow sceptically and say, 'Yeah, right. So really what's wrong?' but he didn't. He gave Michael a long look – direct but distant, as though he was behind glass – and then turned away, wiping his hands on his jeans. 'Fair enough.'

Michael felt a rush of disappointment, then anger. Jesus, he was pathetic, he was like a *kid*. Pretending he was doing all this tactical, strategic stuff when all he really wanted was someone to look at him like he mattered and say, 'Come on, Michael, tell me what's wrong.' He felt like he was five years old, telling his mum to go away just so that she'd see how upset he was and put her arms round him. Not that he wanted Francis to put his arms round him – but it was the same thing, really. He couldn't help himself: he said, 'I'd explain, only you can probably guess.' He didn't know why he said it; except that he knew, deep down, he *knew* that Francis would think for a moment and look perfectly, casually baffled, and then the weight in Michael's stomach would lift and he'd want to laugh with relief.

Francis looked up. Just slightly too sharply. Just slightly too warily. Then he frowned and shook his head, and smiled, like, *Sorry, Michael, am I missing something here?* But Michael felt cold, because he'd seen the tension in Francis's neck as he turned his head. He was hiding something. He was *definitely* . . . Michael cleared his throat and swallowed and licked his lips and thought, *Go on, say something. Now.* But the pause carried on. Francis tilted his head back and raised his eyebrows. 'I suggest you just assume I don't know what you're talking about.'

It was almost spot on. It was almost what Francis would have said, if he didn't know what Michael meant. But there was a hostile edge to his voice, a sort of precision. Michael noticed his accent for the first time in weeks: the private-school tone that said, *I'm in control here. Don't mess with me.* For a split second Michael considered hitting him. But this was it. He'd planned it, and this was his moment. Even if, somehow, he already knew there was something wrong. He took a deep breath and said carefully, 'I've been thinking about Evgard.'

What was it on Francis's face? Confusion? Embarrassment? It looked like *relief* – only why would it be? Whatever it was, it was gone before Michael had time to understand it. Francis was looking smoothly away at the pigeons squabbling round the rubbish bin. 'Right.'

'I think I might give it a rest for a bit. I mean, it's basically pretty puerile. Just kids' stuff. I mean, for Chrissake, it's an *imaginary country*.' Michael heard his own voice, heavy with contempt, and thought, *What am I doing? I'm sorry, Evgard, I'm sorry, it's not true . . .*

'Maybe.' Francis's voice was so quiet Michael wondered if he'd imagined it.

'You can carry on with it if you like. But I'm sick of it. You know, when you think about it, it's just really lame. Really sad. Kind of *pathetic*. There must be better things to do at the weekend.' Desperately Michael thought, *He'll look at me in disbelief. He'll say, don't be stupid, what's happened? You were enthusiastic enough last week . . .*

Francis was still watching the pigeons. Michael thought he hadn't heard; but then Francis brought one hand up to his mouth and bit pensively on the thumbnail. After a while he turned his head and smiled. He wiped his hand on his jeans. 'What did you have in mind? Hanging out in the park drinking Strongbow?'

Michael shrugged. 'Anything.'

'Not really your scene, is it, Thompson?' Francis's gaze was level, unsympathetic.

Michael stared straight back at him. 'You mean, I'm the kind of person who stays in all Saturday making up their own rubbish fantasy worlds? You think that's where I belong? With the other saddos and weirdos and losers?'

Francis raised his eyebrows and stared at him. 'Like me?'

Michael thought, *That wasn't what I meant.* But he was too angry to say it. And anyway, Francis *was* a bloody loser. Why else would you bother to lie to someone for weeks and weeks, just so you could laugh at them? He looked at the ground, scared of what Francis would see in his eyes.

When he didn't answer Francis laughed. 'Right. You know what, Michael? I think that's *exactly* where you belong. With the other losers.'

It was so close to how Michael had imagined it that it shouldn't have hurt. But it did. It was like being kicked in the kidneys. Francis thought he was a loser. *Francis*, who had always seemed . . . Michael couldn't speak. He laced his fingers together and stared at them.

Francis took a deep breath, letting the air hiss out through his teeth. He said, 'Sod it. I don't care . . . Whatever you say. God forbid you should do anything *pathetic*.' Michael didn't understand what he meant, but he felt like he was somewhere else, where the words didn't really matter any more, didn't mean anything. Francis rubbed at the knee of his jeans with a fingertip, over and over again. 'But what did I –?' He broke off. 'So, you sussed it. What happened, how did you –?' He glanced up suddenly. He looked oddly young, somehow. 'That's right, I mean, it's because you found out –?'

He didn't need to finish the question. Michael met his gaze and nodded. *So it's true. Jesus, it's true. You admit it. You bastard, you fucking bastard . . .* He saw Francis's face freeze over, saw it go white and rigid and strange. It was like this was the other Francis, the way Michael had changed into the other Michael. And the other Francis looked him casually up and down as though he despised him. One corner of his mouth tightened. 'Well. Now you know. Pleased with yourself, are you?'

Michael couldn't speak. He wasn't sure he could move. He nodded, jerkily, feeling the resistance in his neck muscles. He wanted to say, *Why? What did I do to you? Why would you do that? Do you really hate me that much?* But there was no point, because he

78

knew the answers. Or rather, he knew that there weren't any. *What did I do? You were there, Michael, that's all. You were an easy target. If you're different, if you're vulnerable, if you're weak. If you're a victim. There's no way out.* He felt the inevitability of it sitting in his throat like a lump of dirt. He wanted a drink of water.

Francis got up from the bench and yawned, stretching his arms above his head. Michael wanted it to be theatrical, a sort of see-how-relaxed-I-am gesture, but it wasn't. It was as though Francis was really *bored*. Game over. Time to think of something else. 'Nothing much to be said, then, is there?' He wasn't expecting a response. 'Shall we go home?'

Michael glanced up, surprised – what, walk back to the station *together*? – and Francis smiled, without warmth. 'Oh, come on, Michael, get over it. I thought you didn't want to be *pathetic*?' His voice was loaded with malice. It made Michael wince.

'Fine.' Michael had won. He'd done it. He'd got Francis to admit it; he'd seen the look on his face when he realised he'd been sussed. But he felt humiliated and confused, like he'd lost, like he hadn't even been playing the right game.

They started walking back, in silence. There wasn't anything to say. Part of Michael wanted to ask: *Who sent me those notes, then? Who else has seen Evgard? Were you laughing at me all along, or only recently?* Or just, *What did I do to you? What did I do?* But he knew he didn't really want to know, because he had to keep something intact. Somehow he had to start again; he had to get out of bed tomorrow, and Monday, and the day after, and on and on and on. He didn't want to know more than he had to.

They stopped at a pelican crossing. Francis stood off to the side, leaving an exaggerated space between them, like Michael was contagious. The lights were taking ages to change. Michael watched the cars going by. They were pretty fast, for a main road. Normally on a Saturday they were almost at a stand-still. Jesus, he was tired. The cars went *swoosh* . . . *swoosh* . . . *swoosh* . . . like the sea. He almost closed his eyes. He turned his head and stared down the road to where it curved. Blue BMW. White Ford Fiesta. Black two-seater. Red 4x4. He felt like he was actual-ly falling asleep. *Swoosh* –

He didn't mean to step forward. He really didn't. It was just that the lights were taking so long to change, and he was dead on his feet, and the cars weren't going *that* fast. And it wasn't a huge step – down off the kerb, not even far enough to cross the path of the 4x4, or only just. And it wasn't like he was running out into the road. He was actually moving really slowly. So slowly that he felt like the whole world had stopped spinning and was holding its breath, waiting for his foot to hit the ground. He was just crossing the street.

He was jerked back, almost off his feet. There was a car horn blaring and a sort of shriek, like there was an animal under the tyres of the 4x4. There was red metal in front of his face, close enough to touch. And Jesus, the *noise*, filling his whole head. His heart was pounding like someone was hitting him in the chest, again and again, and he was gasping for breath. His upper arm ached and burned. He stumbled back-wards, found the railing and held on with a slippery

80

hand. His knees, where had his knees gone? He slid down until he was crouched on the pavement, gasping. Someone was shouting at him. His trainers were dirty; they blurred and wavered like they were underwater. He heard the breath catching in his throat. His face was wet. Either the ground was shaking or he was. He held on tight and waited for everything to calm down. One of his shoelaces was fraying at the end. Someone was still shouting. He didn't know if it was the same person or not; he just let them get on with it. More car horns. Consonants spitting at him, whtthfck, jststppdtntthrd . . .

The first voice that meant anything was Francis's. 'You OK? Michael, are you OK?'

He managed to nod. 'Yes.' His voice wasn't very steady.

'Then what the *hell* were you *doing*?' It was Francis's hand on his arm that was hurting. It hurt now, because Francis shook him, hard. 'You could have *killed* yourself, you could have been *killed*.' He was so close Michael could feel his saliva on his face. 'You *idiot*, Michael. *Christ*. What the hell were you thinking? I mean, *Jesus*. Didn't anyone ever teach you how to cross a road?' He was still shaking Michael, but not so violently. Michael heard him breathe out heavily in a long rush of air. 'You're meant to wait for the little green man. Not walk under a bloody car.'

'Sorry.'

'Michael. *Fuck*.' Francis laughed jerkily and let go of his arm. 'Don't do that again, OK? I don't think my nerves can stand it.'

'I won't. Sorry.' He looked up. The traffic jam was clearing. The 4x4 had gone; a string of cars was

81

waiting for the last stationary car to drive off. There was a woman waiting to cross the road; she met his eyes and then looked away, embarrassed.

'If you're going to kill yourself, do it some other way, all right?'

'All right.'

Francis stood up slowly, shaking his head. 'You're a bloody psycho, Thompson. If you'd been on your own you would have *died*.'

Michael wiped his face with the palms of his hands and tried to smile. Francis grinned at him reluctantly, like, *I don't know why I like you*, and held out a hand to help him up.

Michael nearly took it. Then he pulled his hand back. He looked up at Francis and saw him understand. Francis shook his head slightly, like he didn't believe it; his mouth moved as if he was about to speak. Then his jaw clenched and he let his hand drop to his side. He watched as Michael drew himself shakily to his feet and started to walk away. Michael heard him swallow.

'I think I just saved your life, Michael.' It was a statement of fact – but colder than that. Measured, not giving anything away, the way you'd speak to someone who had betrayed you. Michael wanted to laugh at the injustice of it. The sheer bloody *balls* of it. He stared at his trainers, the place where his jeans had frayed at the bottom. But Francis waited until he had to look back and meet his eyes. Then he smiled, in a weird, pinched way Michael had never seen before. 'You owe me. Remember that. You owe me your *life*.'

'Bollocks.' Michael felt sick. The idea of it . . . He'd

rather die. He wished he *had* died. He stared at Francis, at that strange, horrible, triumphant look on his face, and turned and stumbled away. He ran blindly, trying desperately to get away, not knowing where he was going.

At least, he didn't think he knew where he was going, until he found himself at the entrance to the cathedral grounds, digging around in his pocket for the entrance money. He was struggling for breath; he could feel sweat down the small of his back. When he gave the man the money for the ticket his hand was trembling.

He went in and sat on a bench in front of the altar where Thomas à Becket was killed. He sat forward and put his head in his hands. He closed his eyes. Suppose he could just fall asleep here, and wake up not knowing who he was, like someone out of a film. Or wake up in Arcaster, open his eyes and be there . . . No. His throat ached. He took deep breaths and let himself fade away. There were people moving around, tourists . . . Once someone came down the steps behind him, talking loudly about the sculpture on the wall. He stayed still and ignored them and they left.

When it was quiet again he didn't know how long he'd been there. Maybe half an hour, maybe three hours . . . the light from the window had changed, but maybe that was the weather. Something was different. The voices from the crypt had faded. He opened his eyes and stared at the sculpture on the wall in front of him. Swords like lightning, like scrap metal. There were worse places to die.

He glanced to his left. Francis was there, sitting at

the end of the bench. For a split second he thought he was dreaming, then he blinked and saw how the sunlight outlined the hair on his neck in a coppery S-shape. He wouldn't have imagined that. He wanted to say, *How long have you been here? How did you find me . . . ? Please, leave me alone, you've done enough, please just leave me alone.* But he was too tired. He met Francis's eyes and looked away again. He waited for him to say something.

Francis said, 'You're very predictable, Michael.'

Michael said nothing.

'I was just thinking . . .' Francis leant forward and put his chin on his hands. 'I had a thought about Evgard.' Michael was about to shake his head, or stand up to leave, or say, 'Just piss off, Harris . . .' but Francis carried on speaking, raising his voice slightly as though he knew how Michael was going to react. 'You probably don't want to hear it, but I'm going to tell you anyway. I was thinking about it on the train, and I don't see why it should go to waste. I think you'll like it. The idea is, right, there's this substance that they mine in South Evgard, say in Sangarth. It's called Tempus's silver. It's like silver, only more precious. But it's also called lightlead, because they can make glass out of it. And it has the property of slowing down the speed of light. So, it takes half an hour or so for the sunlight to get through a window made of it, but then it holds the light for longer, too. So if you have a west window made of lightlead glass, it's still light inside when outside it's been dark for half an hour. You can watch the sunset outside and then go inside and watch it again, through the window.' Francis glanced at him, then back at the altar. 'And

84

mirrors . . . if you make a mirror out of it, it shows what was going on an hour ago. A whole hour, because the light has to go through the glass twice, through and bouncing back again . . . So you can look in the mirror and see no one, or someone else, or whatever. Someone having sex, or a murder, or anything.'

Michael said, 'Why are you telling me this?'

'I guess they'd have a lot of lightlead mirrors in brothels. So the next customer could watch. And the Duke of Arcaster probably has one on his ceiling. But they wouldn't just be for time-lag porn or surveillance – I mean, you couldn't really use them to spy on people, because you'd need to keep sneaking into their rooms an hour after you thought they were up to something, and that would be sort of pointless. You could use them to send messages – like sending a video, I suppose – and, I dunno, look at the back of your head.' He added wryly, 'And other useful stuff like that. But it's precious, anyway. It's the most expensive thing there is. And jewellery – because you could put it in a lighted room and then half an hour later when you were in the dark it would start to shine.'

'It's a good idea.'

'It's bloody brilliant.'

'But I'm not interested.' Out of the corner of his eye Michael saw Francis turn his head to look at him. He stared resolutely at the swords on the wall. 'You'll just have to tell your friends.'

He heard Francis take a deep breath. 'Michael. You're being childish. Why don't you just grow up and get over yourself?'

Michael spun round to face him and hit his shoulder on the back of the bench. 'Yeah, all right, I'm *childish*. But I hate you, OK? I *hate* you. So why don't you just go and fuck yourself?'

Francis blinked. 'That's a bit extreme.' He stared at Michael, as though he was waiting for him to apologise, or laugh. Then he narrowed his eyes. 'For God's sake, Michael, you're overreacting. Seriously, what's your problem?' He tried to smile and reached out a hand, maybe to ruffle Michael's hair, maybe to touch his shoulder. 'I mean, Jesus, I haven't *done* anything to you.'

Michael knocked his hand away as hard as he could. He heard Francis's shocked in-breath as it hit the back of the bench, and the dull sound of bone on wood. '*Haven't* you? Haven't you *done* anything to me?'

Francis stared at him, utterly, utterly still. There was silence, a pause that felt like it spread out into the whole cathedral, cold as stone. Then a blush spread up into his cheeks, staining his whole face the colour of blood. He looked away and swallowed. Michael stared at the skin over his cheekbones, the deep scarlet that looked uncanny on Francis's skin. It was so strange he almost didn't have room to be angry. Then Francis put his hands over his face and his hands were white, except for a long stripe of red where one of them had hit the bench. *Red and white*, Michael thought, *like the Wars of the Roses* . . . Francis stood up, slowly, carefully, like an old man. He gave Michael a long look of contempt as he walked away.

Michael closed his eyes. He could still see Francis's face, that crimson flush . . . Francis never blushed. He was always pale and cool and calm. But at least Michael knew, now. It was as clear as a mark on his forehead. And he'd won. You couldn't argue with it. He'd won, and Francis had lost. Easily. Checkmate.

He should have felt triumphant. But he didn't. He felt empty, adrift, like he wasn't really there . . . He looked up to his left, to the window, and gazed into the blazing sunlight. He let the light hit the back of his skull. He tried not to blink, and squinted, as though he was standing somewhere high up, staring into a dazzling, blinding abyss. Black stars swam across his vision, like something starting to surface. It was like the beginning of a dream. He felt dizzy, as though he was fighting vertigo, as though he was somewhere else.

He thought, *Evgard*. It was there, pushing at him, not letting go. He thought, *No, please, I don't want to feel anything, I don't want to . . .* but it was *there*. He couldn't argue with it. And anything was better than the real world.

The light flooded into his face, stinging his eyes like acid, bleaching everything. Michael thought, *OK then. I won't fight it. I'd rather be anywhere than here*. He kept his eyes open and tried not to look away.

EF

non ciccus sed cor . . .

The sun's so bright it's almost like being blind. It's all I can see: light and light and light, dazzling, colourless, filling my head like water in a bowl. It's like a blazing fog, dropped across the landscape. If it wasn't for the sunlight I'd be able to see for miles. There are black stars growing in front of my eyes, unfolding like fists and closing again, but I keep staring, forcing my eyes to stay open, because somewhere behind that glare of silver there are frozen marshes and a crumbling coastline, there are black-thatched villages and people that speak Mereish. Somewhere under that shining pall there's Ryn and my father, my grandparents, there's my village. My *heird*: my hearth, my home, my heart. They're so far away it would take days to get to them, but that doesn't matter. I know if I look hard enough I'll see them. If I can keep my eyes open, if I can stare at the sun without blinking . . . then I'll see them. Just for a second, maybe, before my eyes burn out; but it would be worth going blind for.

It's no good. I blink and blink again. My eyes are stinging and I can feel water on my eyelashes. I put my hands over my face for a moment, and when I look up again, towards the sun, I can't hold my gaze for longer than a second. So I look down, instead.

At the base of the tower, a long way away, there's a narrow walkway of grey stone, with a high wall on the other side. The shadow from the wall makes the stone look almost black. Beyond that wall there are a few shabby buildings, made of wood and daub, huddled closely together, a barterplace where a few people are already building bonfires and setting up stalls, and then the long lines of warehouses. I've been inside one of those, years ago, when it was my father's turn to bring the wool in for trading. I remember how much it frightened me: the long rows of blue-grey bales of wool, the bitter smell, like blood, the high dark roof – as though it had been built by something not human, something too big to live in a house. But later that afternoon my father found me, so he says, curled in a nest of new-dyed wool, fast asleep, with the marsh-reed dye coming off on my face. He would tell the story sometimes, laughing at me. 'Had a purple cheek for days afterwards, you did . . . And when I brought you back, everyone looked askance. They thought it was a bruise, you see. And I was that worried to have lost you, I *could* have hit you . . .' Then he'd draw his hand back in a big exaggerated motion and I'd hear it whistle through the air. I'd grin and stand my ground and my father would stop his hand before it touched me, letting it tap on my cheek so softly I could hardly feel it, and he'd pretend to grunt with the exertion. Now I suppose my face must look like it did then, stained lilac-blue from temple to jaw. Only this time it *is* a bruise. If he could see me my father would be furious, half mad with anger and helplessness and shame. Ryn would look at me in wonder, that I'd let anyone do it to me. And my grandmother . . . It hurts too much to think about what my grandmother would do. I'm glad they think I'm dead, because it would only make it worse, to know they were worrying about me. There's an old Mereish saying, *ester yuin halb, ester solon liever by*: when you're beyond help, it's better to be on your own.

And I am on my own. For the first time in days. As I sneaked out of the Duke's apartments it felt like an escape – the sudden, raw relief of being alone – but it isn't, not really. There's no one hitting me, or taunting me, or telling me in lip-smacking, brutal detail what happened to the others in the Winter Games, but I can't get out of the castle. And when the Duke gets bored he'll send people to find me. They'll call to their hounds to follow my scent, sound hunting horns in the galleries, and drag me back to him like a prize. If I struggle they'll hit me until I stop. I can't escape. I know that by now, and the Duke knows that I know. The guard caught my eye as I left the Duke's chamber this morning, and shrugged. He didn't need to stop me. He knew there wasn't anywhere for me to go.

Except here. The top of this tower. The only escape there is.

And it's as though nothing exists but me and the dark paving-stones at the foot of the tower. Nothing else matters: only the ground, and gravity, and the space in front of me. I don't need to look down. I can feel it there, the way you can feel your way round a place you've lived in all your life. I can stare into the light and the clean, cold air, the fresh early-morning winter silence, and step out, knowing it's underneath me. No one can take that floor away. It's ready to catch me, impersonal and cold and sure.

I'm not scared. Not any more. It's as though there's nothing left to be scared of. I take a deep breath. When I breathe out I'll walk forward.

Behind me someone says thoughtfully, 'It's the *falling* that would frighten me. Not the landing – only the falling.'

His voice is so like the Duke's it brings a bubble of nausea into my throat. I nearly step forward just to get away from it. But I stop myself, just in time, and turn to look. After all, I'm so close to the edge that he wouldn't be able to prevent me from jumping if I wanted to. And there was something in his voice, in spite of the dry Evgard consonants: something warm, almost as though he were human.

I've seen him before somewhere. For a second I can't remember where. Then it comes to me: at the feast, that first night. He was the boy sitting at the high table, the one who never looked up. He was the only person in the room who wasn't watching when Thurat fell, who didn't lean forward in excitement before they blindfolded me. I remember suddenly that he was the last thing I saw, before I crossed the floor: pale as a statue, staring down at his hands, knotted together on the table in front of him. Now his face is quizzical and cool, as though someone's just given him a shek problem to think about. He frowns. 'I mean, what if you changed your mind on your way down?'

'I wouldn't.'

He nods, as though he believes me, and shrugs with one shoulder. 'I just think there must be a better way. So there wouldn't be any danger of it. And that would hurt less.'

I shift my weight so that he can see both sides of my face. 'I'm not scared of how much it would hurt.'

He moves his head sharply, as though he wants to get a better view of my bruise; then he checks himself. He presses his lips together and looks down. 'No.'

'Please go away.' There's no point saying *please* in Evgard. I know that now. But I've got nothing to lose. If he laughs and says something obscene I can jump.

He nods slowly. He starts to turn. I look back down at the walkway. From here it looks as though it's the width of my hand. He says, 'I can give you poison, if you want.'

It's a sick Evgard joke. It has to be. When I look at him he'll laugh, throwing his head back. But he doesn't. He hunches his shoulders awkwardly and looks at the ground: as though he really means it, as though he feels guilty for offering. I take a step towards him, keeping one hand on the edge of the window. 'You don't mean that.'

He meets my eyes. 'You'd have to take it some-where else, on your own. You couldn't die in my rooms. My father would kill me if he found out.' He grins wryly. 'But it might be . . . better. You'd just go to sleep and not wake up.' His gaze flicks to the window and back to me. 'At least you wouldn't be all spread out like an egg.' Tentatively he reaches a hand out to me, to help me down from the ledge.

I don't take his hand. But I do jump carefully down off the ledge and step towards him. It's like the beginning of a fight: if he makes a false move that's it. No second chances. But he stays very still, the way you wait for an animal to approach. And he keeps a decent distance, turning on his heel to lead the way before I get too close to him. I walk behind him warily, wondering at myself. Why didn't I jump when I could? There's something about him that makes me uneasy. But I follow him anyway, remembering the way he offered his hand, casually, as though it meant nothing.

When we get to his rooms he lets me catch up, so that the guards won't challenge me, and rests the palm of one hand on my back as I go through the door; but he drops his hand as soon as the door closes behind us. He goes straight to a chest next to the fireplace and unlocks it with a key hanging round his neck. When he turns to me he's pulling a knot of black fabric undone in his fingers. Then he holds out a little dark nub of something. 'Somnatis. Otherwise known as king's mandragora. Completely painless. In small doses –' he rubs the ball of his thumb over the pellet and licks it, 'it induces a sort of deep relaxation, which is quite pleasant. It's pretty valuable – you can get ten *liae* of gold for something this size. A lot of people take it every day. But if you take enough you go into a deadsleep and die.'

'How much is enough?'

'This would be, easily.' He reaches out and drops it into my hand. It's black and greasy, like old leaves squashed into a paste. It smells pungent and sweet.

'I don't have ten *liae*.'

He laughs, then bites his lip. 'I didn't mean – never mind. You're welcome to it. You need it more than I

93

do. Only . . .' He pulls absently at the chain round his neck. He's looking at me the way Ryn's father sometimes did, when he was worried I was a bad influence. 'Only – don't take it all unless you're sure.'

'I am sure.'

'Of course.' He turns away and scuffs around in the rushes on the floor with his foot. 'It's up to you.' He smears a sprig of hartwort into the stone with the toe of his boot. 'I know what it's like for you. Maybe if I were you I'd do the same. If you have to, then you have to . . .' He glances up and away again. 'It's just . . . my father, he'd probably do this. He'd give you poison, just to see your face – for the power. He'd enjoy it.' His voice is cold but there's a sudden colour in his face. 'I think it would turn him on.'

'Your father . . . ?' He looks up for a moment, as though he can't help it, and I see the likeness in his face. Of course. The Duke . . . the eyes, like glass catching firelight, the thin mouth. And the voice. His father . . . It's so clear I wonder how I didn't notice it before. Because if I'd known . . . I stare at him, struggling against the panic, the hatred that rises in my gut like icy water. I shouldn't have trusted him. I shouldn't be in the room with him. I should be at the bottom of the Ghist Tower, spread out on the walkway like – what was it he said? – spread out like an egg. He *is* the Duke, thirty years younger. Except for the look in his eyes . . . I'm shaking. I can't speak. I have to get out. I have to get out *now*.

My mouth tastes bitter. I clear my throat and feel the bile on the back of my tongue. Then, suddenly, the fury makes me reckless. I meet his eyes, holding his gaze for as long as I can; then, deliberately, I lean forward and spit on the floor at his feet. I throw the bulb of poison back to him and turn to leave. Just now, just for this moment, I'm not scared. But I know I should be. The penalty for spitting in his presence must be death, at least.

'Wait.' He reaches out one hand to catch the poison, but his eyes are still on my face, and it slips through his fingers. But he doesn't bend to pick it up. Instead he's there at my elbow, pulling me round to face him. 'Don't go. *Don't*. I'm his son and I don't have any choice about that. But what I'm trying to say is – I'm sorry. I'm really sorry. I want to help.' I try to pull my arm away, but he's strong, stronger than he looks. 'Listen. Listen to me.'

He grabs my other arm and pulls me round to face him, roughly, so a wave of black sickness goes through me, a kind of furious horror at his touch, making me reel backwards, weak at the knees. It's hard to breathe. For a second his grip tightens; then, suddenly, he drops his hands and steps away, putting a *hycht* of space between us. His expression has changed. There's a silence. He swallows. 'My father is . . . I hate my father. Honestly. Whatever he's done . . .' He takes a deep breath, watching me. It's almost a question. I don't answer; but when he starts to speak again, it's as if my silence was enough. 'He's a – a *varesh mordyth meidburuchtts*.' A bloody murderous virgin-ravisher.

I hear myself make a noise that's almost a laugh. And for a moment it almost *is* funny: the way he shapes the words so carefully, keeping his eyes on my face, as if he's expecting me to correct his pronunciation. Then I look away, feeling an ache in my throat and a tight grin on my face that isn't quite a grin.

He doesn't say anything. When I look back, he's still watching me, as if he's waiting.

I swallow and say, as carelessly as I can, 'You speak Mereish?'

'Not really. Only some of the swear words.' He narrows his eyes thoughtfully. 'And he's a *ryglyng*,' he adds, for good measure: a man with only one testicle. It makes me laugh; a helpless, jolting, uncomfortable sob of laughter, like crying – but a laugh, all the same.

He smiles back. For a moment we look at each other. Then he bends to pick up the nub of poison. I expect him to give it back to me, but he puts it carefully on the wide stone ledge of the window. He turns back, then, unexpectedly, he bows to me. It's a proper, courtly bow, with his right hand over his heart, not the sketchy flourish I've seen the Evgard courtiers give to each other. It takes me completely by surprise; I catch myself looking over my shoulder to see who he's bowing to. He says, 'Columen, of the house of Nitor, at your service.'

I suppose I should bow too, but I'd only look stupid. In Marydd we nod to each other and offer both hands. I say, 'I'm Argent.' And because I can't think of anything else, I add, 'From Skyph.'

'I know who you are.' Columen walks to the window and picks up the poison. He tosses it into the air and catches it again. With the other hand he pours wine from a green-glazed jar into two heavy silver cups. His movements are so smooth it looks like a performance, but I don't think it is. He turns to face me, the black stub of poison held between his finger and thumb. 'You won't need all of this.' He holds it over one cup and rubs it with his fingers. A few dark flakes fall into the wine. Then he does the same with the other cup. He puts the poison down, picks the cups up, one in each hand, and takes a gulp of each in turn. There's something theatrical about the way he does it; as though this is an Evgard custom I don't know about, as though he's making a point. I suppose I'm looking blank, because he grins and inclines his head towards me. 'Just so you know I'm not poisoning you, Argent.' Then he holds one out to me. 'There's only a tiny bit in it. Less than I normally take.'

The cup's cold and heavy and must have cost as much as our entire reed-harvest. I hold it in both my hands, wrapping my fingers round the smooth silver. I don't drink until Columen takes a gulp from his cup; then, very slowly, I take a sip and let the wine sit in my mouth for a moment before I swallow. My throat's tight: I don't know what he's given me, I don't know whether I trust him. Maybe he's built up a resistance to it; maybe I'll go mad or die in agony. But I don't have any choice. If he wants to kill me he will. And it's just – *just* – possible that he's as honest as he seems.

The wine tastes of salt, and something else, an elusive fragrant hint of spice or leaf mould. It doesn't taste *wrong*, the way seaberries do, or bad meat . . . I take another sip, suddenly daring. Columen watches me drink it, deadpan. 'Why the Evgard name?'

I shrug. 'My mother was from Thornwell, near Petra Caeca.'

'It suits you.'

'I'm Mereish.'

97

He's just taken a sip of wine, so he has to swallow, shaking his head, before he answers. 'I know. That wasn't what I meant. The name. Argent. Silver.' He peers at me. 'Your eyes are silver, actually, aren't they?'

I look away deliberately and take another mouthful of wine. I don't need him to tell me what I look like. I've heard it from every man in the castle: *pisciculi albus*, fish-belly white, when they were being kind; *color seminis*, when they weren't. There are more words for *freak* and *weird* and *disgusting* than I can translate. I know I'm not a freak. I just look Mereish. But I'm starting to see Ryn in my head – darker eyes than mine, but clear pale skin and bright colourless hair – and wonder how I thought she was lovely. I look at myself in the mirror and think, *They're right, I look like something that's crawled out from under a stone.* Except now, of course, there's a bruise down half my face. The Duke laughed at how pale I was and pretended to be anxious. Then he hit me. 'That'll bring some colour into your cheeks,' he said.

Columen puts his hand on my chin and turns my face back to look at him. It's as though I'm some object that he wants to get a decent look at. It's not how the Duke would touch me; it's the way you'd look at a carving. *I do exist, you bastard, I'm here.* I push Columen's arm away so hard that he takes an involuntary step backwards. His hand goes to the dagger sheathed in the small of his back. Mine goes automatically to the same place, where my own knife should be; but they took it away the day they captured me. For a moment we're caught there, ready to jump, watching each other's eyes for the smallest flicker. Then Columen shakes his head as though he's trying to clear it. He runs both hands through his hair and steps back. He's dropped his wine. Mine's still in my hand, my knuckles round it white as ivory, white as milk or ice, white as my skin. I make my fingers relax. He goes silently to the wine-jar and pours himself some more, grating the poison into the cup with his fingernail. He doesn't look at me. 'I've never seen someone like you before.' He stands very still, his head bent, with his back to me. 'You look . . . extraordinary. Different.'

'The colour of semen, you mean?'

He laughs, suddenly, as though he can't help himself, and turns to look at me, still grinning. 'I was going to say *beautiful*.'

I think I've misunderstood. Maybe my Evgard isn't as good as I thought . . . or it's a special, idiomatic use of *beautiful* that I don't know. It must mean something else. But he's looking at me as if to say, *No, that was what I said*, and suddenly my heart's pounding. I think he's laughing at me, but I'm not sure. I drink a long draught of salty, earthy wine, dipping my nose further into the cup than I need to, clenching my hands on the metal; but when I look up he's still watching me. The unease comes back in a wave, sucking at the ground under my feet. *Beautiful* . . . I put the cup down and start walking towards the door, slowly, as though he might not notice.

'Relax, Argent. I'm not my father.' I look straight at him and he shakes his head, very slightly. I stand still, wanting to trust him. There's so much sympathy in his gaze that I have to swallow. Then he drinks his wine, all of it in one go, and puts the cup back heavily on

99

the trestle. He picks up the poison and slips it deftly up his sleeve. Then he goes to the other end of the room and opens the door there. I catch a glimpse of the room beyond: hung with dark green silk, glowing in the light from a fire. He's about to leave me on my own. That's it. Whatever he was trying to offer me . . . Somehow I've blown it, and all I can do is go back to the Ghist Tower and try again to screw up the courage to jump. But as I feel the misery come flooding back he beckons to me. 'Coming?'

His privy chamber's warmer than the first room, and darker, full of green tarnished-copper shadows and surfaces that gleam like gold. Before I was captured I'd never seen wealth like this: linen and silk and heavy furs on the bed, woven wool on the floor, carved chests and chairs and a screen of painted vellum across the window. But Columen ignores it all and sits on the floor in front of the hearth. He gestures to the chair next to him. I sit down obediently but it feels odd; in our house in Skyph the adults got the stools and I always ended up sitting on the floor. And I don't like being told where to sit – although I'm not stupid enough to argue, not any more. Stupid enough, or brave enough . . .

Columen looks into the fire for a few moments, holding out his hands for the warmth. He doesn't hold them out flat to the flames, the way I would, but with his palms together, as though he's swearing allegiance. Then he looks up at me. In the light from the fire his face is almost his father's. It makes my gut twist with something that's not quite fear.

'Do you know *trecho*, Argent?'

'Trekko?'

'A game. Like shek. The traitor game.'

'I know shek. I played that in Skyph. The priest taught me.' And I was good at it, although I don't say that. I could see patterns that most people couldn't, all the separate possibilities stretching into a web that you could catch the other person in. I understood how it fitted together. 'But not – whatever it was. I don't think so, anyway.'

'I'll show you.' Without waiting for me to answer he reaches for a carved box at the side of the fireplace. I feel an irrational pulse of anger that I don't seem to have a choice; then I want to laugh, because if someone had said an hour ago that the worst the Duke's son would do to me was teach me to play a game, I'd have been weak with relief. Columen upends the box, so that a pile of wooden pieces falls on to the hearthstones, and then flicks a catch somewhere and unfolds the box into an elaborately carved board. He sets the pieces out carefully in two triangles, black and white, facing each other. I bend forward, curious in spite of myself, but I can't see properly. He looks up, faintly mocking. 'You don't *have* to sit in that chair, you know.'

I feel the side of my face that isn't bruised go red. I lever myself awkwardly out of the chair – my ribs are still stiff down one side – and sit on the floor opposite Columen. He sets the last piece in place and smiles at me.

'It's like shek, really – it's the same kind of game. The main difference is . . .' He picks up a black piece and turns it over so that I can see that the base is hollow. Then he reaches over to my side of the board and pulls a little white peg out of the corner. He slides the peg into the base of the piece he's holding. 'There's always a traitor.' He holds it out to me and I take it, not knowing whether I'm supposed to understand what he's talking about. 'At the beginning of the game, you see, you choose one of my pieces and you put your marker in it. That makes it a traitor. And I do the same with one of yours. You still control yours and I still control mine. We don't know which one it is. But we know it's there. We know one of our pieces can't be trusted.' I nod. 'There are three ways to win the traitor game. One, you can win the way you'd win a game of shek, by checkmating my king.' He points to the piece at the apex of the triangle, which has a crown running round the rim of its top edge. 'Two, you can win when your opponent loses, if they use the piece you've marked, the traitor-piece, to occupy one of these squares –' he points to a band of darker squares across the middle of the board – 'or to checkmate your king. Are you following so far?'

'I think so.'

'And three, if you guess which of your own pieces has been marked. If you guess wrong, you've lost. But that's the best way to win.' He smiles, and for a brief, brief moment he's got the Duke's lupine grin. Then it fades into something warmer.

'How do you know?'

'Just the look in your opponent's eyes.' He picks up one of the white pieces and turns it over in his hands. 'It was designed to make shek more interesting, to introduce an element of chance. Just like rolling a die. If you wanted to gamble you could try to guess the traitor, but the odds were thirteen to one against you.

But then people realised there were tactics you could use for that, too. If you know your opponent well, it's often quite easy to read them. You have to get good at lying.'

'I can see why it caught on.'

His eyes flick to my face as though he doesn't know whether that's a joke. Then he relaxes and laughs. 'The best way is probably to show you.' He holds out his hand for the black piece and puts it on the board. It's got a tiny hand carved into the top, and as I look more closely I realise that all the pieces have their own emblems: a star, an eye, a knot, a ship . . . Except one. Columen follows my gaze and points to the blank piece. 'If you choose the blank as the traitor you have to declare it, but then you can move that piece behind your enemy's lines as though it was one of yours. My grandfather invented that rule. But people don't do it much any more.'

I nod. It's easy to see why. Intrigue comes naturally to these people. As far as they're concerned, honesty just isn't as much *fun*.

Columen leans forward and starts to tell me how each piece moves. I watch him, trying to listen, trying to concentrate, but all I can think is, *What will happen if I'm no good? Will he send me away in disgust? Do I want him to?* And suddenly I'm sleepy. I want to let my head drop forward and close my eyes, but I feel like I'd never wake up. I force myself to focus on Columen's finger, noticing the way it gleams in the firelight, like pale gold. Every time I take an in-breath I feel like I'll never need to breathe out. I mustn't let myself go to sleep. I dig my nails into the palm of my hand and blink again and again.

A door opens behind Columen, so that the draperies billow out in a flood of green, and a draught of cold air hits my face. For a second it's a relief: that should help me keep awake . . . Then a girl steps into the room, and the relief changes into a sort of heart-stopping, wonderful fear. She's beautiful. She's fair, for an Evgard girl, but with a lambent quality to her skin that's completely different from mine; her hair is like dark copper or red bronze, in a heavy cloud round her face, a dark halo. And her eyes are like embers. I know I should drop my gaze, but I can't. It's as though my eyes have a will of their own.

Columen looks up, over his shoulder. 'Iaspis.' He curls one finger at her, and I realise he's beckoning her over, nonchalantly, as though she were of no account. I want to stand up, or bow, or kneel, but it's hard to move. Columen looks at me. 'Argent, this is my sister, Iaspis.' He turns his head and smiles at her, without warmth. She looks at him silently. He raises his eyebrows. 'As far as I'm concerned, Argent is our guest.' It's an order.

They stare at each other, and for a second I can see how alike they are: the hair, the firelight eyes. Then Iaspis looks at me for the first time and I'm dazzled. She holds my gaze insolently, and curtsies like ice deigning to melt. 'Iaspis, of the house of Nitor, at your service,' she says, and I can't even imagine what she'd sound like if she meant it. I wonder if I should reply. The thought of it makes me want to wince in advance. But she doesn't wait for me to say anything before she turns back to Columen. 'Are you teaching him the traitor game? How appropriate.'

'I assume *you*'re trying to teach him manners,'

Columen says coolly, and one of her hands clenches on the silk of her dress. 'What do you want?'

'I have a favour to ask.' Her voice is low and quiet, but it has an edge to it that makes me think of a knife.

'To hear is to obey, my sister,' Columen says. I can almost taste the sarcasm in his words, like grease. He sounds exactly like Ryn bickering with her cousin.

But Iaspis ignores it, inclining her head as though he were being sincere. 'I need some – I mean, do you have any somnatis?'

Columen sucks air in through his teeth as though it's a monumental request. 'I'm not sure. How much can you pay for it?'

She gives him a long look. 'How much are you asking?'

Columen's face is grave, but somehow I can tell he wants to laugh. He frowns innocently. 'I'm not sure,' he says again. 'How much can you pay?' This time Iaspis doesn't say anything; she just puts her hands on her hips and looks at him coldly, her chin tilted. He screws up his face and nods. 'All right. I'll go and look.' As he gets to his feet and goes into the antechamber he glances at me, so briefly I wonder if I've imagined it. Then I'm alone in the room with Iaspis.

'Get up.' I stand, automatically. She walks round me, looking me up and down. I want to look back at her, but she's so beautiful I don't dare. Instead I watch the hem of her dress swirl hypnotically round her feet, kingfisher-green. She's walking in a spiral, closer and closer to me. She's regarding me as though I'm a statue, and I feel like one: a clumsy, melting snow-carving, or a rough-hewn bit of wood. I can smell ambergris, rich and sweet. 'Lift your chin.' Suddenly I'm staring into her eyes. I'm breathless from the colour of them, like autumn leaves, the intensity of it. She frowns and peers closer. Then she turns away, snorting delicately. Whatever the test was, I've failed.

Columen comes back in, tossing a little phial from hand to hand. 'No somnatis. But there's this. Aqua quietis. Just as good – unless you're thinking of trying to poison someone.'

She looks at him contemptuously. 'Given the last of it to your *guest* here, have you?' She flicks her finger at me as though she's trying to get something sticky off her fingernail. 'Have you seen his eyes? He can hardly keep them open.'

'I don't see how it's any of your business.'

She shrugs. 'It isn't. But Father wouldn't like it.'

Columen looks at her sharply and lets the phial fall through his fingers. Quicker than thought she reaches out and pulls it from the air beneath his hands, as though it was just hanging there, like an apple. Columen watches her slip it into a pouch at her belt. Then he says softly, 'I'm not sure about that.'

She tilts her head to the side; a soft coil of hair swings delicately past her ear. 'Shall we put it to the test?' She turns to go, as though that's the last word, as though she knows he won't argue.

'All right.'

She turns back to look at Columen for a moment and then laughs, keeping her mouth closed. 'Oh. I'll tell him, then, shall I? Daddy, did you know Columen took your little Mereish slave to his room and drugged him out of his mind?' She looks at me. 'You know what he'll do, don't you? It won't be just a bruised

106

face. You know what he'll do to your little pet –'
She uses a word I don't know.

'Shut up, Iaspis.' And to my surprise she does shut
up. Columen sits loosely on the end of his bed and
looks up at her. 'You should wash your mouth out.
But no, to answer your question, you needn't tell him,
because I will.' He turns to me. I stare back, because
I'm not sure I understand what he's saying. He meets
my gaze without smiling. I don't know if he's even seeing me, or whether he's just staring into the middle
distance.

Iaspis makes a little noise of disbelief. 'You'll tell
him you gave him somnatis?' She shakes her head
incredulously. 'I mean, do you even know how much
that *costs*?'

'Of course I do. I sell it.'

'And you'll tell him –'

'*Yes*, I'll tell him. Or maybe –' Columen smiles. It's
a slow, calculating smile that makes me uneasy. 'No.
No, you're right. I think I'll just ask a favour.'

She bends forward to look at him, raising her eyebrows. 'You are *joking*?' He shakes his head, still
smiling, and she steps backwards. 'Oh. Of course.
You're high too. Shall I come back when you've
crashed?'

Columen gets up, swiftly, in a smooth movement
that my eyes can't quite follow, as though there's something slippery about it. His sister moves automatically
out of his way. 'I mean it. You've given me an idea.' He
walks to the door, straight past her, and pauses there to
beckon me to follow, the way you'd click your fingers
to a dog when you're taking it for a walk. Iaspis
watches him coolly, with her head on one side.

I don't move; my heart is stuttering now, beating loudly in my ears. What's he going to do? What does he want?

He holds my gaze. 'Argent. Come with me.' There's a tone in his voice that I want to obey, in spite of myself: partly because it makes me want to trust him, and partly because I'm afraid not to. Finally I get up and go to him, silently, because there's nothing else I can do. I don't have a choice; not if I want to stay alive.

Columen goes out into the corridor – a little, dark, winding corridor, that's more like a tunnel than anything else – and I follow at his heels. Iaspis walks after us, with a sort of it's-not-that-I'm-curious-I-just-think-you're-crazy insouciance that makes me think of Ryn. The door behind her swings shut and clicks into the wall so that you wouldn't realise it was there.

Columen doesn't take any notice of her. Or of me, for that matter. He moves swiftly to the end of the corridor and leads us through a series of passages without looking back. When I'm outside, my sense of direction is quite good – even in a sea mist, I know how to get home, how to find the path, how to get round the patches of rotten ice where the adders nest – but inside the castle I'm lost. I try to concentrate, but I can't; the corners of my vision fizz darkly and blur with tiredness. It's as much as I can do to put one foot in front of the other. I haven't even got the presence of mind to count the turnings. I just follow mindlessly, like I've got no will of my own. Like a dog, or a slave, or a ghost.

But when we turn left into a big pillared gallery I know where he's going. It's the way I came this morning. The Duke's apartments are at the end of the hall.

The tiredness vanishes like a flame that's been blown out. No. *No.* What's going on? He can't . . . I don't understand, I can't . . . I stop dead, feeling my pulse in the roof of my mouth, struggling against the panic. I'd rather die . . .

Columen's in front of me, so I don't know how he knows I've stopped, but quicker than green he turns on his heel and grabs my arm above the elbow, gripping right down to the bone, like a bird of prey. I flinch, and he drops his hand. But he still says, 'Argent.' It's a command.

My mouth is too dry to speak. I think about running, but there's nowhere to go.

Columen gives me a long, steady look. Then he walks between the guards, who glance at him briefly and then go back to staring rigidly in front of them. He gives another flick of the wrist in my direction, to say, *Follow me, come on.* And I do.

I go through the archway, into the smoke and the noise of men gaming and drinking and joking, the harsh over-muscular sounds of lots of people speaking Evgard. Except that now, as they look up, they go quiet, until there's only the Duke finishing his sentence, and then there's silence. The familiar knot of terror gathers in my stomach as he looks up, slowly, from the dice he's just rolled. He sees Columen. Then he sees me.

He leans back, stretching his hands out on the arms of the chair, like a cat showing its claws, and tilts his head back, looking at us. It makes me feel cold. But in front of me Columen shifts his weight slightly, mirroring his father. It's so subtle that it's hard to say exactly what's changed, just a tiny alteration in the

109

angle of his chin or his back. Whatever it is, though, it makes them look the same: staring each other out, balanced, reflecting each other. It reminds me of the moment just before a fight starts. It feels dangerous.

Then the Duke grins. 'Columen . . .' he says silkily, and turns to me. '*Vermiculus* . . .' It means *grub*. Like one of the white squidgy maggots that eat dead animals. Columen lets the silence hang for too long. Then he drops to one knee and bends his head. 'My lord.' The Duke waits. So does everyone else. Columen looks up, straight into his father's eyes. For a strange, frozen moment it's as though there's a sort of tenderness in the way they look at each other. Then he says, 'I have a favour to ask.'

'Indeed . . .' It's hard to know if it's a statement or a question.

'This slave . . .' Columen flicks a finger over his shoulder without looking at me. 'I want him to teach me Mereish.'

The Duke doesn't show surprise. His face is very still. But somehow I know he's taken aback, caught off-guard. He glances up at me and then quickly away, almost as though he doesn't want to catch my eye. 'I see. And why should I give him to you?'

Columen shrugs. 'Because I'm your beloved son?'

The Duke's mouth twitches. 'Not beloved enough, I'm afraid.'

'Then because I should learn Mereish. Please. I only know the swear words.' He leans forward and says again, 'Please.' It sounds funny, coming from him.

'No.' The joke's over; the Duke looks away, picks up his cup. Columen's been dismissed. But he stays where he is.

'I'll buy him from you.'

The Duke frowns. 'No.'

'*Please* –'

'No.' His voice is so cold it makes the back of my throat ache.

Columen rocks back on his heels. He starts to get up – at least, I think he starts to get up, his shoulders sagging – but then he drops slowly back to his knees. His expression has changed. He leans forward and says softly, 'I'll throw dice for him.'

He's joking. Isn't he? You don't throw dice for *people*. Of course, to these Evgard bastards, I'm not a person – but I thought he was different, I thought he was on my side. He seemed . . . Then I want to kick myself for being so stupid, for being taken in so quickly.

The Duke's eyes narrow; he licks his lips. 'And what will you bet with?'

Columen glances round briefly, as though he's look-ing for ideas. 'If you win,' he says slowly, 'I'll go on the next raid to Marydd.'

'You want to gamble with slaves you haven't even got yet?' The Duke laughs, as though he admires Columen's audacity.

Columen looks back at him without blinking. 'Yes.' He could be talking about my father, or Ryn, or my grandmother. He'd be there, hunting them down, the way I was hunted down. I want to kill him. I can't move.

The Duke nods. 'All right. Highest roll takes all.' It's happening so quickly that I can't take it in – what will happen if he wins? If there's another raid? – but already he's picking up the die sitting by his hand, and rubbing it in his palm. Unexpectedly he throws, so quickly it makes Columen jump. He smiles. 'Eleven. Not regretting it, are you?'

The atmosphere has changed, in the blink of an eye, unbearably. Now everyone's leaning forward, excited, hungry, the way they did that first night. I feel sick, sick all the way to the inside of my bones. This is what it's like to be nothing, to be worth absolutely *nothing*. They're gambling with me as though I were an object. I'm a game they can play, that's all.

Columen's hand is shaking. When he reaches forward for the die he can hardly hold it. Then suddenly his whole arm twitches, and I see the die fall out of his hand on to the stone floor. He says, 'Wait – that's not my throw – I just dropped it –' and starts to scrabble for the die. The Duke laughs, leaning back in his chair. The men swap glances. When Columen kneels up again he looks flushed and shamefaced. He deserves it. He deserves more than that. I hope he rots in hell.

He grimaces nervously. Of course he's going to lose. He'd have to roll a twelve. And you can see that he knows he's already lost, pretty much, because he drops the die on to the table as though it's not even very important. As though he's given up. He doesn't even throw it properly – like he can't be bothered – just drops it. He hardly even looks at how it lands.

Twelve.

Silence. Silence that settles on everything like snow. Until the Duke says, 'I see. Congratulations, Columen.' He means the opposite.

'Thank you.' Columen stands up swiftly and inclines his head.

'Take the *luridus* and get out of my sight.' It means

sallow, sickly-pale. 'And you, boy –'

I look him in the eye. 'Me?'

'You have extraordinary luck. Don't push it.' He turns back to Columen, who's on the balls of his feet, ready to leave, like a runner before the beginning of his race. 'What you want this pathetic specimen for I can't imagine. Except the obvious, I suppose.' This time when he looks at me I look away, in spite of myself. The hate rises in my mouth like bile. I promise I'll kill him, one day. I'll kill them both. 'I thought you had higher standards. This boy is a traitor, you know. He'll never be more than that. Just a *ciccus*.' The men laugh, nodding at me maliciously.

Ciccus. An apple-core. A nothing. A nought.

'Oh,' Columen says coolly, 'I'm not sure about that.' He lets the pause lengthen for a split second. 'Don't be a bad loser, Father.' And then, before anyone has time to wonder – *did he really just say that? Is he out of his mind?* – he turns and walks past me, pulling me after him. He walks without hesitation past Iaspis, through the archway, and back down the gallery towards his own rooms. I go with him, because there's nowhere else to go; but I'm so angry I'm shaking as though I've got a fever. I almost reach out for the knife sheathed in his back. *Shudfargtte. Varesh ryglyng. You think I'm nothing. You* threw dice *for me*.

He flicks a latch somewhere to get back into his room, looks away, turns back to me, easily, about to say something. This is the moment.

And before I've even thought about it his dagger is in my hand, fitting into my fingers as if it was made for me. It's light, and sharp. It catches the light. It's at his throat. I hold my hand there, steady, feeling the blade just start to draw blood.

He looks so *surprised*. As though he doesn't understand what he's done.

'You bastard,' someone says, and it takes a moment to realise it's me. I sound hoarse, fierce, unfamiliar. 'You think I'm *nothing*. You gambled with my life. You said you'd go out and get more slaves from Marydd. You said –' Something cracks. My voice. I stare at Columen. I swallow and try again, forcing against the harsh edges in my throat. 'You think I'm . . . *ciccus*. That's what your father called me.'

His eyes narrow and widen again. 'Argent . . .'

I press harder and there's a tiny red flower expanding on his collar. 'You *threw dice* for me. You were *playing* . . .'

'Wait.' He brings one hand up gently to the knife. There's something in his eyes. I let him push the blade away from his neck, but I keep it up, in front of me, at the level of his face. 'Watch. Just let me . . .' His face is very calm, very still. Deliberately, he holds his arm in front of his body, as if he's showing me something. He shakes his hand, and a little dodecahedron rolls out of his sleeve into his palm. A die. He drops it on the floor, at my feet. Twelve. Slowly he crouches, picks it up, rolls it again. Twelve. Again. Twelve. I meet his gaze, and he grins, slyly, inviting me to grin back. 'It's weighted, Argent. It's a trick.' He watches me.

I don't say anything. I don't know what to say.

'You're right. It would have been an awful thing to do.' He stands up, quickly now, and takes the knife easily out of my hand. He sheathes it in the small of his back as though nothing's happened. 'But I knew I'd win.' A beat. 'Did you really think . . . ?'

I still can't say anything. But he doesn't wait for a reply. He pushes the door open with one hand and beckons me through.

'Oh,' he says, 'and as for thinking you're an apple-core . . .' He doesn't look at me; he smiles into the middle distance like it's a friend. '*Non ciccus, sed cor*,' he says, quietly, so quietly I almost don't hear it.

It's a pun. It means, not a core, but a heart. Not a nothing, but an everything.

SEVEN

Everything went in the black plastic bag. Everything. The Book and the papers and the Latin dictionary Francis used for names sometimes and the mapping pens and the special silver ink. All of it. Everything. Michael junked it all.

Once, ages ago, right at the beginning of the stuff at the comp, he'd come home and told his mum what was happening. He didn't mean to; it just came out. All the stuff about them taking the mickey (he wasn't going to say *piss* to his mum) and calling him names and saying he was clever, and the way they'd push him sometimes in the corridor and 'borrow' money and not give it back. It wasn't that bad – he found out later how much worse it could get – but at the time he thought it was awful. And when he ended up telling his mum he couldn't stop himself starting to cry, so that there were tears and mucus and spit everywhere and it took him ages to calm down. He hiccupped his way through the whole story, like his body was trying to stop him talking about it. He could remember how

116

salty his mouth tasted, how difficult it was to swallow. He could remember the smell of his own snot.

His mum had hooked a lock of hair behind her ear, smoothing it back over and over again. She'd rubbed his back and put her arms round him and told him to drink his tea. She'd waited until he could breathe in properly, until he wasn't sobbing any more. Then, very gently, she told him not to let it upset him. 'They're just jealous of you, darling. If you ignore them they'll get bored. They're probably just worried about *not* doing well in tests. They must be unhappy themselves, and they're just taking it out on you. Try to forget about it.' She smiled at him. 'You know, sweetheart, a lot of people wouldn't think being called *clever* was an insult!'

Michael looked at her. He stared into her eyes until he had to blink. Was that all she could say? That *couldn't* be all . . . *Please, Mum, help me, you've got to help* . . . She smiled back at him, reassuring and loving and totally, utterly *useless*. She couldn't do anything. *They're just jealous of you. Try to forget about it.* She didn't have a clue. And suddenly, horribly, it hit him, as if someone was wringing out his stomach like a flannel. He was on his own. He always had been, of course – but somehow it was worse, because now he *knew* there wasn't anyone to go to. He shouldn't even have told his mum. He looked away and stood up, quite calmly. He put his mug in the dishwasher, picked up his bag and went upstairs. 'You're right,' he said flatly over his shoulder. 'I'm fine, really. I'll just ignore it.' She said something else as he closed the door, but he couldn't hear the words.

The stupid thing was, he actually tried to do what

she said. Then, and later, when it got really bad. He ignored them, he tried not to let them upset him, he tried to walk through the school wide-eyed and empty and non-existent, as transparent and slippery as a jellyfish.

And when he came home, he sat and ignored himself. He pretended he wasn't there; he was just an empty Michael-shaped space, just air and dust. But he had to try harder and harder. He had to sit for longer and longer before he felt himself fade away. After that last day at the comp he sat like that for hours, with his head on his knees and his arms braced over his head like a passenger on a crashing aeroplane. Maybe, if he did it properly, he'd be able to forget about it. He'd be like everyone else. He wouldn't be a loser any more.

Sometimes it worked, just for a bit, and he went numb. He could function then. It was a sort of relief, that weird airless gap when you could fold up your pyjamas or make a cup of tea. But mostly, even then, you could see it all coming back, rising on the horizon like a tidal wave. And then it was there again, and – well, you might have made a cup of tea, but you couldn't *drink* it, not without throwing up. You could stare at the TV, but everything you saw would be through a filter, like there was coloured plastic over the screen. Everything was in shades of you're-a-loser. And he'd always be a loser. He was *nothing*.

He'd grab on to the arm of the sofa and breathe, just to get through it. *Don't let it upset you . . .* but it was too late, he was already upset, the way a glass of water gets upset. That was him all over the floor. All he could do was hold on, and wait for the misery to recede. It had to, eventually. Sooner or later he had to come out the other side.

It was funny, really. He *had* come out the other side. He'd made it to the surface. He'd come up, blinking, into . . .

Into Evgard.

Now he sat, exactly where he used to sit, at the foot of his bed. He stared at the black bin-bag and waited for the flood to hit.

In Ghist Marydd there's a custom called *sterdark*. Sometimes it's a punishment; but mostly it's something people choose to do, as a kind of mourning ritual. Normally you'd go *sterdark* if your twin died, or your firstborn. Once you're marked as *sterdark*, you're invisible. As far as other people are concerned, you don't exist. You can go anywhere you want, steal food, dance and scream for help and cry, and no one will take any notice of you. It's as though you're a ghost.

Michael would have liked to go *sterdark*. He almost felt like he had; as though Evgard was the real world, and he didn't really exist. It made it easier, if he could close his eyes and be somewhere else, someone else. He could blot himself out, and Francis, and Shitley, and his mum; he could let Evgard carry him like a river. On Monday morning, as he was walking down the fifth-form corridor to his locker, he was thinking, *I'm not here. Not really. I'm not here. I'm sterdark*.

Francis was there, standing at his locker, tapping his fountain pen against his teeth. Michael felt a jolt of hatred, like electricity; for a second he lost the untouchable feeling. He *was* real. He didn't want to be, but he was.

Then Francis looked round at Michael; and straight through him.

Michael thought madly, *Christ, I have, I have gone sterdark . . . He can't see me. I'm invisible*. He felt the shock of it, the disbelief, the weird humiliation. For a split second he felt like he could stand in the corridor stark naked and no one would take any notice. He swallowed. Francis had seen him – Michael knew that, he'd swear to it – but he carried on getting his books out of his locker as though he were on his own.

Michael's first instinct was to hit Francis. The way he stood there, calm, cold, acting like Michael had done something unforgiveable to *him*. It was infuriating. And the way he slid his books into his bag – precise, competent, utterly self-assured. Michael had a vision of smashing Francis's head into the locker door, the face-shaped dent it would leave, the blood . . . He took a deep breath and walked over to his own locker. He had to stand next to Francis to open it, and he felt himself flinching away as though Francis was twice as wide as he really was. That was when Francis did notice him: he gave Michael a swift, contemptuous sidelong look, like, *I'm not infectious, tosser*, and then turned away again as though even that was too much energy to spend on him. Michael felt that look in his gut; he didn't want to care, but he did. He wanted to grab Francis's arm, turn him round, say, *You bastard, what did I do? I really thought you liked me* . . . God, he was pathetic. He stared at the grey metal of his locker door. In his mind's eye he saw the black bin-bag of Evgard stuff that he'd put next to the bin at home. He couldn't move. He felt, more than saw, Francis shut his locker and swing his bag up on to his shoulder. *Go on, then, Harris, piss off . . .*

Behind him, someone said, 'Hey, Harrisss . . .'

Michael knew it was Shitley even before he looked round. There was something about the voice that made his stomach twist.

Francis turned sharply, then leant back against his locker as though he were perfectly at ease. 'Hey, Shitley,' he said, the mockery in his tone so subtle Michael wasn't sure if Shitley would even notice it. 'How's tricks?'

'Not trying to pick up any third-years today?' Shitley leered meaningfully at Francis. He was standing in the middle of the corridor, blocking the exit.

For a moment Francis looked completely blank. Then he glanced away; a muscle flickered over his jawbone. He said, imitating Shitley's inflection exactly, 'Not torturing any third-years today?'

Shitley laughed, with a sort of nasty gurgle that set Michael's teeth on edge. 'Don't take it all so seriously, Harris. Your friend Bent Dick's used to it.'

'Right, and that makes it OK? Go to hell, Shitley.' Francis turned to pick up his bag and started to walk towards the doorway, but Shitley moved to block his path. 'Get out of my way.'

Shitley leant back on his heels and stayed where he was. 'Why are you so worried, anyway? He's just a little faggot, Harris. Just a little bender-boy. He's not worth worrying about. You seem very . . . *protective*.' He drew out the consonants.

'What's that supposed to mean?'

Shitley smiled, curling his lips obscenely. 'Well – you and Thompson here . . . you're pretty *close*, wouldn't you say? I just wondered if you had, well, you know, a *fellow feeling*.' He slid a malicious glance at Michael.

'Screw you, Shipley,' Michael said. He turned back to his locker and pretended to be sorting through his books. His hands were shaking. He had to fight to keep them steady.

'Sorry,' Shitley said, a bubble of satisfaction in his voice, 'have I touched a nerve?'

Silence.

'Wow. So you two *are* . . . not that I'm surprised. Everyone knew.'

Michael punched the locker door so hard that the whole block rocked back against the wall with a clang. He swung round; Shitley and Francis were both staring at him. '*Fuck* you. Go fuck yourself. Go to hell.' He hardly knew what he was saying. He looked straight at Francis. 'And you can fuck off, too.' Francis held his gaze: neutral, uncompromising.

Shitley whistled softly. 'Language . . .'

But it was like Shitley wasn't even there. Francis tilted his chin slightly, so that he was looking down at Michael; they stared at each other. Then Francis shrugged. 'Oh dear,' he said coldly, 'I hope nothing's *bothering* you.' When Michael didn't answer, he laughed. It sounded painful. He said, 'My God, you're a wanker, Thompson.'

Shitley said gleefully, 'Lovers' tiff?'

Francis turned, wearily. 'And you're a cock, Shitley. Christ, I don't know why I'm wasting time on you. Either of you.' He spun on his heel, and this time Shitley let him past.

Michael's hand hurt. He had to pick up his bag with his left; there was a smear of blood across his knuckles. He flexed and unflexed his fist without looking up, hoping that Shitley would just go away. Jesus, he felt awful, like he was about to cry. That was the last thing he needed: but he kept seeing Francis, that look on his face, *My God, you're a wanker, Thompson* . . . He said to himself, *Don't think about it. Don't think about it.* And the worst thing was, he just didn't *get* it. It didn't make sense – even though he knew what was going on. It didn't add up. It was horrible, and it was all *wrong*.

Shitley said, 'So, *is* he a poof?'

'No, of course he bloody isn't,' Michael said. He almost added, 'He's a complete shit, though,' but something stopped him. Francis might be a shit – well, he *was* – but that didn't mean he was as bad as Shitley. He kept his mouth shut.

Shitley moved aside to let him pass. 'He's not too keen on *you* any more, is he?' His tone could have been friendly, except for the look on his face. The Shark Look: he'd scented blood.

'Get stuffed, Shipley.' Michael was determined not to look at him. He kept his gaze on the carpet. He watched a dark brown stain, unblinking, until the edges of his vision blurred.

'What did you do? Steal his boyfriend?'

Michael looked up; stared straight into Shitley's eyes. 'Look, piss off, will you? Leave him alone. Just because he stopped you bullying that kid . . . It's none of your business, anyway.' For a moment he heard himself – sad middle-class accent, crack in the voice, stumbling over the words – and felt a pulse of pride even so, that he'd said it, when it needed saying . . . and it took another few seconds before he remembered that it was pointless. Because Francis wasn't his friend, hadn't ever been his friend. He wasn't worth defending.

Shitley looked away, glancing over his shoulder. Then he turned back to Michael, head on one side. 'Ah . . . how touching. What loyalty.'

Michael didn't answer. He hoisted his bag on to his shoulder and walked past Shitley without meeting his eyes. He didn't bother to look where he was going.

He walked straight into someone. He felt the impact of his shoulder on their chest and threw himself back like he'd walked into an electric fence. He said, 'Sorry, sorry . . .' before he realised it was Francis, coming back the other way. He stepped to one side, to get past. Francis didn't move.

'Did I scare you? Or are you frightened of catching something?' Francis's voice was icy. 'I thought only fleas jumped like that. Fleas, and other vermin . . . But then, maybe that's pretty appropriate.'

'Sorry . . .' Michael said again, helplessly.

'Not at all,' Francis said. He still didn't move. 'I hope I'm not interrupting anything.' His eyes flicked to Shitley, then back to Michael. 'After all, you're going to need some new friends.' It sounded like an accusation.

'I wasn't . . .' Michael didn't know what to say.

'Please. As if I'm interested.' Francis went to his locker, opened it, got out a book, put it in his bag. Michael and Shitley stood in silence, watching him. When he turned back, he looked Michael briefly up and down, ignoring Shitley completely. For a second his face was sort of regretful – almost *pleading*, Michael thought, although it didn't make sense. 'It's a pity you're such a loser, Michael. If you weren't so spineless . . .' There was a long pause, as though Francis had asked a question and was waiting for the answer. Then he shrugged, tightly, and walked past Michael.

It must have been as an afterthought, the way he turned, just as he'd got clear of Shitley. The way he looked at Michael, met his eyes, and waited for a split second, until Michael was on the point of saying something. The way he said it, so offhandedly, as though it hardly mattered, just loud enough for Shitley to hear. The way he *said* it.

'I expect that's why you got battered at your old school. Not surprising, really.'

Silence.

Michael waited for his ears to tell him he'd heard wrong. He waited for the words to mean something else. Francis hadn't said that. He just *hadn't*. That was all there was to it. Francis couldn't know – Michael had never told him – and anyway he wouldn't, he just *wouldn't* . . . except that this was a different Francis. Who hated him; who obviously *did* know, somehow . . . But Michael still waited, too incredulous to be angry.

Francis closed his eyes. When he opened them again his face was blank; he didn't meet Michael's look. He walked away. Michael watched him go.

Then the fury hit him, as suddenly as an express train, so hard he wouldn't have been surprised if it had lifted him off his feet. Jesus, Francis had really *said* that! *Bastard, bastard, bastard* . . . Michael couldn't think straight. As if the stuff at the comp was just – as if Francis knew – as if – and – *not surprising*

– as if Michael had *deserved* . . . And in front of Shitley . . . He was paralysed by it, breathless, winded. So Francis knew, he'd known, all the time, he *knew* – and he said *that* . . . *You fucker, Harris, you evil bastard shit* . . . Michael was so angry he didn't know what to do. He had to concentrate to take a deep breath. *OK, calm down, Thompson. Go and get a coffee. Don't punch anyone.*

Shitley said slyly, 'And normally he's such a nice guy . . .' He laughed, pushed his hair off his forehead, put one hand on Michael's shoulder. 'Guess you really got to him.'

Michael almost turned and hit Shitley. Instead he pulled away, roughly, and started to walk. Then, without really meaning to, he turned back. Suddenly he felt absolutely calm. He wasn't going to let it upset him. He heard himself speak like he was talking about the weather.

'Actually, Shipley, he *is* gay. Made a move on me. I said no, of course. That's why he's in such a paddy. He said not to tell anyone – but I think it's disgusting, frankly. I think he deserves all he gets.'

Shitley looked confused for a second. Then it was like Christmas had come early. 'So he *is* a poofter? I knew it!'

Michael felt sick. What was he *doing*? He thought, *Stop it, Michael, shut up, what the hell . . . ?* But he was still talking, like he didn't have any choice. 'Yeah, well, I should have guessed, I suppose. Bloody pansy.' *Jesus, Thompson!* He wasn't even homophobic, for God's sake. He didn't even know why he'd said it – except it was the worst thing, the only thing he *could* say that would make Francis's life a total misery.

Especially in this school. And then *Michael* could say, *Expect that's why you got battered. Not surprising, really.*

Shitley chuckled. 'Yeah. Bloody perverts. Repulsive.'

'Right.' *Just walk, Michael. Left foot, right, left. Don't let yourself think.*

Shitley said warmly, 'You know, Thompson, you're OK. I have to say, I thought Harris had you exactly where he wanted you – but actually you're all right.' He grinned at him artlessly. 'Don't worry about Harris, he's a loser.'

'I know.' Michael didn't look at Shitley; he stared at the wall across the corridor and thought, *Evgard. Francis betrayed Evgard. He pretended to be my friend. Now he's acting like he hates me.*

He thought, *So I haven't betrayed anything. There wasn't anything to betray.*

I haven't betrayed anything.

For the rest of the day he kept his head down. He just looked at his exercise book and tried to ignore the space next to him where Francis normally sat. He didn't let himself look round to see who Francis was sitting with. He didn't care. He was fine, sitting on his own. He even got through lunch; he played a mindless, infuriating game on his mobile until the bell rang and it was time for afternoon lessons.

In Maths he worked quicker than normal, but when he finished the questions Father Markham had set he went straight on to the next chapter without even looking up. He almost didn't have time to think: *If Francis was here we'd be pissing around.* He turned over another page and tried to forget that it would have been his turn to ask the Timewaster Question and that he needed four minutes thirty-three seconds to beat the record. That was over now. He had to pretend all that stuff had happened to someone else, ages ago. Not him.

And it worked, kind of. He felt OK. He got through the lesson, anyway. He stayed at his desk for as long as he could after the bell rang, but in the end he had to leave, wandering lazily after everyone else like it was just lethargy that had stopped him rushing out to get a coffee the way he normally did. He strolled along behind everyone else. He stopped to tie a shoelace. As he knelt he was thinking, OK, *five minutes at the drinks machine, five minutes for a cigarette* . . . He said to himself, *Yeah, OK, that should be enough. I hope. Then English, and I can go home.* He straightened up – not quickly – and carried on walking.

He wasn't really paying attention to anyone else. But as he went into the main building he saw Francis going up the stairs and he felt his gut twist. Shitley was slouching artistically against the banisters. Michael knew Francis had seen him – his jaw was clenched, and his freckles stood out against his temples – but he was acting like Shitley didn't exist. He walked carefully up the stairs, looking straight ahead, not meeting Shitley's gaze. Michael didn't want to stand there and watch him, but somehow he couldn't help himself. There was something in Shitley's eyes as he looked at Francis – a steady, gleeful light – that made Michael feel sick. He saw Shitley stretch one leg out to stop Francis getting past and told himself not to care. *Relax, Michael. It's not your problem.* But he couldn't stop himself staring.

Francis barely glanced up. He stepped over Shitley's trainer in one smooth movement like it was always there. He knew how to handle himself, you had to give him that. He gave Shitley the briefest of glances; then he carried on walking. Michael felt his heart give a tiny treacherous leap. Nothing was going to happen. He was just being paranoid.

Then Shitley said, 'Pervert.' It was almost under his breath. Michael could tell Francis had heard, because he flicked a casual, contemptuous V-sign over his shoulder, but he didn't stop walking.

Shitley turned to look after him. 'At least, that's what Thompson says . . .'

A fractional pause. Then Francis turned so quickly it looked like he'd stumbled. For a second Michael thought, *He's going to hit him. Jesus, Francis is going to* hit *someone* . . . but Francis was stock-still, staring straight at Shitley. Michael saw him swallow. He said, 'What did you say?'

Shitley smiled, letting it hang in the air. He whistled softly between his teeth. Michael counted five, slowly, before Shitley said, 'Sorry about that . . . 'Fraid Thompson spilt the beans. Told me everything . . . That's right, isn't it? You're a poofter?'

Michael felt the words drip into the pit of his stomach like acid. *Oh God, oh Jesus, what did I say?* Shitley leant back even further against the banister, his hands in his pockets.

Francis blinked. Michael stared up at his face and waited for him to come back with something clever and disdainful. *Go on*, he thought bitterly, *you do a*

129

great line in effortless contempt. Just pretend Shitley's me. At the very least you can tell him to screw himself. But Francis just stood there, face blank, as though he'd misunderstood.

Shitley started to laugh. And you could see why, because in a bizarre sort of way it *was* funny – Francis standing there with that look on his face, like he'd died standing up . . . Shitley leant forward. 'What's the matter, Harris? Not come out yet? Trying to keep it quiet?' His tone was insinuating, confidential. It was weird, the way he made it sound worse than *poofter* or *pervert*. It set Michael's teeth on edge.

Francis said, 'No.' It wasn't an answer to anything. It was like he was talking to himself, about something else.

Shitley looked momentarily confused. Then his face went back into the feral grin. 'Oh *no*,' he said, and flapped a limp-wristed hand. 'Have I spoilt your *surprise*?'

Francis looked straight at him, as though he'd only just remembered he was there. 'Get lost, Shitley.' But he sounded defeated, like his heart wasn't in it.

Michael thought, *Come on, Harris, you can do better than that, for God's sake, don't be so pathetic.* Somewhere in the back of his mind he heard Francis's voice, cold, precise, *I expect that's why you got battered . . . not surprising, really . . .* but in spite of himself he didn't want Francis to get rattled, didn't want to see that odd, lost, deadened look on his face. Especially when it was his fault. It was all *wrong*.

Shitley cowered back, mock-afraid. 'Oooo. I'm *scared*.' Then he stood up straight and laughed, brushing his hair back with one hand. He could smell blood: now he could relax. Magnanimously he beckoned him through. Francis turned his shoulder away and slid past, quickly, without looking at him. Michael didn't believe it, somehow, the way Francis walked past Shitley, eyes on the ground, like he'd lost in a fight. Jesus, what was *wrong* with him? He'd called Shitley a sadistic bastard, for God's sake, he'd called him Shitley to his face, just that morning he'd told him to go to hell, and now he was slinking away like . . . well, like something had changed. It didn't make sense. It made Michael uneasy. Just because Shitley had said, *Thompson says* . . . It was strange. But anyway, no one could say he didn't deserve it. Francis was probably going to see his mates now and laugh at Evgard, laugh at Michael, the way he'd been laughing for ages. He was even more of a bastard than Shitley. Anyone who could betray you like that . . . He had it coming.

Michael looked up at the staircase. Shitley was still there, slouched in his vantage point, ready to trip people up as they went past. For a second Michael felt a pulse of hatred so strong it actually knocked him forward, off balance. *You'll pay for this, Shitley. And you, Harris. It's your fault too. I hope you both rot in hell.* He felt his face go blank with the force of it.

Shitley caught his eye and waved.

EIGHT

Thompson's Third Law: don't bunk lessons, because someone will notice.

So he went to English. He opened his book at the right page. He put his hand up, once, to ask a question. He didn't meet Francis's eyes across the room; he didn't try. When the bell rang he packed his books mechanically; he had to get his stuff from his locker. Then he could go home. Thank God.

He clung to the feeling of unreality. *I'm not really here.* None of this was really happening. He concentrated on summoning the willpower to get up the stairs and to the fifth-form corridor. By the time he got to the top of the stairs he was fighting his way past first-years going in the opposite direction and he felt less real than ever.

He stood there for a moment. In the corridor beyond, Dan Holdstock was on his mobile, talking loudly, and Murray was weaving round him, throwing mock punches, dodging out of reach. Holdstock said, 'Oi – tosser! Piss off –' and then added hastily, 'No, not you, sweetheart . . .' He hissed, 'Piss *off*, Murray,' and then went back to the phone. Michael felt his face move like he was smiling. *They're* real. He caught a glimpse of someone behind them, leaning forward to put something into a locker. Francis. Michael turned, ready to bolt, hating himself. Running away – *because that's what you always do, isn't it, Thompson? You coward*. He shot another glance over his shoulder, poised to leg it to the common room, and then he stopped, frozen. He'd seen a flash of white paper, skinny hands slipping it through the gap in a locker door. Michael's locker. A piece of A4 paper, blank, folded over. Jesus, the notes . . . *I'VE SEEN EVGARD* . . . He felt his heart pause. He couldn't breathe. He held himself still, because if he moved he'd trip or just collapse at the knees like a girl. What was going on? He didn't get it. *Francis?* And – how had he got there so quickly, ahead of Michael? He waited for Francis to straighten up and turn towards him.

But it wasn't Francis. It was Luke.

Michael stood still, watching him, letting every-thing fall into place around him like a ceiling starting to crumble. *I'VE SEEN EVGARD*. Even before Luke turned to look at him – even before Michael saw his expression – he knew. He thought, *So it was Luke, it was Luke all along, the malicious little sod* . . . but he wasn't exactly angry yet, just curious, sort of wonder-ing. He couldn't think clearly; it was like swimming through crude oil. *Why would he do that? Why would he bother? And why would Francis show Luke, of all people? What's going on? Do they* both *hate me?*

Wait. He caught himself. *If it was* Luke. *If it was Luke, then –*

It was like someone punched him. He felt it in his gut, immediately, before his brain could get there. It winded him. Oh *Jesus* –

Michael closed his eyes. He made himself think slowly, carefully, as though he was writing it down; but he already knew . . . He thought, *Suppose Francis took something home to work on. And he left it on his desk. In his desk, perhaps, doesn't matter which, because he always moans about not being able to lock it. Anyway. Doesn't matter. Luke looks at it. And Francis hasn't shown him, doesn't even know that he's seen it, maybe. Until he gets the note that's meant for me. And then – of course – he just chucks it, Christ, of course he does, he chucks it in the bin, he doesn't mention it, because it's just his kid brother, he's just irritated, and that means, oh Jesus, so he hasn't done anything wrong, he hasn't betrayed Evgard, he never hated me, he's still my mate, he hasn't betrayed anything, but I've, shit, oh shit, what have I done, I've told Shitley –*

He had Luke pinned up against the lockers before he even knew he was going to move. He'd kill him. He'd fucking kill him. He felt the smack of Luke's head against the metal, heard a dull knock as one side of his head struck the lock. Luke flailed, caught off-guard, and tried to twist away, but Michael held him tightly, fingers dangerously close to his larynx, pushing him backwards with all his strength. He felt like he could push him right through the wall if he wanted to. 'You little – you *evil* little – you –'

'What? What?' Luke scrabbled at Michael's hands. 'Let me go! I haven't done anything.'

'Yeah, right.' Michael was calm, suddenly in control.

He let his hands tighten slightly on Luke's collar. 'You've been writing me anonymous notes, haven't you?'

'No.' Luke's eyes flickered away. 'Don't know what you're talking about.'

'Tell me the truth, you vicious little bastard, or I'll strangle you.' Michael heard himself speak and thought, *My God, I mean it, I actually mean it. I will strangle him.*

'I haven't –' Luke choked and pushed frantically at Michael's chest. 'Stop it, you psycho! I haven't done anything!' He tried to wrench himself away. Michael braced his feet and let his hands take the weight of his body. He felt the sinews in Luke's neck under his thumbs. Luke gasped for breath and shook his head. 'All right, all right, stop, I'm sorry –' He coughed, his eyes watering. Michael relaxed his grip, but only a bit, not enough to let him get away.

'Tell me what you did.'

Luke had stopped struggling. He cleared his throat and coughed again. 'It was only a joke. Just a joke. What's the big deal?' He stared sullenly at Michael as though he expected him to look away first. Michael held his gaze, levelly, until Luke's eyes dropped. He muttered, 'There's no need to get all queeny about it.'

Michael opened one hand, like a pianist stretching for an octave, until the ball of his thumb was on Luke's larynx. He pressed gently. 'A joke?'

Luke swallowed. Michael felt his throat bulge and contract under his hands. 'Just so you got a bit rattled, you know. Like, nothing serious. I mean, chill out. It's not like anyone got hurt.'

Except me, Michael wanted to say. *Except your*

brother. Except that you've screwed up the only thing in my life that I could bear to think about. You vile, obnoxious, poisonous little bastard. You don't have a clue, do you? But he couldn't speak. His throat constricted as though he wanted to laugh.

Luke pulled ineffectually at Michael's fingers. 'Now will you let me go?' His voice was high and hoarse. 'Let me *go*. You're crazy.'

'Right.' Michael let him struggle. It was like someone else was holding him there, at arm's length, digging their thumbnails into his neck; Michael was just watching. 'Let me get this straight.' He waited for Luke to stop squirming and meet his eyes. 'What did you see? A map of Evgard? And did Francis show it to you or did you steal it?'

Luke had given up trying to get loose. Suddenly he was a dead weight, limp and unresponsive; only his eyes were alive. He tilted his chin mulishly. 'I dunno. Just a map. Francis left it on his desk. Anyway, why would I steal it? It's, like, so *sad*. You and my brother are real losers.'

So why bother to screw up our lives? But Michael knew the answer to that. *Because we're there, that's all. Because he can.* He stared at his thumbs and thought, *If I brought my hands seven centimetres closer together . . .* With an effort he loosened his grip. He said, 'So the notes haven't got anything to do with Francis.'

Luke shrugged. Now he could breathe properly the cocky glint was coming back into his eyes. 'You should leave him alone. He was cool before you came along.'

It was true. Michael knew it was true. He couldn't even have a mate without it going pear-shaped. He stared at Luke, wishing there was something he could say to defend himself. 'So you thought you'd just try and – what? – scare me off?'

'Maybe.' It was a challenge.

'Well, tough. I'm not going anywhere. So get over it.' It would have sounded good; except that Michael knew how lame it was. It was too late, he'd already gone somewhere. Somewhere he didn't want to go. He pushed the thought away and looked straight into Luke's eyes. They were so like Francis's he felt sick. The same odd metallic brown, the same shape. God. He blinked and forced himself to keep looking. 'From now on, you leave me, and Francis, alone. Got it? You fuck off like a good little boy and never come near me again. If you ever, *ever* do anything else like this –'

'You'll what?' Luke tilted his head back belligerently.

'I'll kill you,' Michael said, and meant it. 'Understand?' And there must have been something about the way he said it, because Luke just bit his lip and nodded briefly. Slowly Michael let go of him, feeling the blood start to tingle in his palms as he unclenched his hands. The collar of Luke's blazer still held a web of creases where Michael had pulled it. He started to turn away.

Luke muttered, 'Tosser.'

Michael looked back at him. Jesus, those eyes, it was uncanny. 'You think so?' He waited, staring at Luke until his face blurred and he could have been someone – anyone – else. 'Maybe you're right.'

Then he smacked Luke across the face, as hard as he could.

* * *

He had to find Francis.

He knew – rationally – he knew the best thing was just to wait by the lockers for Francis to turn up. Chances were Francis would need to pick up some books or something for his homework. So he stood in the space between the corner of the block of lockers and the wall and waited; a couple of people clocked him and said hello, but then there were too many people around for anyone to notice him properly. And it was just as well, because he could hardly breathe, let alone talk to anyone. He thought, *This is stupid. This is really stupid. What if he doesn't turn up? I have to talk to him. I have to explain.* He was jumping around like an idiot, craning to check that Francis wasn't somewhere in the scrum of people round the lockers, looking from side to side like he was watching a tennis match. *Come on, Harris, come* on . . . He waited there, until pretty much everyone had gone, and there was just Tom Townsend and one of his mates pissing around with a ball of screwed-up paper, and then they left too, and he was on his own. By that time he knew Francis wasn't going to turn up. He must have gone straight home. *Shit.*

It was OK. He'd just tell him tomorrow. He'd make sure he cornered him tomorrow morning. After registration, if he had to. It would be fine. Michael tried to ignore the urgency that sat like a supernova in his stomach saying, *You have to tell him, you have to tell him* now . . . Jesus, what could happen between now and tomorrow morning? He said to himself, *Stop being a tosser. Chill out. It'll be fine.* He pushed aside the thought of Luke's face, and what Francis would

138

think of him when he saw it. *For God's sake, Thompson, don't worry about that! Luke* asked *for it, the little bastard. Forget it. He had it coming.*

But Michael would have done anything, anything in the world, to be able to explain to Francis. He couldn't get rid of his own voice, ringing in his ears like a dream: *Actually, Shipley, he* is gay. *Made a move on me . . .* It haunted him. Francis hadn't done anything to deserve it. And it was the worst thing, the absolute worst thing he could have said, especially to Shitley. *Oh, bloody hell.* If only he could talk to Francis now, if only he hadn't gone home already . . .

It was a mad, irrational hope. But all the same Michael swung his bag on to his shoulder and started to sprint down the stairs. Maybe, just maybe, he'd gone to have a cigarette before he went home. He did that sometimes. Michael had seen him occasionally down in the belt of trees after school; he couldn't smoke at home because his mum would have gone mad. Maybe that was why he hadn't come up to get his stuff yet. Maybe he was there. Michael started to run, thinking, *Please, come on, please, Harris, don't have gone home already, please be there, I can explain, I can explain everything . . .*

He pelted down the stairs, swung himself round to his left and through the door without slowing down. He hurried across the lawn, then broke into a run towards the music block. Francis would be down by the trees. Michael knew he would. He had to be. Michael felt relief like a wave, catching up with him, pushing him forward, because they could talk properly there. They'd be on their own; no one could overhear and take the piss. He could explain everything. It was going to be all right. He ran as fast as he could, past the music block, past the cricket pavilion. Almost there.

If he hadn't stumbled, catching his shoe in a tangle of long grass, he might not even have noticed them. It was as he fell, twisting awkwardly, that he caught sight of them, just out of the corner of his eye, and it took him a second look, pushing himself up on his hands, before he was sure. Shitley and his mates. He struggled to his feet. They were a long way away, the other side of the music block – too far away to notice Michael – but all the same he didn't like having them there, at his back. He carried on towards the trees, but slowly now. The fear in his chest uncurled like a hand, digging into him. There was something nagging at him, wordlessly. *Pull yourself together, Thompson, stop being such a girl* . . . But what *was* it? There was something. Something about Shitley, about his gang. Had he seen . . . ?

He slowed down. He tried to make himself keep going, one foot, the next, but there was a kind of dread, dragging him backwards. Just suppose . . . Francis. *Had* he caught a glimpse –? No. He was being paranoid. Francis would be down by the trees. Michael could see it, as clearly as a photo. He'd be smoking. He'd have his jacket hung over a branch. And when he saw Michael, he'd look round, with that expression of, *What do* you *want?* Michael squeezed his eyes shut as he walked, *willing* Francis to be there, on his own, cool and solitary and self-sufficient, the way he always was. *Please, Harris,* please . . . but all he could think about was Shitley's gang in a straggly, ominous circle; the flash he'd seen of dark red hair, a familiar turn of the head. He opened his eyes again. He was close enough to see the space where Francis should have been, between the trees, silhouetted by the sun. There wasn't anyone there.

He closed his eyes again, opened them. As if he could magic Francis into existence. Please. *Please*. But it didn't work.

He turned; ran back the way he'd come, sprinting like his life depended on it. The dread in his stomach was burning him now, pushing up, filling his lungs with fire. He flung himself forward, half sliding on the grass, struggling to keep his balance. He'd got it wrong. He was seeing things. He had to be. This wasn't happening. But even before he got there, throwing himself round the corner towards the music block, he knew what he'd seen, knew he hadn't been imagining it. His heart was going like mad: go *on*, go *on*, go *on* . . . He had to force himself to slow down, so he didn't run straight into Shitley's gang. He walked carefully, fighting for breath, over to the corner of the building, and peered round. *Please, God, let Francis not be there. Please. I'll do anything. Let Francis not* –

But he was. He was there.

Michael could see him now, almost surrounded, standing stiffly with his hands in his pockets. Shitley was standing in front of him, smoking, just too close. And the gang. Michael saw, with a kind of sick horror, that there were more of them than before, like this was a bigger deal. They were standing around, ready to close ranks, still waiting for the signal. Before they moved in for the kill. For a second Michael wanted to turn and run. It wasn't Francis in the middle of that

141

circle, it was *him*. He had to get away. He could taste his own fear. But he held himself there, hanging on to the edge of the wall with his fingers, because he knew if he ran away he'd hate himself for the rest of his life. He gritted his teeth and made himself hold on.

Shitley rocked back on his heels, staring at Francis. 'So, gay boy, shouldn't you be on your way home? Or did you stay late to suck a few dicks?'

'Piss off, Shitley. Stop being such a creep.' God, his *voice*. It was so close to the way Francis normally talked: except for the strain underneath the casual tone, the strident note that said he was scared and trying to cover it. Michael thought, appalled, *He's really* afraid. *He's shitting himself.*

'Not denying it, then.' Shitley laughed; a ripple of mirth spread out through the gang like a disease. 'Or don't you even get that far? Maybe you have to get your kicks on your own.' Shitley took a long, pensive drag of his cigarette. 'I heard something about a faggot once. He put a hamster in a freezer bag, right, and shoved it up himself. Apparently as it dies it's very *titillating* . . .'

'That's disgusting.' Francis met Shitley's gaze head-on; suddenly you could see he was angry. 'You're repulsive, Shitley.'

Shitley smiled. 'But it's not people like me that do things like that, Harris. It's people like you.'

Francis gave a weird, tight, incredulous laugh. 'I don't have time for this.' He glanced round as though he was going to make a break for it, but as he looked the gang moved subtly together, blocking his path. He set his jaw and stared resolutely forward. 'For God's sake, Shitley. What's your problem?'

Shitley tilted his head to one side and regarded Francis thoughtfully. His eyes were half closed. He took another drag of his cigarette. 'It's not *my* problem, Harris. It's not me that's queer. It's not *me*,' he added, breathing out smoke, 'who's been coming on to other blokes and getting turned down. I mean, how sad is that?' He smirked.

Francis frowned. Then his eyes widened. 'What the hell are you talking about?' But his voice was flat, as though he'd already understood.

Shitley tapped his cigarette delicately with one finger, watching the ash fall. Then he glanced back to Francis as though for a moment he'd completely forgotten he was there. 'Your *friend* Michael Thompson. That's right, isn't it?' An infinitesimal silence. 'Told me all about it. He seemed to think it was all pretty grotesque. What was it he said about you ... ? *Repulsive*, I think.' He smiled, showing his teeth. 'Must be disappointing, being turned down like that. Bet you're kicking yourself. Especially now Thompson knows what a hideous little pansy you are.'

Francis swallowed. His face was very white. 'That's not true.'

Shitley laughed. 'Oh, really? Isn't it?' He flicked his cigarette over his shoulder and one of his gang flinched out of the way. 'Thompson seemed pretty certain.' He watched Francis's face with a sort of avid malice. 'Mind you ... why anyone would want to come on to *him* is beyond me.' For a second his voice was almost sympathetic. 'That must make it even worse. To be turned down by *Thompson*, of all people. What a loser.' He added, as though it was an afterthought, 'Actually, I'd be surprised if he had a dick at all.'

'Shut up.'

Shitley raised his eyebrows lazily. 'Wow. Sore spot, is it, Harris?' His tone was lewd, like he wasn't talking metaphorically. 'Seriously, though, you must be desperate. Sounds like you don't care who you suck off. As long as there's *someone* . . . And at least with Thompson there wouldn't be much to lick clean afterwards.'

Michael heard the punch before he understood. He registered the sound of bone on bone, saw Shitley lurch back clutching his face, even saw the blood start to flow, before he actually believed that Francis had hit him. Bloody hell. *Francis* had hit someone. And as he saw the other members of the gang advance on Francis he was still making sense of it, still rerunning the moment like film in his head. Jesus. Francis *hit* Shitley. And it was a proper punch, too, straight on Shitley's nose with all Francis's weight behind it. There was blood everywhere, now, over Shitley's face and trousers and the grass. He was spluttering and spitting great gouts of it. Michael watched Shitley gasp and splash red on the ground and thought, *Good man, Harris, well done, he deserves it*.

Then someone hit Francis. And the others joined in.

Michael sensed it in his own body, the force of it, the damage, like someone had swung something hard into his chest. He felt the separate punches, the moment when Francis dropped to his knees, the kick that knocked him forward, scratching for breath. Francis raised his arms to protect his head, just taking it now, not fighting back, and cold haemorrhaged into

Michael's stomach, burning him. *Christ, make them stop, make them stop* . . . They were battering him. They'd kill him. *Stop, please, stop, make them stop* . . . But he couldn't move, couldn't run forward. He was stuck there, like in one of those nightmares. He couldn't even breathe. *Please, God* . . . But there was nothing he could do. He waited.

They didn't stop all at once, but slowly, very gradually, they started to drift away. It seemed to take hours. Shitley was standing, now, bloody hands cupped over his face like a mask; once he saw they'd started to get bored he picked up his bag and walked away. A couple of kids exchanged looks and followed him. One of them lit a cigarette; another one got out his mobile and started to jab at the keypad with his thumb. There was only one boy standing over Francis now. He glanced up like he'd realised the fun was over and gave Francis a last vicious kick in the small of his back. Michael saw his shoe leave a mark on Francis's blazer. Then he jogged off to catch up with Shitley and the others, limping as he ran as if he'd stubbed his toe.

Michael watched them leave, strolling unconcernedly back towards the cricket pavilion, and took a deep breath. His hands ached from trying to hold on to the wall. He thought, idiotically, *Thank you, thank you* . . .

Now there was only Francis there, folded over himself on the grass. Relief rose in Michael's throat like nausea. He swallowed. He was weak at the knees. He could move, now. He stepped forward.

Francis stretched his hands out in front of him without looking up, pressing his palms into the ground like he was checking he was still there, still

145

alive. Then slowly he stood up, rolled his shoulders, explored his face with his fingertips, raised an arm and checked his ribs with the palm of his hand. He had blood on his shirt, and smeared across his tie. He took a deep breath and winced. Michael stood and watched him. He was OK. Thank God.

Francis turned. He saw Michael.

Jesus, his *face*. His expression . . . an expression that would have been blank if there hadn't been a bruise across it. The skin was already darkening. There was a vertical runnel of blood from his nose over his top lip. The bottom lip was beginning to swell. One eye socket was outlined in scarlet, but the eyes themselves were steady, and cold, and unreadable. Michael met his gaze and felt something inside him die. He forced himself to meet Francis's eyes; thought desperately, *Say something, for God's sake, Thompson, say something* . . . But nothing came. It was like someone had turned the sound off. There was no noise, anywhere. The whole world had gone quiet. Francis's face was utterly still, watching Michael: a long relentless look of – what? Hatred, and resignation, and fatigue, and maybe something else, something Michael didn't understand. Francis blinked. Then he turned his head to one side and spat. He lifted one hand to his face and wiped his mouth. Michael saw the spittle glint redly in the grass.

I'm sorry. Please. I can explain. I didn't mean, really, I'm so, so sorry . . . but he couldn't say it. He stared at Francis and thought, *Please, you can't think I did this on purpose, please, Francis, you* can't *do, you know I'm not like that* . . . Underneath it all, *sorry, sorry, sorry*, pounding in his head like a pulse.

Francis turned his head away, breaking his gaze. He started to walk, slowly, aiming just past Michael's shoulder, as though he didn't exist. For a second Michael almost believed he'd disappeared, and Francis really was on his own.

'Francis . . .'

Francis turned, wearily, stiffly. He didn't say anything; just waited for Michael to carry on.

'I didn't mean –'

'Save it.' Francis shrugged with one shoulder, and winced.

'I can explain –'

'I said, *save it*.' His voice was so cold, so *final*, it took Michael's breath away. It said, *Don't even bother, Thompson. There's no point*. And Francis turned away again, deliberately, like a door closing. Then, unexpectedly, he turned back. For a moment Michael's heart expanded – *he's going to listen, it's going to be OK* – but as soon as he saw Francis's face he knew he was wrong.

'I don't want to speak to you ever again, Michael. But there's just one thing.' Francis's eyes flicked away, then back to Michael's face. 'How did you know?'

'Know – what?'

Francis looked to his right, turning his whole head to one side in a strange, precise gesture of contempt. When he met his eyes again Michael could feel the anger coming off him like a thick, hostile fog. 'For God's sake . . . you slippery, treacherous *shit*.' He swallowed and took a deep breath. 'How did you know I'm gay? What did I do?'

'But you're not gay.' He wasn't. He couldn't be. Michael had just – it was just something to say, something to tell Shitley . . . 'You're not gay. You're *not*.'

Francis narrowed his eyes. 'What are you talking about?'

'You're not – gay.' A dreadful slow-growing panic started to tug at Michael's heart. 'You're not. Gay. Are you?' He couldn't be. Except that it would explain – *oh God, that's what he meant when – in Canterbury – what he was talking about when – no. No.*

'Jesus, Thompson . . . what the fuck . . . ?' Francis gave a harsh, painful-sounding laugh. 'What do you think this is all about?'

Not that. It wasn't about that. It was about Evgard, and Luke, and – wasn't it? *I thought you betrayed Evgard*, Michael thought, *it was always about Evgard, I didn't mean . . .*

Francis shook his head. 'I don't know what you're playing at, Thompson. Frankly I don't much care.' A tiny, tiny pause. 'Have a nice life, Michael.'

He started to walk away again. This time he didn't turn back.

LLAS

– *I am not faithless, sir, but over-true,*
And lieganced to more than one affection.
– *Why, 'tis the same thing . . .*
(from The Counterfeiters' Tragedy, *trans.*
MT)

He turns back to look at me, and his face is so innocent, so childlike, that it makes me catch my breath.

The daylight from the window is blue-grey, dim, so
that the shadows on his skin are the colour of slate,
and his eyes are so dark you can't see what colour
they are. But it's not the light that gets to me, or even
the sudden beauty of his silhouette against the sky, the
arch of stone behind him. It's the expression on his
face: pure, absolute delight – wide-eyed, excited,
open. It's the way Ryn looked, the first time she
climbed the woolbarn roof; how I suppose I must
have looked, the first time I won at shek. It's so unlike
Columen's ordinary manner that I almost want to
laugh.

'*Nix*,' he says. His voice is so jubilant that at first I
don't hear the word; only the tone, the excitement
that reaches out to me like a hand. Then I catch sight

149

of the sky behind him and it makes sense. Snow.

Snow. It's just started to fall, a few sly flakes floating towards the ground. If you weren't watching for it you'd hardly notice. It isn't settling yet, but the flakes that fall on the window sill stay white for a long heartbeat before they fade into water. By tomorrow it'll be deeper than the breadth of my hand. The first snowfall: the advance guard of the winter, the gate that shuts you into months of misery and boredom and fear. I draw back into the room, as far as I can. I can smell the chill on the air, the kind of cold that picks you up by the scruff of your neck and shakes you into bits, the kind that gets into your bones. I pull my clothes round me, more thankful than ever for the furs and padded silk, even if they do smell of Evgard, the musty, buttery smell of too much wealth. My hands are already tingling, remembering old chilblains. But Columen turns his whole body back to the window, leaning out into the freezing air, face upturned and eager. He reaches out with one hand, as though he's offering something to the sky, and pauses for a moment, suspended. Then he whips round, showing me his open hand and the grain of white where the lines meet on his palm. It melts before I can focus on it and he laughs and shakes the water off his skin.

'*Snow*, Argent!' he says again. His eyes are shining.

'I know.' I glance to the window again and try to summon some kind of excitement, some enthusiasm, to mirror his. But outside there's only the snow, heavier now, swirling down in a great bewildering swarm. If you fell asleep in that you'd never wake up.

'I love it . . .' Columen tries to catch another

150

snowflake, cupping his hands together like Ryn's little brother after a butterfly, his face creased with concentration. I've never seen him so unguarded. I've never heard him use the word *love*. Then, as he turns back to me, showing the droplets on his hands, laughing at himself, it comes to me. Of course. He's never actually been *cold*; the way he's never been hungry or tired. Not properly cold: only chilly, only enough to make him pull his furs closer round himself, to make him grateful for the fire in his hearth. For him, the snow's a toy, a novelty – sometimes, maybe, a nuisance. But that's all. It's never killed anyone he knows.

Now, staring at the blizzard, I can imagine what it must look like to him. It *is* wonderful, I suppose, the way it silences everything, the way you almost see shapes rise towards you through the flakes: a face, a ship, an eagle . . . And you *could* love the endlessness of it, the patterns that come and go, the great blank lovely mercilessness of it. It's *clean*. It shocks me, somehow, that I can understand him so easily. As though we're not that different. I turn away, gaze into the shadows in the corner of the room. I can still see snow whirling and eddying like dust in front of my eyes.

Someone's at the door. As soon as I hear the latch my heart clenches in a sudden surge of fear, but Columen's hand is on my shoulder, pressing down. It says, *Relax, you don't need to move*. His touch is firm, matter-of-fact, so impersonal that I don't flinch away. He clears his throat, and I hear the steel come back into his voice. 'Come.'

It's Iaspis. She's in the room before he's finished speaking, pulling the hem of her dress clear of the door as she closes it behind her. From the way she walks towards us it's clear that she would have come in whatever he'd said. Columen's hand is still holding my shoulder, forbidding me to move. I look down, at my feet, anywhere but at her eyes. She sits down on one of the cushions on the sill next to Columen and her dress flares out in a puddle of bluebottle-coloured silk.

'What are you doing?' She uses *te*, the singular form; she's not including me in the question.

'Watching the snow.'

Her eyes flick to the window, to the delicate curtain of flakes that's started to blow in. Suddenly she smiles, and for a moment she looks human. 'Snow!' Her voice has the same breathless delight as Columen's.

Columen smiles back at her, and she laughs, a lovely unexpected chuckle, and looks at me, still smiling. I wait for her expression to change to disdain, but it doesn't. It's the first time she's ever looked at me without scorn in her eyes. I feel a deep swell of warmth start in my gut and push upwards, and I know I'm grinning at her like an idiot. She spins round, her skirt twisting out in a flare of blue, and runs towards the door. 'Come on!'

'Where?'

She swivels round again impatiently to face us, half laughing. 'Outside, of course!' She holds out her hand, the way you would to a child or a lover. Her rings flash in the winter light. 'Hurry – before it stops!'

'It won't stop any time soon,' Columen says, but he's already swinging himself down from the window sill, landing lightly on the rushes. Even so, Iaspis has gone by the time he gets to the door. He looks each way down the corridor and says over his shoulder, 'She'll have gone to the North Tower. Bet you. Come on, let's go.'

The North Tower isn't as high as the Ghist, but all the same I'm out of breath by the time we get to the top. For the last few *hycht* I'm only concentrating on the next breath, trying to keep up with Columen, who's going up the steps in front of me. My heart's pumping. I stare at his feet, his gleaming leather boots striding inexorably up the stairs two at a time, and make myself keep the same rhythm. That's all I can think about, so that when we come out on to the top of the tower it's so different it feels as though I've stepped on to the moon. The world swirls and glitters, beautiful and bitterly cold. Everything's white: the ground, the sky, the air. You can see right over the North Quarter of Arcaster. The buildings appear and disappear through a fog of snowflakes, as though they're not quite real. I blink, letting my eyes adjust from the half-dark of the staircase, the dull glow of torches on stone walls.

The top of the tower's as big as Columen's antechamber and privy chamber combined. Already the snow's deep enough to show footprints, but we're the first people here and the space stretches out in front of us, white and white and white.

Columen breathes out a sigh of delight. '*Hiu* . . .' I don't know if that's just a sound, or if it means something; it sounds like Ryn, the way she'd clutch my arm and say, '*Gesh* . . .' when there was lightning or summer stars or my father brought home a whole silver piece.

We stand there for a few seconds, still, silent, watching the snow. This is how the sky would fall, gently, interminably . . . I'm not cold any more. I could watch it for ever.

But suddenly Iaspis is at my side, materialising out of the blizzard like a *sheehan*. I turn to look at her, and she swings her arm up, fast, pushing a fistful of snow into my face. I reel away, gasping with the blind out-of-nowhere cold. I can't see anything. There's icy water running down my face and down the front of my shirt. She laughs. I splutter and try to clear my eyes, and before I know it I'm laughing too and crouching to scoop up snow in my bare hands. I'm about to throw it into her face but she turns and runs a few steps, yelping and shrieking with laughter as though she's ten years old. Then something cold hits me on the side of my neck and I whirl round to see Columen smirking at me, already stooping for another handful of snow.

'Hey –!' It comes out in Mereish, *hoi*, but he's ducking away, dodging my flung armful of snow, giggling like a child.

I haven't played in the snow since I was tiny. At home it's something to hide away from, to endure, like a siege. But somehow it still comes naturally. Before I even think about it, I'm shaping a rough ball of snow in my hands, packing it loosely, ignoring the bite of the cold. Columen's holding his hands in front of his face as a shield. I wait until he relaxes and lowers them slightly, peering through his fingers to see what I'm doing. Then I lob it. It lands smack on his cheekbone, exploding into a dense swarm of white powder. He jumps back with an exclamation. Then he stoops and straightens, flinging two handfuls of snow at me without bothering to pack them into spheres. They hit my tunic, leaving white streaks. We're both laughing now, hooting with merriment like children. I'm fighting for breath as I scoop up a whole armful of snow and chase him, dodging away from Iaspis as she tries to grab my collar to put snow down the back of my neck. I score a direct hit on the back of Columen's head and yell, '*Ybreda!*' He springs round to face me, one arm outstretched, and suddenly I've got a mouthful of snow, clean-tasting, squeaking between my teeth. He punches the air.

Iaspis calls, 'Over here!' Like a fool I turn to look. A snowball glances off my shoulder and another one skims my ear. She's crouching behind a little pyramid of snowballs, her splendid dress wet and grimy. There's no time to retaliate; I turn on my heel and run, uselessly, because there's nowhere to go, scuffling and zigzagging, kicking up snow like water, brushing snowflakes out of my eyes. I feel a couple of snow-balls hit my back, but when I look back, panting, she's run out of ammunition, and there are little marks around me in the snow where she's missed her target. She brushes her hair out of her eyes, giggling. Her face is wet, and pinker than usual. I lean forward, catching my breath, and for a moment we're laughing at each other, easily, unselfconsciously, like friends. I can't take my eyes off her. It's only when she looks down, finally, and her giggles subside, that I notice Columen standing behind her. His grin has faded a little. Now he looks more like his usual self, although he's still flushed from running and his hair is plastered to his forehead. I catch his eye and he smiles coolly. After a while he glances away.

The snow isn't as heavy as it was. At the moment it's just a few drifting flakes here and there, glinting like grains of salt. As I stand still, letting my heart slow, Iaspis pushes herself awkwardly to her feet and goes to the battlements. She stares out over the whitened city towards the north and the marshes. Columen follows her without a word and stands silently at her side. It's as if the snowball fight hasn't happened. As if I've just imagined it.

It's so quiet. Below us somewhere, in the streets, someone calls and a cart goes past, but the sound's swallowed up by the snow. Columen and Iaspis are motionless, bending forward over the battlements like figureheads. I'm beginning to feel chilly again. I go and lean on the battlement next to Columen and follow his gaze, to the dull white plane of the Flatlands and the low-hanging sheet of cloud. Nothing moves. The road leading to Than's Lynn is just a faint seam of shadow, hardly visible. I turn and look ghistwards, away from Columen, towards Skyph. I stare until the whole world goes out of focus. Ryn. My father. My grandmother. My *heird*.

But – I don't know why – it doesn't hurt as much as it should. Maybe because it seems so long and so far away. Or because Columen is there at my back; or because Iaspis smiled at me, only a moment ago, as though she liked me. Or maybe it's because I'm wearing silk and fur and I'm warm and dry and I'm not hungry. The thought makes me sick. Ryn's out there, somewhere, wearing her wet linen and soggy wool, aching with cold: and I'm here, wearing clothes that the Duke's son gave me. I fix my eyes on the space where Skyph would be, if I could see it, and try to summon the misery I used to feel, the helpless rising emptiness that almost lifted me off my feet. But it's like pressing on a wound that's already closed. It just doesn't hurt as much as it should.

There's a wind rising, tugging at us in little gusts that flick up snowflakes around our feet. Columen hunches his shoulders under his cloak and starts to move back towards the staircase. 'Let's go back down.'

I follow him, turning away from Skyph. Deep in my gut something tugs at me, but I ignore it. Because, after all, inside there'll be a fire and hot food, spiced wine, a nub of somnatis to help me sleep. And it's easy, horribly easy, to go with him. As though Skyph never really existed. As though this is where I belong, with these rich, brutal, spoilt people. It makes me despise myself.

We're almost at the archway that leads to the staircase when Iaspis says, 'Look.' Her voice is so strange, so taut and flat, that it doesn't sound like her.

Columen looks back over his shoulder. 'What?'

Iaspis is bending forward, her hands clenched on the stones of the battlement. 'I saw something. A light, outside the walls.'

'*Outside* the walls?' When Iaspis nods, Columen snorts gently. 'In this weather? And the gates'll be shut, anyway. It's past curfew.'

'I know. But there was something. Something moving.'

'Just a stray animal. Or a beggar.'

'No.' Iaspis shakes her head, like a child that won't back down. 'I saw a light.'

Columen frowns, walks back a few steps and casts

157

a cursory glance down towards the walls. He shrugs. 'There's nothing –' Then he looks down again. He cranes over the battlement and purses his lips in a sort of noiseless whistle. 'You're right.'

Iaspis is on her toes, leaning precariously out across the battlement, bracing herself with her arms. 'I *said* there was something. People.'

Columen swings himself up on to the wall and sits with one leg dangling over the forty *hycht* drop. He holds on with his hands and tilts himself over, bending forward at such an angle it makes me swallow and look away.

Iaspis says again, 'There was something. I saw something. There's definitely –' But Columen holds up a hand and she goes quiet. A damp lock of hair falls across his eyes but he stays still, looking down so intently it's like the world has frozen solid.

'There was a raid yesterday, wasn't there?' He's talking to Iaspis but he doesn't look round.

Iaspis laces her fingers together and shrugs jerkily. 'I'm not sure . . . yes. They went to Minnon, I think. But they'd be back by now. Wouldn't they?' She looks up at him, suddenly eager. 'Of course! It's just the raiders coming home! They must have been delayed by the snow.' She laughs. 'For a moment I thought . . . They're breaking curfew. I wonder if the gate-keepers will let them in.' She leans over the battlements again to look, poised extravagantly on one leg like a dancer. 'Cousin Aper will be livid if they don't. Especially if they've captured any rebels.'

Captured any rebels . . . She means *slaves*. Mereish villagers, men, women, children. Hunted down and trapped, brought to Arcaster in chains, and then sent across the Judas floor or murdered in the Winter Games. Maybe they're out there now, shivering, ankle-deep in snow, waiting to be shepherded through the gate. Maybe they're people I know.

Iaspis pulls her cloak more tightly round herself, her hands sinking into the fur. 'Come on. Let's go in. I'm cold.'

But Columen doesn't move. He's grimacing to himself, still staring in the same direction, still leaning over the edge of the tower.

'Come *on*. It's only the raiders.' When Columen doesn't answer, she sighs. 'Fine.' She turns and strides towards the staircase, lifting her skirt clear of the snow. She shoots a glance over her shoulder. 'I think I saw Aper's cloak. The red one, with the gold thread embroidery. I'd know it anywhere.'

'Yes.' But he's not agreeing, exactly.

I clear my throat. 'Have they – are there any – prisoners?'

Columen shakes his head. 'Not that I can see.'

Iaspis hisses between her teeth. 'None at all?'

'No.' Columen's voice is steady and thoughtful. He hasn't moved. There's no reason to think he's afraid, but there's something about the concentration on his face, the force of his gaze, that makes me uneasy. 'Not a single one. It's unusual.'

'Father won't be pleased.'

'No . . .' He's leaning forward, so still, so oddly, *unyieldingly* still that I can't help thinking of a sail in a storm, stretched against the wind until it splits. 'You're right. It *is* Aper's cloak.'

'So let's go in.' Iaspis hugs herself and rotates in a circle. 'I'm freezing.'

'They're letting them through the gates,' Columen

says, in a strange, pensive tone. He breathes out slowly. 'They've let them in. I expect they recognised Aper's cloak.'

'Well, why shouldn't they?'

'No reason.' Except that the words are so slow, so dreamy and distant, that they don't mean what they should. They mean: *they shouldn't have let them in.* They mean: *something's wrong.* 'The snow,' he says, still in that strange detached tone, as though he's reciting poetry. 'The snow's only just fallen. It wouldn't have delayed them.'

Iaspis puts her head on one side and wrinkles her nose. 'You know what I mean.' She heaves a great theatrical sigh. 'I told you. I saw Aper's cloak. It's only the raiders. Why shouldn't the gatekeepers let them in?'

'I'm not sure. It's just – odd.'

Iaspis swings one foot, making a long shallow ditch in the snow. 'Not really. Anyway, I'm going in. I'm hungry.' She turns and walks briskly back towards the stairs. I watch her go through the archway, the hem of her dress leaving a brief smear of damp on the top step. I will her to look back at me, but she doesn't. I close my eyes and try to see her face, the way she looked when she smiled at me; the way her eyes lit up, like amber, like firelight, like polished bronze.

Columen gasps.

When I open my eyes he's already staring at me, face almost blue in the twilight, a hand clutching my wrist so hard it's like the grip of a hawk. And the noise he made . . . I step forward, towards him, reaching for his shoulders, panicking, because it's the grunt that men make when an arrow hits home, the surprise, the soft horrified in-breath of a man who sees a shaft coming out of his breastbone without understanding how it got there. Columen isn't hurt, I can see that; but his face has the look of someone who is. I babble something frantically in Mereish, *Eir du gweuthed? Min lyshe, hath er badh?* but before I can say it again in Evgard he's running towards the stairs, pushing himself away from me so hard I stumble back against the wall behind me. I can hear him swearing, in a strange, pleading undertone that sounds more like a prayer: *Oh foeda meretrix, oh cunnus, oh copulatus cunnus* . . . He tears down the stairs so fast he skids on the third step and throws his arms out for balance, not pausing to grab the rope strung along the wall.

I'm running after him, calling out in Evgard now, 'What's wrong? Columen? What's going on?' But he doesn't answer. I propel myself down the steps after him, fighting to stay on my feet, but I can't catch him up.

It's not till we're halfway down the spiral staircase that I start to understand; and even then it's only because he pushes past Iaspis and says, 'Get my father, Iaspis, get him *now* – I don't think those people were raiders –' without looking back at her, so that the words bounce back off the stone.

'*What?* Columen! What do you mean?' She grabs for him but he's already out of reach. She hurries down another few steps, then she comes to a halt, pressing one hand against the wall beside her. Her other hand is spread on the front of the bodice of her dress, the tendons white under her skin. She calls again, 'Columen . . . ?' but there's no reply.

161

I don't dare to push past. 'Excuse me, my lady.' I wait for her to move, but instead she turns to me, with a sort of helpless, wondering stare. 'Let me get past. Please. I have to go with Columen.'

'What's happening?'

'I don't know. Please. I need to get past.'

'What does he mean, they're not raiders? Who else could they be?'

'I'm not sure.' But as I'm saying it the answer comes to me, and a little treacherous hope uncurls in my mind like a leaf. What if . . . ? They could be Mereish. They could be one of our companies. But in *Arcaster* . . .

'Well, what did he say? Why does he think there's something wrong?'

'I *don't know*. Please –'

'Why should I get our father? What should I tell him?'

'Iaspis. Get out of my way. *Now*.' I'm half horrified, half excited by the power in my voice. I can't imagine talking to Columen like that. But Iaspis doesn't flinch. Unexpectedly she moves out of my way without saying anything. I'm so close to her I can see a pulse beating in the dent above her collarbone, as fast as an insect's wings. 'Thank you.'

'Argent –'

I'm already three steps below her, but there's something in her voice that makes me turn. For one thing, she's never said my name before.

She clears her throat. 'Come back. When you know what's going on. Come and find me.' It's almost an order – but not quite.

I swallow. 'Iaspis – you should do what Columen

said. Go and find your father. Tell him what's happened.' I still expect her to look disdainfully at me – *who are you to tell me what to do, slave?* – but she nods and gives me a tiny, unbelievable smile. For a moment I'm tempted to run back up the stairs, put my arms round her, reassure her. But I haven't got time. I have to find Columen.

I don't know where I'm going to look – I don't know where he was going – but when I come out of the stairwell I take a turning at random and I'm in luck. I'm on the lower level of the castle walls, and a long way ahead of me I can see Columen sprinting though the flurries of snow, a man-at-arms at his heels. They're going towards the keep. I run as fast as I can, trying to ignore the scrape of cold air at the back of my throat, the ache in my calves. But even though I'm pushing myself as hard as I can, they disappear into the keep before I can get to them. When I finally reach the door and push it open, Columen's in the middle of a sentence, surrounded by a group of soldiers, some in chain mail, others still half-dressed and bleary. He breaks off and whips round to face me. Then, as one of the soldiers reaches out to grab me, he gestures with one hand. 'Leave him alone, idiot! He's one of ours.' He turns back without meeting my eyes. 'I want men on the battlements. Archers. And boiling lead, hot sand, dropping-stones, you all know the drill. Anything you can think of. Kill them, maim them, whatever, as long as you stop them. If the keep falls, the whole castle falls. Clear?'

The men nod, exchange glances, shuffle a little. One of them clears his throat. 'What about the town?'

'It's too late for that. But they're only peasants. If

we can hold the castle, there's nothing to worry about. They'll be sloping off back to Marydd before the week's out.' Columen's voice has a kind of casual authority that I envy in spite of myself. It's as though he's *enjoying* himself. 'Any questions? Good. Get to your places. I'll send a messenger as soon as I know more.' He holds one hand in the air, not dismissing them yet. 'Just – keep them *out*. Whatever it takes. That's all.'

A pause, full of the rank smell of the hearth and men's bodies, new snow, bloodlust and fear. Then Columen turns on his heel, easy now, as though he's done what's needed. He walks through the door without looking back.

I turn to follow.

'Mereish traitors.' The man who's spoken is only a *hycht* away, and he's looking at me. He grimaces and hawks a great gobbet of spit into the rushes by my feet. 'Thieves and murderers, all of you.' He jerks his head in the direction of the town. 'Proud of them, are you, white boy? Out there, massacring innocent people, raping virgins? Like the idea of it, do you?'

'Are they –?' But I can't ask. I'm shaking, but not with fear. Does he mean –? *Is* it a company of Mereish fighters? I stare at him, speechless.

His mouth curls; he wipes a fleck of spit off his chin with the back of his hand. 'They won't get in, *cimex*. We'll see to that. You heard the Captain – we'll pour molten lead on them if they try.' He leans closer. 'Ever seen someone with burning sand inside their clothes? You should see them dance.'

I walk blindly back out into the snow and run a couple of steps to catch up with Columen. My

164

stomach's churning – with fear, and dread, and something else, something that could almost be excitement. I lick my lips and try to say, 'Columen – who is it? What's going on?' but he starts to speak before I do.

'They murdered the gatekeepers, Argent.' He's looking straight ahead, into the falling snowflakes, as though he can see someone there. 'That's what I saw. The gates opened, and stayed open. Then I saw them throw out a couple of bodies . . . something red on the snow. And more of them, all in white, coming out of the shadow at the base of the city walls. Like maggots when you turn a corpse over. Swarming. All in white. To blend in with the snow, I suppose.' He turns to look at me now, one hand against his forehead, wiping away the drops of melt-water in his hair. 'I don't know how many there are. Enough to take the city, I think.' He waits, as if he's asked a question. When I don't answer he shrugs. 'It's not a bad plan – ambush the raiders, take their clothes, rely on the gatekeepers' incompetence to get you through the gate.' He laughs, without amusement. 'Aper's cloak – Iaspis was right. Everyone in the city would know it a mile off. And in this weather no one looks at your face.'

I look at him sideways. 'Are they – they're Mereish, aren't they?'

'I think so.' He chews his lip. 'That's a point, actually. Father should put all the Mereish slaves in the dungeons. Stop anyone opening the gate from inside.'

'In the dungeons?' A swift blade of panic stabs under my ribs. *No.* I've seen those dungeons. I'm not going back there. My eyes go to Columen's back, the place under his cloak where he keeps his dagger.

He reaches out, a brief touch on my arm. 'Not you, fool. You can stay with me. I won't let them lock *you* up.' He smiles, narrowing his eyes. 'Anyway, someone who knows Mereish might be useful.'

We duck through a low archway and along a low, chilly gallery. If I concentrated I could probably work out where we're going, but my head's too full of other things. A company of Mereish fighters. In Arcaster. In my mind's eye I can see my father, the day Ryn's brother went away to join the White Company, shaking his head. *Whatever makes you happy, lad. Just don't tell yourself it'll do us any good* . . . and later, when he thought I was asleep, *Boys with iron swords, that's all they are. Rabbit-hunters* . . . But he was wrong. They're here; somehow they're powerful enough, or desperate enough, to attack an Evgard fortress. And if the keep fell – they'd be here, in the castle, to free the slaves, to depose the Duke . . . My heartbeat roars in my ears.

Columen unlocks a little door behind a curtain and pulls me through. I come out, blinking, into a wide windowless hall, smoky and bare. In the middle of the room there's a huge, detailed model of Arcaster – the castle, the School, the Quarters . . . like the most elaborate toy in the world. But I don't see it at first, because the room's full of people, mainly men, in small groups, talking in harsh whispers. The Duke is there, bending over the streets of the miniature Arcaster. He looks up, beckons Columen over, and this time Columen gives me a small cautionary push to warn me not to follow him. I stand near the wall, in the shadows, trying to listen to the conversations going on around me. The news must have spread like the water-sickness, but all the same no one knows exactly what's going on. I catch fragments of speech: 'Rebels – got through the gate – how many days' stores do we – waited for the snow to . . .'

A little oily man slides past me in a draught of cold air from the door. No one looks up; he slips through the clusters of people like a shadow. Hardly anyone seems to notice the way the Duke turns his head, sharply, or the way Columen doesn't even wait for him to bow before he says, 'What news?'

The little man speaks so softly it's as if he's only pronouncing the consonants, without any vowels at all. They're speaking Evgard, of course, but I can just about read his lips. It's easy: because somehow I already know what he's going to say.

'A band of Mereish traitors, my lords.'

The Duke nods. 'And?'

'They are occupying all of Arcaster, except the School. There are fires in the Ghist Quarter and one Trade Street is impassable. We estimate their numbers at something between fifty and two hundred.'

Columen glances at his father, then back at the man. 'That's as precise as you can be?'

'I'm afraid so. The matter is complicated by the possibility of female fighters.'

'*Women?*' The Duke snorts. 'In that case . . .'

'I believe they are not to be underestimated, my lord.' He clears his throat, addressing Columen as much as the Duke. 'Although the attack is unprecedented, it isn't entirely unexpected. Sooner or later we anticipated that they would launch some kind of attack. And the Mereish can be extremely clever and unconventional opponents.'

'I see.' The Duke jerks a thumb over his shoulder, dismissing him. Then he turns to Columen. 'Give orders for all Mereish workers to be held in the dungeons, preferably in solitary confinement.' Columen nods, running a finger along the wall of the model castle. 'Check our supplies. Set guards in place to watch for anyone trying to scale the battlements. Set basins of water by the walls to show up vibrations from tunnelling. Make sure the women are safe.'

'Yes, Father.' Columen bows to him and turns away, but the Duke puts one hand on his arm and wrenches him back.

'Your Mereish slave – where is he?'

Columen gives the briefest of glances down to his sleeve, at the Duke's fist pulling the embroidery out of shape. Then he looks straight into his father's eyes. 'My slave? He's already in the dungeons.'

The Duke lets go of him. 'Good. Make sure he stays there.' He clicks his fingers to a little huddle of armed men and they hurry towards him. 'Now. I want an observation post on the Ghist Tower . . .'

Columen catches my eye as he walks towards the door. He inclines his head very slightly – *come with me, don't let anyone notice you* – but doesn't speak until we're safely back in the gallery. Then he breathes out a long, slow sigh. He pulls me over to an alcove, where we'll be out of sight. It's got dark; there's snow blowing in through the windows, settling on the floor like drifts of sand, glinting in the torchlight. He leans close to me, so near I can see the texture of his skin. 'Argent, I have to carry out my father's orders. I want you to go and find Iaspis – but *stay out of sight*. I've told my father you're already in the dungeons.' He smiles, searching my face with his eyes. 'I know she's insufferable, sometimes – but look after her, will you?' I nod, without speaking. 'Thank you.'

There's a noise behind us as someone comes through the door, and Columen pulls me back against the wall. Once the coast is clear he looks at me again. 'One more thing.' He reaches round to the small of his back, pulling his cloak out of the way. His hand fumbles for a moment underneath the cloth. He's looking down, with the concentrated look of someone who's trying to locate something by touch. He tugs impatiently at the cloak, as though it's in his way.

His dagger. Oh, *shud* – he's getting out his dagger.

I try to step back, but there's a wall in my way. I wait, frozen, feeling the stone press against my shoulder blades. The way he's fumbling . . . he isn't normally clumsy. Any moment now, he'll have the blade in his hand. I feel cold wash over me, and the flat unyielding stone of the wall behind me, holding me there. I'm trapped. I should hit him, punch him in the windpipe, knock him out, before he has time –

But it's too late.

He's got it. I see his hand come round, the flash of a blade, and feel the raw clutch of panic in my gut. Has he – did he –? How does he know –? I don't understand, but there's nothing I can say. I squeeze my eyes shut and think, *Go on, then. Do your duty*.

When I open them again, he's staring at me. He raises his eyebrows and shakes the knife at me as though he's trying to attract my attention to it. He's holding it in his left hand, hilt towards me. 'Take it, idiot.'

'What?'

'You don't have one. And I don't like the thought of you going unarmed.' He glances round, biting his lip. 'I don't think the castle's in any real danger – but just in case. Go on. Take it.'

I reach out and take it. I want to laugh. I can feel how expensive it is just from the weight, the way it fits into my hand. It feels *right*. 'Thank you.'

Columen grins briefly and shakes his head. 'It's good to know you've got it.' I look down at the snow eddying round my feet and wait for him to leave. But instead, unexpectedly, he puts the heel of one hand on my forehead. 'Be careful, Argent.' He pushes, so I can feel the bones of his wrist against my skull, a firm, enigmatic pressure. Then he drops his hand and turns, without waiting for me to reply.

I watch him leave. My heart gives a funny jerk, like regret, or shame. Then I turn in the opposite direction, towards the corridor that will take me out on to the walls.

The city's burning. As I come out on to the battlements I can smell it: the heavy, harsh smoke of burning wool and blackwood. I wipe snow off my face and my hand comes away dark grey with ash. You can even see the glow of the warehouses, off to the ghist, staining the sky red. There are men on the walls, pointing, yelling back to each other, loosing off arrows at things I can't see. No one stops me as I go past.

The keep is surrounded by guardsmen, looking uneasy. You can hear the sounds of the siege more clearly from here: yells and screams, the rumble of the fires in the distance, a regular banging, an occasional clang. The men look at me suspiciously as I approach;

but they've already seen me with Columen, and when I say, 'Message from the Duke,' – my voice hardly shaking at all – they shift aside without challenging me. I've still got Columen's dagger in my hand. The hilt is slick with sweat and I can feel my pulse beating in my fingers. I ignore my fear and make myself walk into the gatehouse as though I have every right to be there.

The siegers are using a battering ram. It won't work – the gate is far too thick, and anyway there's a portcullis – but the noise makes the whole keep ring and echo unbearably. As I go down the steps towards the gate I can see things shake, blurring round the edges as they vibrate.

It's too loud for the men on duty to talk to one another; they sit stolidly on benches at the side of the room. They don't flinch at the sound of the battering ram, but the swords leaning against the wall opposite them shudder and ring at every blow. A couple of the men look at me curiously as I walk past, and I force myself to meet their eyes, the way Columen would, with that cool assumption of superiority. It works: they look away. I don't know exactly where I'm going – I haven't been through the main gate since the night they brought us here – but I follow the noise, making sure I don't frown or look round too much. Now I'm getting closer it's hard to distinguish between the battering ram and my heartbeat: my whole body is jolting.

There are only a couple of men on guard in the space directly in front of the gate. They're pacing, axes slung over their shoulders, but somehow they look less jumpy than the men in the chamber I came

171

through, and you can see why. The noise is over-whelming, a continual dull thud that sets your teeth humming, but the door is hardly moving. And in front of that there's the portcullis, rooted in the stone. Even the lever that raises it is as sturdy as a broadsword. The keep won't fall. The castle's safe. The gate could last out the winter.

Unless someone opened it from inside.

The men look up as I approach. One of them stops pacing and stands in my way, legs spread. He looks down at me, chin tilted back, axe balanced on the leather pad on his shoulder. I say, 'The Duke wants you. In the inner room.' I have to shout to make myself heard; it makes me feel breathless.

The man runs his tongue along his front teeth and flicks a quick look at his partner. 'Can't leave our post, sonny,' he says. 'Captain's orders.' It takes me a moment to realise he's talking about Columen.

I nearly say, 'Please – it won't take long –' but I realise just in time that's wrong. Instead I shrug. 'The Duke said to go.' I ought to turn and start to leave, but I can't bring myself to.

He frowns. 'More than my life's worth, boy.'

I shrug again, but this time my shoulders are too tight to move properly. 'He said to go. That's all.' My voice is too high; I sound like a girl.

'Desert my post? I don't think so.'

'It was an order.'

He shakes his head. He says, with more conviction, 'You'll have to tell the Duke I've been told to stay here.' He swings his axe off his shoulder and starts to pace again.

I clench my fists, feeling the nails bite into my

172

palms. I don't know what to do. I can't just go. Not now. Not while I can hear the battering ram, not while I know that the Mereish rebels are just the other side of the wall, a few *hycht* away. I may not get another chance. I start to say, 'But he –'

Unexpectedly the other man speaks. '*Tell* him, mate? You don't *tell* the Duke anything. Least of all that you won't do what he says.' He shoots a look over his shoulder, at the door, the trembling portcullis. 'You'd better go. I'll stay here.'

The man whistles unhappily through his teeth. 'The Captain said *two* of us. At all times, he said –'

'And the Duke's saying he wants to see you. So scarper.' The second man winks at me. 'This young 'un can help me keep watch. He's one of the Captain's men, too.' He aims a casual kick at the portcullis. 'Nothing happening here. Except getting a headache.'

'You sure?'

'I said, didn't I? Go on. Shog off.'

I swallow. 'I think – I think he meant both of you.' But as soon as I say it I know it's a mistake. They turn to look at me in unison, suddenly suspicious.

'What, and leave the gate completely unguarded?'

'Oh – well, maybe not. I wasn't sure. No, of course, he can't have done. Sorry.' I'm stammering, trying to pretend I'm just a kid who's got confused. I've given myself away. I've messed it up. 'He just said – the guard . . .' If they guess . . . I'll end up in the dungeons. Or worse.

But unbelievably they swap a glance and relax. The first man shakes his head. 'Next time you take a message, you make sure you're clear what it means, all right? You could get yourself into trouble like that.'

'Yes.'

'Right.' He hefts his axe again and gives a sort of salute to his partner, punching the air in front of him. 'Back as soon as I can. Don't do anything I wouldn't do.' Then he's out of the door, and I'm left with the other man and the merciless, incessant pounding of the battering ram against the gate. There must be hundreds of them, to keep that up this long. A whole company.

The man looks at me, working his jaw from side to side. 'You *are* the Captain's man, right? You were here with him, when he was giving orders?'

'Yes.' I can feel the fear rising now. I swallow and stare him out; in the end he looks away, but he's still frowning.

'And what did the Duke say, exactly?'

'That he wanted to see the man on guard at the gate.'

'Nothing else?'

'No.' My heart is beating so fast it's painful. The air feels too thick, like freezing soup: it's hard to breathe in.

'Right.' He takes a few steps away and runs a flat rough palm across the grille of the portcullis. He shoots a quick look back at me. 'You – you're the Mereish kid, aren't you?'

Now. I should do it now, while he has his back to me . . . but I don't. 'Only half,' I say. 'My mother was from Petra Caeca.' My hands are cold and clammy. *Go on, go* on . . . but I can't move. There's a new, deeper note to the banging, a kind of scraping, straining groan.

He nods and rubs at his hair. Then suddenly he

swings round and smashes his fists against the metal bars. 'This bloody noise! It gets inside your head. I can't hear myself think.' He leans his forehead on the portcullis, letting his hands droop over the bars to the other side.

I walk towards him, clutching Columen's dagger so tightly my fingers have gone numb. I see him notice the movement and start to turn round. I see one of his hands twitching for his axe. I see him try to back away. I see the look on his face.

And then there's nothing, only the noise, the pounding that goes on and on, and the blood. So much blood, on my hands and the floor and his clothes. And someone making a noise like they're drowning, and at first I think it's him – impossibly, appallingly still alive – until I realise it's me, retching and choking and whimpering like an animal. I try to stand up, but somehow I can only get to my knees and then my legs don't work any more. I crawl away, smearing blood across the paving-stones. Something clinks as I move. It's the dagger, still in my hand, dark and stained and sticky. I put it down. I push at the floor with both hands, taking deep breaths. I have to stand up. I have to raise the portcullis. I have to open the gate.

I stand up. I'm shaking, but I'm on my feet. I step over the body and pull at the lever for the portcullis, dragging the handle down. It's counter-weighted but all the same it takes all my strength to get it to move, and I heave at it urgently, because I know I don't have much time. But when the mechanism bites it rises up smoothly, without even grazing the wall on either side. Now there's only the gate.

It's hard to lift the bars. I hadn't realised how heavy

175

they are. And every time I try to get hold of one, the door crashes and judders inwards, knocking me back. I wrench at the bars with hands that stick to the metal, hearing my own voice saying, 'Please, please, please –' I'm almost sobbing with desperation and tiredness. If they find me here, like this, before I've opened the gate . . .

I link my hands around the lower bar and push it up, straining every muscle, holding my breath – and just as I'm about to give up I see the edge of the metal ease over the top of the bracket that holds it in place. I muster all the force I can and drag it towards me. It's too heavy to hold and I drop it on the floor with a resonant thump that sounds like it's cracked the flagstones. But it's out. I've done it.

I set my hand to the other one, ready to summon the last of my energy. But without warning the wood splits under my hand, tearing itself apart. I'm knocked backwards, off my feet; my head hits the wall and I'm on the floor. There's shouting, and the noise of something cracking. The pounding stops. Suddenly there are people filling the room, pouring through the broken gate.

I hear my own language, surrounding me, like I've come home.

I open my eyes, and they're there, the Company, flowing into the keep like floodwater, yelling to each other. A couple of them look round, or up at the raised portcullis, but most of them have disappeared before I can pick them out, sliding in single file into the stairwell or through the door, swords drawn. Mereish words come out of the babble – *varesh, warrim, gweuthed* – and I want to cry. I've done it.

I've let them in. I shut my eyes again and my face is wet. I don't wipe it because of the blood on my hands.

'*Argent!*'

I look up, blinking. In the torchlight it's hard to see faces clearly, but the voice . . . I'd know the voice anywhere, even if it wasn't saying my name. My heart gives a little frightened jump, because I don't dare to let myself hope, to let myself believe –

Ryn.

Neither of us moves. Then, inexplicably, we're in each other's arms. I must have got up from the floor. She must have stepped forward. But it's as if there was nothing in between seeing her and touching her, as if whatever brought us together was something else, like a blade and a lodestone leaping towards each other.

I'm crying properly now, closing my eyes and pressing my face into the warmth of her shoulder, and her hands are digging into my back, pulling me even closer, as though she'll never let me go. 'Argent, *min levthe, min heird* . . . we thought you were dead, Argenshya, you *shudfargtte*, we thought you were *dead*.'

'Who are you calling *shudfargtte*, wormface?' I say, and we laugh helplessly, both of us still fighting tears.

Ryn pulls away and looks into my face, keeping hold of my arms. 'What are you doing here, anyway? How did you – what happened – should you be –?' She puts her hands on her forehead and shakes her head. 'I mean . . . oh, *ageirt*, there's no time to talk now.' She glances round. We've been left behind; we're the only people in the chamber, except for the body on the floor. 'Why are –?' She grimaces, staring at the blood. Then she looks back at me and her face

177

changes. I see her take in the stains on my hands, the dark red smears on my clothes that could be rust or marsh-reed pollen. '*Varesh meither*, Argent . . . you opened the doors for us?'

I nod.

She gives me a long, steady look. I can't read her expression. Then she takes my face in her hands, as if I'm a child, and kisses me deliberately on the mouth. She steps back. 'You did well.'

'Did I?'

'Of course.' She looks at my hands again and adds, 'You killed the guard?'

'Yes – I –'

'That's all right. You had to.' She nods at the dagger beside the corpse. 'You should keep that. You'll need it.' When I don't move she bends, picks it up, offers it to me. 'Take it, Argesha. We'll show these bloody murdering bastards a thing or two.'

She turns and walks towards the doorway that will take her up the staircase on to the walls. It's only then that I notice the stains on her clothes, the patches of dirt and ash and blood. There's a clot of something in her hair, something yellow and fatty, like tallow; her boots have a tidemark of dark above the ankles. And her knife is as dull and wet with blood as mine is. A kind of dread begins to gnaw at my breastbone, chewing at me.

She looks back. 'Come on.' She spins her dagger deftly in her fist, grinning at me. Then she turns and starts to bound up the stairs. 'So. Who do you want to kill first?'

I stand very still.

TEN

Michael stood still; frozen, trying not to breathe. Even after Francis had gone round the corner, out of sight, and he was on his own. He wondered foolishly if he could just stay there. Maybe if he didn't move no one would notice him and he'd just fade away.

But he couldn't keep the world out indefinitely. In the end it started to leak in, swirling up round him like cold water. He took a deep breath by mistake, and suddenly he was back, his head filled with Shitley and his gang and Francis's face, his gut filled with a tight knot of shame and hatred and disgust. If he looked down he could see the tiny flecks of blood on the grass, the long string of red mucus where Francis had spat. Oh God. He thought, *Why wasn't it me? I wish it had been me* . . . Except that he couldn't get rid of the picture in his head – the vicious cluster of Shitley's gang, Francis's back curled to protect his groin – and the relief, the horrible greasy relief that it wasn't him. Jesus, how could he be so cowardly? How could he have let it happen? He dragged his fingers over his scalp, hard enough to hurt, then dug his fingertips into his eyes. For a moment all he saw was a fizzing tide of orange, like the beginning of an explosion. He thought, *I want to kill someone. I want to die.*

Then, in spite of himself, a cold calm voice in his head said: *Francis didn't betray Evgard. Francis didn't do anything wrong.*

He said back, *I know, but I didn't realise – please, I swear I didn't mean –*

Francis didn't do anything wrong. And what they did to him was your fault.

I know. I know that.

And he thinks you did it because he's gay.

Shut up. Shut up. He opened his eyes, but it didn't help. He could still see Francis, the blood, the bruise across his face like a map. He thought desperately, *But anyway he isn't* really – *I don't believe* – *I know he said, but he can't really be, surely I would have* – *I'd never have said it, I swear I wouldn't have, not if he really* was –

No. Francis couldn't be gay. He just couldn't. That was all there was to it. Michael thought, *I would have known. He's my best mate. I would have* known.

The voice said, *Yeah, right, the way you knew he hadn't betrayed Evgard? For God's sake, Thompson, you're pathetic. You don't know anything about him. You don't know* anything.

He wanted to argue; even if the voice was only in his head, he wanted to say, *No, you're wrong, he's my mate, I know him better than anyone.* But he didn't believe it himself. He *didn't* know anything about Francis. He never had done.

But even if . . . He still couldn't get his head round

it. He said to himself experimentally, *Francis is gay. Francis is homosexual. Francis fancies blokes. Francis is* gay. *Surely I should feel* something . . . But it was too big for him to get hold of; it didn't mean anything. It was an excuse for Shitley to beat Francis up; it was the worst thing you could say about someone. That was all. Unless –

Michael thought, *Jesus, what if he fancies* me? There was a split second when the world lurched drunkenly, when he didn't know what he felt. What if – dear God, Francis couldn't possibly – could he –? But before he even had time to think it Michael knew it was stupid. Francis was hardly going to fancy him *now*, was he? That expression on his face: *You slippery, treacherous shit . . . And I deserved it*, Michael thought. *I told Shitley Francis had come on to me. I deserve worse than that.*

A kind of fatigue punched into him, unexpectedly, like concussion. Suddenly he could hardly keep his eyes open. The world went blurry and distant and submerged; everything started to get fuzzy round the edges. He thought, *I have to go home. I can go to sleep and stop thinking. I need to go home, before I* . . . He started to walk.

And he made it. Just. Once he'd got through the front door it was as much as he could do to get into his bedroom before he collapsed on his bed and went straight to sleep like a little kid. He had time to think, *Oh, thank you, thank you.* Then he was unconscious.

He was dreaming about Evgard. There were people with swords, and a sunset, and something good – but then there was a phone ringing somewhere, insistent, shrill, and he felt the noise suck him back into the real world. He opened his eyes and stared into the half-dark, hating whoever was ringing, hating himself for waking up. He couldn't get back to sleep, even when his mum answered it. He rolled over and stared at the wall. Fragments of words drifted up the stairs: *what? when? . . . but . . . I'm sure he didn't mean . . .*

His door banged open. Someone turned on the light. Michael sat up, blinking, protesting automatically, but then he saw the look on his mum's face.

'What the hell is going on, Michael?'

'What?' He shook his head, looking at her wide-eyed. But he already understood, in spite of himself. She knew, somehow. She knew.

'That was Mrs Harris on the phone. About Luke.'

Michael pressed down on the duvet with his hand, watching the way the fabric dented round his fingers. 'What about him?'

'Did you hit him today? At school?'

He thought about lying to her. He could say, 'No. Why would I? He's making it up. He's got it in for me, I don't know why . . .' Half of that would be true, at least. But he wouldn't get away with it, not for long. 'Yes.'

He heard her breathe out. He didn't want to look at her, but he had to. She was staring at him, so white and tense that it was like he'd hit *her.* 'How could you, Michael? How *could* you?' Her voice was odd. It didn't sound like her.

'Luke –' It would be so easy to tell her. But he couldn't. Evgard was sacred. It was all he had left; all he'd ever had. And how could he explain it, anyway? *Me and Francis have this imaginary country . . .* He shrugged stiffly. 'He deserved it. He's a poisonous little bastard.'

She tilted her head to one side, as though she wasn't sure she'd heard properly. Michael tried to hold her gaze, but it was too much for him. That disbelief, that shock – as though Michael wasn't himself any more, as though she didn't recognise him . . . She said softly, 'He *deserved* it?'

He couldn't stop himself. 'Yes. He did.'

She pressed her lips together and took a deep breath. 'Did he hit you first?'

'No – he –' But what could he say?

'Did he . . . he took something? He stole something from you?'

'No – Mum – it wasn't . . .'

She nodded slowly. 'He was picking on someone else. You stepped in to help someone else.' God, it was horrible, the determination in her voice, like just *saying* it would be enough.

Michael forced himself to look her in the eye. 'No.'

'Then . . .' She was pushing at her hair with one hand, pushing it back over and over again. 'Then, what happened? Why did you do it, Michael?'

'Because –' For a long, mad second he thought, *I'll tell her, she'll understand. I'll tell her.* But a voice in his head said, *Yeah, right, because it worked last time, didn't it? When she went to the comp and told the teacher you were being bullied – that really made things better, didn't it? You know what happened then. You remember that last day . . . That's what happens when you tell the truth.*

Michael stood up and walked past her to the window. He could feel his heart pounding. He tried to

183

keep his voice level, deliberate.

'Because he asked for it. That's all. Because he deserved it.' He didn't turn round. 'I hit him because he's a horrible nasty little kid.'

She gave a small incredulous gulp. 'Michael –'

He spun round to face her. 'What?' Half of him couldn't believe that she'd think that, that she'd believe he'd just hit someone for no reason. *I'm not like that, Mum, you know I'm not, you must know there's more to it* . . . But the other half was so angry he could have hit anyone. 'I hit him because I *could*. Why shouldn't I? What's wrong with that?'

She shook her head. Jesus, the look on her face. 'My God, Michael. You of all people. *You of all people* should know what's wrong with that.' She moved towards him; he felt himself back away automatically. 'What about what those kids at the comp did to you? They did that because they could. Didn't they?'

Michael pressed his back teeth together. He wasn't going to think about that.

'Michael, for heaven's sake! I don't understand – can't you see . . .' For a moment it was like she was pleading with him; she reached out to touch his arm. 'That poor little boy. *Why* did you hit him, Michael? There must have been a reason, darling.'

Evgard, he thought. *Evgard. And I'll never betray it, I'll never tell anyone, because I don't* have *anything else. I'd rather Mum hated me.*

He took hold of her hand and detached it from his arm. She clutched at his fingers and he shook her off. 'No. There wasn't any reason. I just don't like him.'

'That's not *enough*. No one – you'd have to be mad, to think that was enough –'

'I'm mad, then, obviously.' He wanted to say, *Wow, that's what Luke said:* you psycho, Thompson . . . *You two must have a lot in common.* 'There you go. That's why. Because I'm mad.'

'Stop it! Michael. Please. Talk to me. Tell me.'

He didn't know what it was, about her face, about her voice, that made him want to hurt her. Maybe it was the way she didn't *want* to hate him. 'Tell you? Why? So you can fuck my life up even more? The way you did when I was at the comp?' He watched her face change. 'That's why all this gets to you so much, isn't it? Because you know you just make it worse? Because you know that everything that's happened – it's all your fault. If you hadn't been such a stupid, meddling, interfering *cow* –'

It was almost a relief when she slapped him.

Although it hurt. Christ, it really did hurt. His whole head turned to the side with the impact. It took him a second to feel it, but then it spread across his face like a burn. When he opened his eyes his mum was staring, not at his eyes, but at his cheek. As though she could already see a handprint there. He wouldn't be surprised if she could. He felt like it was branded into his skin; he'd be walking round for the rest of his life with his mother's hand in red on the side of his face. *Well, that makes three of us*, he thought, *me, Luke and Francis . . .*

'Oh Lord,' she said helplessly. Then she started to cry.

He didn't know what to do, so he left her there, standing in the middle of the carpet, with tears running down her chin.

*　　*　　*

The thing was: when you didn't have anything to lose, you could be brave.

He didn't know what it was – desperation, courage, that dream of Evgard, as though it wouldn't let him go – that made him stumble down the stairs. But that didn't matter. All he could think was, *Francis, I must explain to Francis* . . . He blocked out that memory of Francis's face, *you slippery, treacherous shit,* and forced himself to believe there was a chance. Just a chance. If he could explain – and Francis knew what he was like, better than his mum did. Francis would forgive him. He had to. Michael thought, *I'll do anything. Because if it's over, if Francis really does hate me* . . .

He thought he'd left the bag of Evgard stuff in the alcove next to the bin in the kitchen, but it wasn't there. He couldn't think straight. *Oh, come* on, *Michael* . . . of course. It'd be in the wheelie bin outside the back door, ready for the bin-men tomorrow. He was in luck: there it was, slumped at the bottom of the bin. He hoisted it out as he went past, and staggered out of the back gate. The bag smelt sickly, like it had been in the bin for too long. Michael knew he must look stupid, sprinting with a bin-bag in one hand, hair all over his face, in his slept-in school uniform. His cheek still felt like it was bright red. But he kept on going – past the girls' school, the traffic lights . . . All the way, he was thinking, *Evgard. Francis might care about Evgard.*

Then he was standing outside Francis's front door with his finger on the doorbell, wanting to turn and run. But he didn't.

The little ginger one (Catherine, was it? Elizabeth?)

opened the door. The hall light wasn't on, so he could barely make her out – only her eyes . . . She gave a great mucus-filled sniff. Then she said, 'Hello, this is the Harris household,' like she was answering the phone.

'Is Francis in?' Michael heard his voice shake.

'Yes.'

'Can I see him?'

She put her hands on her hips and stood on tiptoe to look into his face. 'Who are you?'

He wanted to say, *Come on, you know I'm his mate. You've seen me loads of times.* 'Just say it's Michael. Please.'

She tilted her chin and regarded him sternly. 'Michael *Thompson*?'

Jesus, she was going to ask for ID next. He felt his other cheek begin to tingle under her stare. 'Yes. Michael Thompson.'

'You hit Luke.' She narrowed her eyes even more, until Michael could hardly see her pupils. 'Luke said Michael Thompson hit him. And Mum's On The Warpath. And Francis fought someone and I think he lost. Was that you too?'

'No, look, can I just – is he here? I need to talk to him.'

She put her head on one side. 'Mum says you're a selfish evil bully.'

'Right.' It was like a slap in the face. *Exactly* like a slap in the face. He hated himself for how much it hurt.

'She says you should be ashamed of yourself, hitting someone who's smaller than you. She says you're vicious and mareverent –'

187

'Malevolent,' Michael said automatically.

'Yes, and you must be full of hatred and misery.'

There wasn't much he could say to that. It was true, after all. He *was* full of hatred and misery. 'Thanks for telling me.' He thought, *And am I really vicious and malevolent? Jesus, what if I am?*

A voice behind her said, 'Mary. Get out of the way. Go on. Scat.' She turned reluctantly – like she hadn't finished with Michael – and left, scuffing one foot against the skirting board.

It was Francis. He waited until Mary had shut the door of the kitchen at the end of the passage. Then he flicked the light on.

God, his *face*. It looked worse, even, than when it was covered in blood. His eye had gone a shade of purple that clashed with his hair, and his mouth was swollen on one side. There was a dark scab capping the bulge on his lip. Michael wondered wildly how he'd managed to pass it off as a *fight*. Surely even his mum could see . . . ?

He leant sideways against the wall and looked at Michael. 'What do you want?'

'I just . . .' Michael struggled for words and gave up. Did *Francis* think he was vicious and malevolent? *Of course he does,* his brain said. *Of course he does.*

'Right.'

Michael suddenly realised he was clutching the bin-bag of Evgard stuff so hard his hand hurt. He thought, *Say something, please, mate, say something, anything,* you bastard *would do . . .* but Francis didn't say anything else, didn't even meet his eyes. As if he was waiting for something. But Michael didn't know what. He said in a rush, 'I need to talk to you –' and knew he'd blown it.

'Don't come back, Michael. There's really no point.' Francis started to close the door.

'Wait – Francis – please –'

'What?' A pause. 'Oh Christ, Michael . . . what could you possibly say?'

'I'm sorry. Really. I'm so, *so* sorr—'

'Shut up.' Francis turned his head to the side and started to play with the chain on the front door. Michael felt a mad urge to rub his hand across Francis's face, as though he could wipe the bruise away like paint. 'Is that all you can think of?'

'No – I mean, I can –'

'On second thoughts, forget it.' Francis looked him straight in the eye and mimicked his intonation. 'Sorry.' He stepped back and started to close the door again.

'Please – Francis – I can explain –' The door shut in Michael's face. *Shit.* He pressed his fists against the wood. 'Francis – I brought the Evgard stuff – d'you want it?'

Nothing. He thought Francis had gone away. Then he heard the latch. He pulled himself back just in time to stop himself falling forward as the door gave way under his hands.

Francis glanced at the bin-bag at his feet. Then he looked back up at Michael and shook his head slowly. 'I don't get you at all, Thompson. I just . . . I really don't. You're a complete fucking mystery. Why didn't you just throw it away?'

'I thought . . . I didn't want . . . maybe, we could still . . .' Francis's eyes flicked to Michael's face; his expression was so odd Michael couldn't bring himself

189

to finish the sentence.

'Go back, you mean? Forgive and forget?'

'Not – yes, but – no, I don't mean . . .' God, surely he could do better than this? He took a deep breath and started again. 'I know it sounds lame –'

'Damn right.'

'OK.' He stared at Francis. 'Yes. It's lame. It's really lame. But I'm sorry. I didn't mean to – I can explain – if you'll let me – please – I'm sorry –' *Oh yes, great one, Michael. A brilliant bit of rhetoric. Well done.* But what else was he supposed to say? 'It was a mis-understanding, I never actually *meant* to screw your life up irrevocably'? 'Forgive me, O lord and master'? 'Please, Francis, I'll do anything you want, please just be my mate again'? Christ . . . He bent and picked up the bin-bag at his feet, holding it in both arms like an animal. It felt lumpy and awkward. 'Do you want this, or shall I throw it away?'

Michael actually *saw* Francis think, *You loser, Michael, I should tell you to stuff it.* But then he held out a thin white hand. 'Give it here.' His voice said, *This doesn't mean I've forgiven you.* He took it, untwisted the top, and looked into the bag. His face was impassive. After a moment he twisted the bag up again. He shot a glance at Michael. There was some-thing funny in the way he looked at him, something that didn't quite fit: a kind of tension around his mouth and eyes. 'Why would I want this?'

'Because – Evgard –' Michael's throat started to ache suddenly, as though someone was squeezing it. He swallowed.

Francis frowned. Then his face cleared to a sort of neutral mask. 'Oh . . . Evgard. I see.' He dropped the bag on to the doorstep and kicked it delicately with one toe, as though he could hardly bear to touch it. There was a silence. Michael thought, *Please, please. Just let me explain. I'm not vicious and malevolent – really, I'm not . . .*

Francis sighed and looked up, like he'd suddenly got tired. He looked at Michael straight on, unsmiling. Then he put his hands in his pockets, pushed past Michael and walked down the street, towards the corner. He looked back, cocking his head. 'Come on then, Thompson. I want to hear you apologise. Again. Oh –' Francis stopped, as though something had just occurred to him. 'Bring that, will you?' He clicked his fingers at the bin-bag.

Michael thought, *I'm not your bloody slave, Harris.* But he picked up the bag and ran after him.

Francis turned off the pavement into a little dark alley that ran down beside the end of the terrace. It was hard to see anything, after the bright sodium glare of the streetlights. Michael followed him, trailing one hand against the wall on his right. It wasn't like he was *scared*, but there was a voice in his head that said, *If he was going to kill you, this would be the place for it* . . . God, he couldn't see a thing. How come Francis knew his way around so easily? Did he come here a lot? The voice in his head added, *Yeah, maybe it's a cruising ground. Maybe this is where he gets –*

Michael said back to it, fiercely, *Shut up, shut up. For fuck's sake. You're not helping anything.*

Francis stopped so suddenly Michael had to do a sort of awkward sideways jump to avoid walking into him. He heard him shuffling. Then he heard the splutter of a match, and saw a flame and a cigarette-end catching and glowing in the dark. Ah. So he *did* come here often.

Michael thought, *God, I'd kill for a cigarette.* He watched Francis's hand carry the spark to his face and away again, flicking the ash on to the ground.

It wasn't as dark as it was. Or at least Michael's eyes were getting used to it. He could see the outlines of Francis's face now, the smooth pale plane of his cheek on one side, and the bruise that dissolved into the darkness on the other. *It must be painful to speak with a mouth like that,* he thought, *maybe even to smoke. If it were me, I'd lock myself in my room until it had gone down.*

'So. Go on, then, Thompson. *Explain.*' There was a hard, deliberate edge in his voice.

'I –'

But Francis didn't let him finish. 'My mum took Luke to Casualty. To get him X-rayed. In case you'd broken his jaw. But don't worry, she's not going to tell the school. So you can relax.'

Oh God. Luke. As well as what he'd done to Francis . . . He said, in a rush, 'Shit. Francis . . . I didn't – did I? I'm sorry – I mean –'

Francis breathed out sharply, the air hissing between his teeth. 'Christ. So you *did* hit him. I thought maybe . . .' He laughed, without amusement. 'I thought maybe he was lying. That it wasn't actually you. I didn't think you'd do that. But you did.'

'Yes – but –' Michael squinted, trying to see his expression. 'Only because . . .' *Go on,* he thought, *this is where you explain. This is where you tell him about the notes, about Evgard.* Now. But he couldn't help himself; he said, in a rush of guilt, 'I *didn't* break

192

his jaw, did I? I know I really laid into him – but I didn't mean to – not *that* hard –'

Francis swung round, so close that Michael stepped back involuntarily. '*Not that hard?* Hitting him was fine, as long as it wasn't *that hard*?' He shook his head, over and over. 'My God. You are – you're – *unbelievable*. Astonishing. I – I just –' He drew breath; even in the pause Michael could hear the disbelief in his voice. 'What are you –? I mean, is that your idea of explaining? Apologising? Am I meant to say, OK, fine, as long as it wasn't *that hard*?'

'No. No, of course not, I didn't mean – Francis, I –'

'Do you hate me? Is that it?'

'*No* –'

'Because I don't understand. And the other stuff, with Shitley. I mean, *why* –? I don't get it . . . if you knew I was gay, and you thought it was . . . if you thought I . . . I can understand not wanting to be friends, all that stuff. It's crap, but I can understand it. But telling Shitley – hitting Luke . . . I don't understand what I did to deserve it, Michael.' He paused, fractionally, but Michael wasn't quick enough. 'You know what? I really thought we were friends.' There was contempt in his voice; for Michael, or himself, or both.

'Yes – and so did I – until I found out – I mean, I didn't *find out*, I just –'

'Until you found out I was gay.'

'*No* – it wasn't like that –'

'And then you told Shitley I'd come on to you. And *then* you look at me like you've never seen me before and you say *you're not gay* like you really think it. Like you really thought . . .' He swallowed. 'Jesus, I can't even . . .'

193

Michael felt his face burning. His whole body was tingling with shame. He drew in a long breath, trying to keep his voice steady. He said, 'I didn't know you were gay. I really didn't. What happened was – it was because Luke – I mean, I was only – because I thought you'd . . .' *Oh, for fuck's* sake, *Michael!* 'I only said it – because it was the worst thing –' He heard himself just too late. *Oh, Jesus,* no, *that wasn't what I meant, really it wasn't . . .*

'The worst thing?' Such a quiet voice.

'Not like that – I just meant – with Shitley –'

'That's why you said it.' So blank, so relentless. 'Because it was the worst thing you could think of?'

'I didn't mean – not the worst like *that*, not –'

'Not *repulsive*? Not *grotesque*?'

'*No* . . . just because I knew you'd get – that they'd –'

'What? That they'd *what*?'

'It isn't the worst – of course – not for *me* – only – because you'd said – about getting, at my old school, you said you weren't surprised I got –'

'I'm not. I'm not surprised. In fact I'm amazed you've survived this far at St Anselm's.' His voice – it wasn't *sharp*, that wasn't the word, because nothing sharp would hurt so much, so quickly. 'Christ . . . Maybe if we'd known what a little rat you are.'

Yes. This time Michael deserved it. Francis could have carried on, and Michael would have taken it all without arguing. He'd just stand there and nod. But Francis didn't say anything else. He leant back against the fence and finished his cigarette. Michael could hear him breathing.

He had to explain. He had to. 'Francis –'

Francis said softly, 'Fuck you, Michael. Fuck you.'

'I thought – it was about Evgard –'

'And Evgard. Fuck Evgard too.' His voice was so quiet, as though he hardly cared whether Michael heard him or not. But he meant it.

No good. It wouldn't be any good; whatever he said, even if he tried to explain about Luke, the anonymous notes . . . Michael closed his eyes; stood there for a moment, trying to shut out the dark. He made himself say, 'Do you want me to go?'

Silence.

'I'll go. If you tell me to, I'll go.'

Still nothing. He thought stupidly, *What if he's slunk off? Maybe I'm talking to myself.* But when he opened his eyes he could just about see the outline of Francis's face, his head tilted back against the fence, the eyes almost on a level with Michael's. *Go on*, he thought, *tell me what to do, and I'll do it – anything you want. Or you could hit me. I wouldn't mind.* Although he could see Shitley now, after Francis had hit him, could hear the crunch of bone – had Francis actually broken his nose? – and that choking, drowning sound as Shitley spat out his own blood. On second thoughts . . .

He still couldn't get over it, though. Francis had *punched* someone. He'd never seen Francis punch anyone. It wasn't his style. Even now, staring into the dark, trying to make out his face, Michael could feel the shock, and the admiration. It was stupid to admire someone just because they'd hit someone else, he could see that; and most of the time it *wasn't* admirable. Like when he'd hit Luke: he knew, deep down, he shouldn't have . . . But all the same, sometimes . . . It took a kind of bravery. People always said that it was harder to be a pacifist, and maybe it was, but that wasn't the point. *Not* hitting someone, even though you knew you should, because you were scared – that was cowardly. That was what the comp had taught Michael, and he hated himself for it. *Maybe*, he thought unexpectedly, *maybe that's what Shitley will teach Francis, in the end: not to fight back . . .*

He thought he felt bad already. But the guilt hit him at that moment, all of a sudden. There was nothing he could say. *Luke sent me anonymous notes. I thought you'd despised me, all along. I only did it because I thought you hated me . . .* It didn't change what he'd done. He took a deep breath, and then, because he didn't have anything to lose, he said, 'I know it doesn't help. But I'd do anything . . . to put it right . . . if I could. I promise you. I'd do anything.'

He saw Francis turn towards him. 'Oh, really? Would you, Michael? Anything?'

'Of course.' For a moment Michael was glad it was dark. Even his voice was pathetic: eager, sycophantic . . .

'Anything?' There was something very deliberate in the way he said it.

'You know I would.' He added, 'I mean, if it would make a difference –' but Francis had already cut him off.

'So. I could tell you to do anything. And you'd do it.' It was like the way he'd start an argument in English, setting out the facts coolly, making you agree to things that seemed obvious, when you knew that he'd shoot you down five minutes later.

'Yes . . . I mean –' Michael felt a stab of unease. But he could hardly say, *Well, within reason, mate, you know what I mean* . . . He swallowed. 'Yes.'

'Hmmm. Interesting.'

Michael had never disliked anything about Francis. There'd never been anything, not that he could remember, that made him draw back, nothing that put him on his guard. But there was something in his voice when he said *interesting* that made Michael go cold. In spite of himself, he started to say, 'I only meant –'

'So I could tell you to . . .' Francis paused, took another cigarette out of the packet, lit it. 'Yes . . . I could tell you to burn your precious Evgard stuff. For example. Or pick a fight with Shitley. Or – what else . . . ?' The smell of smoke was making Michael feel queasy. 'What about you, Michael? Any brainwaves?'

'Stop it. You know I didn't –'

'*Anything*, you said.' A pause. 'I rather like the idea. There's a kind of justice in it, wouldn't you say?' Michael didn't answer. 'You screw up my life, for no reason –'

'It wasn't – no, wait – I need to *tell* you – explain –' It sounded hopeless, unconvincing, even to his own ears.

Francis didn't even look at him. 'And then you want to make amends. By doing *anything*. All right. Suppose I let you. Suppose I give you something to do.'

He's going to tell me to kill Shitley, Michael thought. *He'll tell me to kill Shitley, and I'll do it*. He waited.

'How about . . .' Francis spoke very slowly, like he wasn't quite sure. 'OK, Michael. How about the

worst thing? I wonder what that would be . . .'
Michael heard him take a drag of his cigarette, a deep
deliberate breath that prolonged the silence. 'What
was it you said again, Thompson, about the *worst
thing*?' His voice was so soft it could have been inside
Michael's head.

'Francis –'

'Shut up.' Another breath; another silence.
'*Anything*. Crikey.'

Michael thought, *Please. Please don't. Please, stop
this . . .*

'I know . . .' His voice trailed off. He took a final
drag on the cigarette and flicked it away; cleared his
throat. 'Seeing as you're my slave, apparently . . .
Kneel down, Thompson.'

'Is that it? Just kneel –' but before he'd even got to
the end of the question he had time to think, *No, oh
Jesus, you idiot, Thompson, he means –*

'No, Thompson, that's not *it*. But it's a start.'

Silence, and the smell of smoke. Nothing else: only
the shadows around him, growing like mould, too
deep to look at, and the night sky. For a moment
Michael felt the world falling through space, felt the
speed, the sickening horrible spin of it. He heard the
roar of the earth's orbit in his ears and thought, *Make
it stop, please, make it stop*. It was hard to breathe.

He said, 'Francis . . .'

'What's the matter? You did say *anything*, after all.'
Francis's voice was clear as glass, precise, unfamiliar.

Oh God, this isn't happening. Not Francis; not this.
Michael's throat was suddenly too tight to speak
properly; he heard himself say, 'Please. Francis. Please
don't . . .' He couldn't carry on. He thought, *Come*

198

on, you shit, say something. Put me out of my misery. But Francis didn't do anything; he just stood there and watched him squirm. Michael took a deep breath. 'Do you mean – you don't – what do you –?'

'I want you to lick my shoes, Thompson. Obviously.' His voice had an edge of something like malice, something like triumph. A tiny, split-second pause. 'Why? Did you have something else in mind?'

'*No*. Nothing. I just didn't understand –' But he couldn't get to the end of the sentence. *You stupid tosser, Michael, you fucking* loser . . . He heard himself stammer and thought, *This is what he wants. The bastard.*

'Go on, then, Thompson. I'm waiting. Lick my shoes.'

It should have been funny. *Lick my shoes . . .* like he was *eight*, for God's sake, like they were both kids. But it wasn't . . .

And he meant it. Didn't he? Michael thought, *No, not Francis, please, this is all wrong* . . . but he saw Francis's face, white and rigid and unforgiving, like a statue in the darkness, and knew he did mean it. Of course he meant it. Michael felt dread rise in his gut, scratching upwards. He'd been here before. He knew how this worked. But *Francis* –

'What are you waiting for, Michael? Go on . . . don't you want to make it up to me? Don't you want me to forgive and forget?'

Nausea filled Michael's whole body now, as though he was breathing it in. He swallowed frantically, trying to quell the sickness, trying to hold on to reality. He could feel the world sliding away beneath his feet, dropping through space like a dead weight. The panic grew deep inside him, swelling like cancer, as familiar as an old enemy. No – *please* . . . But he knew it made sense. He couldn't escape. He had it coming. Like the stuff from the comp, like when – he thought desperately, *Shut up, shut* up. He said, 'Francis . . .'

'Michael . . .' He mimicked Michael's tone, bouncing it back to him like a mirror.

Michael thought, *I can't do this. I'm not going to do it. I promised myself – after that day – I swore I'd never – I* can't –

'What's the matter, Michael? I thought you wanted to be my friend again?' His voice was like snow: gentle, deadly cold.

The earth's orbit didn't slow down. The world didn't stop falling.

Slowly, very, very slowly, Michael started to sink to his knees.

ELEVEN

There are two water fountains in Sangarth Castle. One inside, for the Evgard nobles, and one on the outer wall, for the peasants. It was one of the first places in Evgard to have running water – powered, of course, by a slave on a treadmill in the dungeons forty *hycht* below – and the first by fifty years to have a fountain for the peasants to drink from. When it was built it was held up as an example of the indulgence with which the nobles treated the peasants in South Evgard. The fountain in the courtyard bubbles up into a carved stone wellhead; the surface of the water is so smooth that the ladies of the court claimed to use it as a mirror. The water for the peasants trickles down over a slick mould-encrusted statue of an Evgard lord; the only way to drink from it is to suck at the moisture where it drips off the statue's boot.

Michael didn't know why he was thinking about Sangarth. He tried to push the thought away. Jesus, why was he thinking about that *now*, for God's sake? He shouldn't be thinking at all, about anything. He felt another surge of nausea, of black disgusted sickness – *you* loser, *Michael, you* worm – and thought, *Shut up, keep your mind blank, pretend you're not here, you're not alive* . . . But he couldn't help it; Sangarth Castle was there, suddenly, sitting in his mind's eye like a tiny, perfect model of itself. He could see it exactly, the towers, the tapestries and fire-places and dovecote, the arrow-slits and murder-holes and machicolations. As though he was *trying* to remember, as though he wasn't on his knees in an alley, squeezing his eyes shut against the dark. He fought the vision, the clarity, the mad unnecessary details: *Not now, Jesus, please, not now* . . . but it didn't go away. And at the same time, superimposed, he could see the plan he and Francis had drawn, three pages stapled together, each one showing a different storey; and behind all that he could see the real castle they'd based it on. And he remembered the day they'd spent there, right at the end of the summer holidays, the week before the autumn term started. He tried to push the memory away. *Don't think about it, don't think about it, don't* . . . But it was no use. He didn't have any choice.

It was the hottest day of that summer: blinding blue sky, breathless heat, sunshine that made your skin smell different. They'd walked to the castle from the station, following the path until it gave out, then navigating by the sun and Francis's OS map, wading across a river when they realised they were in completely the wrong place. By the time they got there they were already sunburnt and knackered and hoarse from thirst. They walked the last half-mile in silence, and Michael remembered thinking, *God, he must be really pissed off with me, this was a stupid idea* . . .

but when he sneaked a look at Francis's face he was smiling; he caught Michael's look and grinned back at him without saying anything.

And the castle was almost empty. It was miraculous. Michael thought later that maybe it was because most of the schools had gone back already – but at the time he just couldn't believe their luck. It was like they owned the place. Francis had talked him into buying the National Trust booklet, and they walked round arguing about where things were supposed to go. Michael had said, at first, that maybe they should just use the castle as it was, make Sangarth exactly the same; he could still remember the look on Francis's face as he said, 'No, there's not enough *room* . . . you want an observatory, don't you? And baths? And a torture chamber? Come on, Thompson, this place has hardly got *any* dungeons . . .'

Michael caught his eye and laughed. 'That's true. We do need some more dungeons.'

Francis looked round, his face screwed up into a sort of pensive grimace. 'Right. Let's think about this logically. Where can we expand?' It was funny, the way he was so businesslike about it; Michael half expected him to run a hand over one of the walls and make that sort of whistling sound builders make when they're about to say, 'Dear oh dear, this is going to cost you . . .' And he was so *thorough*. Later that afternoon Michael watched him pacing the courtyard, working out how much they were going to have to add to the length, and he was utterly absorbed, like a little kid playing a game. Michael remembered thinking, *He takes this even more seriously than I do. Maybe Evgard is more his than mine, now*. The odd thing was that Michael didn't mind; actually, he quite liked it.

They had lunch sitting in the shade of the south wall, the National Trust booklet between them; Francis was drawing on the map with one hand and explaining between bites. 'So if we expand here, right – then we can put the baths here –'

'But this wall will be too long to defend properly. We should add a tower here and make the whole thing hexagonal.'

Francis put his head on one side. 'Ye-es. OK. And then the observatory is in the ghist tower –'

Michael snorted through his mouthful of sandwich. 'What did you say?'

'What –? Oh. Yeah, all right. The *east* tower. Put the observatory in the *east* tower.' Francis looked away and smiled reluctantly. 'Oh, shut up, Michael. It's your word.'

Michael leant his head back against the wall and gave him a sideways gleeful grin. '"The ghist tower", Harris? It's not real, you know. Evgard isn't *real* . . .'

'Piss off, Thompson,' Francis said. He took another bite of his sandwich and stared determinedly down at the map.

Michael leant towards him and put on his wise-old-wizard-gives-good-advice voice. 'Beware, my son, of confusing fantasy and reality; for who knows what dangers may lurk at the meeting of two worlds?' Francis didn't look up; but his mouth twitched. Michael leant even closer and intoned, 'Once disturbed, who can restore the Equilibrium? And if you are torn equally between worlds, who will you owe allegiance to?'

Francis shook his head, smiling. 'Shut up, Michael.' He looked up, and they both laughed.

Michael was the first to look away. 'Yeah. Fair enough.' He sat back and closed his eyes. God, he was . . . sleepy. Warm and sleepy and full of lunch. He heard the breeze flip over the pages of the National Trust booklet. *I must suggest a murder garden,* he thought. *In a moment I'll open my eyes again and tell Francis . . .*

But when he opened his eyes, Francis was gone.

Where was he? Michael sat up, blinking, staring round. He was probably just . . . but Michael couldn't see him anywhere. There was just his own rucksack, on the ground, and a little ball of silver foil from his sandwiches. No National Trust booklet. No Francis.

It was cooler than it had been; the shadow at the base of the wall was longer. He'd been asleep. He looked automatically at his wrist, but he didn't have his watch on. What was the time? He wasn't locked in, was he? He looked round again at the courtyard. Surely, Francis wouldn't just *leave* him here? Without leaving a note, or anything? But then – where was he? Michael couldn't see anyone, not even the National Trust woman. He was completely on his own.

He gave one last look round; squinting carefully into the shadows. No. Francis had gone. Michael knelt down, put the tin foil into the front pocket of his rucksack and swung it on to his back. No point staying here, then. The warm, sleepy feeling had dissipated. Francis must have got bored, that's all. He must have decided to go home.

Michael walked across the courtyard towards the keep, without looking back.

'Michael! *Oi!* Michael! *Thompson!*'

He swung round. Where –?

'Michael! Up here!' And Francis was waving at him from the top of the south-ghist, the south-*east* tower. Michael stood and gazed upwards like an idiot. He raised an arm to wave back, then let it drop again. Francis hadn't deserted him. He was glad. Of course he was glad.

'Come up!' Francis beckoned, with an exaggerated gesture, like a spin bowler.

Michael did as he was told. The tower wasn't that high, as towers go, but he felt like the stairs were going on for ever. His T-shirt was sticking to him underneath his rucksack.

Francis was bending forward, squinting at the moat, but he turned round when Michael reached the top. 'Where were you off to? Doing a runner?'

'I wasn't going anywhere.'

'I thought you were going home without me.'

'Of course not.'

'Good.' Francis held his gaze. Then he turned back and peered down at the moat. 'God, it's hot.'

Michael went and leant on the wall a little way off. The water at the bottom of the tower was a dull, muddy green-blue, like jade. You could see grey fish just under the surface. He thought, *How high up are we, I wonder? Fifteen metres? Twenty? High enough, anyway . . .* He looked down at the drop and caught himself thinking, out of habit, *All you'd have to do is jump.*

'Looks good, doesn't it?'

Michael spun round and stared at him. Did everyone feel like that, then? Did everyone look down and

206

calculate the distance and think, *It's good to know I could, if I wanted . . . ?* He started to laugh; he wasn't a freak, then, if Francis felt the same. 'That's just what I was thinking. Not *seriously* – I mean, just, you know . . .' He glanced back down at the murky water, the sinuous fish. 'The moat might break your fall, though.'

Francis turned to look at him; there was something odd in his expression. Michael thought, *What did I say?*

Francis said carefully, 'That's what I meant. I could do with a swim.'

'Oh.' Michael was grateful for his sunburn; it meant Francis couldn't see him flush. He turned away. He thought, *You're a loser, Thompson. You're a loser and a freak. Even Francis thinks so.*

'That wasn't what *you* meant, though, was it?' He couldn't have been more skilful: his voice was perfect, casual and gentle and solicitous . . . but Michael didn't answer. He heard Francis start to say something else, then check himself. There was a pause. 'We should go, I suppose.'

'Yeah.' Michael started to walk back to the doorway.

But Francis hadn't moved. 'I wish . . . Oh, bloody hell, I wish I didn't have to go home.' He ran his fingers back through his hair and clasped his hands at the back of his neck. 'I wish I could just stay here.'

'Right.'

Francis slid his hands back over his head and dragged his fingers down over his face. 'Michael, are you . . . ?' He stopped speaking and took a breath. Then he turned to look at him. 'Are you – happy?'

207

Michael stepped backwards idiotically. He shrugged. 'I guess.' He looked down at his feet and tried to think of something to say to change the subject.

'You don't sound very sure.'

'I dunno.' He put his thumbnail in his mouth and bit it. 'I –' He was going to say, *Well, you know, I could do with a bit more money* . . . But he didn't say it. There was something about Francis's eyes: like he really wanted to know. It wasn't like his mum, just needing him to be OK. It was real *interest*. Michael felt his face go rigid. 'Yeah, I'm fine.'

Francis nodded and peered down at the moat. Michael couldn't tell if he believed him or not. He rubbed at the wall with a finger, like there was writing there that he wanted to get rid of. He said softly, 'I hate being at home. I feel like – like there's no *room*. I mean, physically, but every other way as well. You can't breathe . . . And Evgard – it's sort of the opposite. Like there's more there than I know what to do with. And it's great. I really . . . it's cool.' He took another breath; Michael could see his shoulder blades moving.

Michael said, 'Right.' What was he supposed to say? It was the same for him – that was how he felt too – but he couldn't *say* that. 'That's good.'

Francis turned round and looked at him straight on. 'I've had a really nice day.'

Michael nodded, feeling stupid. 'Great.'

'I really enjoyed it. Thank you.'

'No problem.' He tried to grin, but Francis wasn't smiling. There was another pause, just slightly too long. What was this about? Why was he being so *polite*, all of a sudden? It made Michael uneasy; politeness was a prelude to other stuff. *Nice weather we're having, aren't we, Clever Boy? You don't mind if we walk home with you?* He swung his rucksack off his back and fumbled at one strap.

'Michael . . . I –'

'What?' He pulled viciously at the fabric; it had got twisted.

A tiny silence. 'Never mind.'

He looked up. Francis was still looking at him strangely. He waited for him to say something else, but he didn't. 'Let's go, then.'

Francis nodded, his face sombre, almost stern. 'Yes. Let's go.' And he strode past Michael without saying anything else.

Michael remembered feeling something niggle at him, like he'd missed something. It was like, he thought dreamily, it was like crossing a Judas floor without falling through it – taking the right path, just by chance, so you didn't even realise it *was* a Judas floor. And you might never know that you'd avoided certain death, you might never find out how fragile it was . . .

At the time he'd shaken his head and followed Francis down the stairs, thinking, *You've got an over-stimulated imagination, Thompson. It must be the heat.*

Now, with his eyes closed, dropping to his knees in the dark, sick with disgust and self-hatred, he thought: *Here we go, then. This is what was underneath.*

He felt Francis put a hand on each of his shoulders.

Then, suddenly, he was gripping so hard it hurt. Michael gasped at the violence of it; thought, *You bastard*, tried to pull away – so that it was a second before he realised that Francis was pulling him *up*, dragging Michael roughly back to a standing position. Michael lost his footing, stumbled backwards, and fell against the wall. The pain in his shoulders flared up and faded slowly.

'*Jesus*, Michael –' Francis let go of his shoulders. 'Jesus, Michael, you were going to – you were actually going to *do* it, weren't you?'

Michael couldn't speak. *Yes. Yes, I was going to do it. Yes, I was going to lick your shoes, because you told me to, you shit, you fucking bastard* . . . He swallowed, trying to clear the nausea out of his throat.

'My God. You really thought I . . . didn't you? And you were going to do it.' Francis shook his head. 'Why would you . . . ? Why would *anyone* . . . ?' He carried on shaking his head, as though he couldn't stop. 'I never really thought, for a moment . . . Sweet Jesus, Michael – why didn't you tell me to get stuffed?'

Michael thought, *I'm never going to speak again. I wish I could die here, now, against this wall in the dark*.

'You stupid sod, Michael, what the hell d'you think you were doing? How could you? How could you even *think* –? Jesus Christ . . .' Why was Francis so angry?

'I wasn't going to.' Michael was shaking; he hadn't noticed before, but now he could feel it, like the wall was vibrating under his hands.

'Why the *fuck*, Michael . . . why don't you stand up

for yourself, just once in a while, stop being such a –'
He stopped, like he'd caught himself on the edge of
saying something.

'Such a what? A loser? A victim? A spineless pathetic *target*?' Francis didn't reply; he didn't need to.
Michael tried to keep his voice steady. 'I wasn't *going*
to, all right?'

'Then why –? You didn't say no, did you, like any
sane person would have. You didn't tell me to fuck
off.'

Michael heard himself say, 'It was just a – I was just
taking the piss –'

A long pause. 'I see.'

'I knew you didn't really mean – I was bluffing –'
Michael thought, *Oh, for God's sake, it wasn't a
game, we both know it wasn't a game . . .*

'Right.'

Michael wanted to say, *I wouldn't have done it,
don't be stupid, of course I wouldn't*. But the words
wouldn't come. He turned his face away and spat.

He should go home. There was nothing else to say;
nothing left. He looked at Francis's shadowy, blurred
face, and thought, *He hates me. He's like the others.
He thinks I'm a contemptible, pathetic, vicious,
malevolent, arse-licking –*

He turned to leave. A feeble, childish corner of him
waited for Francis to say something, but all he heard
was a shuffle as Francis shifted his weight from one
foot to the other. As Michael turned his foot kicked
against something; it budged slightly, inert as a corpse.
He looked down. It took him a second to remember
what it was. Oh yes. The bin-bag of Evgard stuff. The
kind of world where you could stop being a victim. He

stared down at it: just a clot of deeper black in the dark. Useless. Worse than useless. He reached for it and then drew his hand back, instinctively, like it could bite him. *Oh God*, he thought, *Evgard . . .*

He jabbed at it with his foot. He was going to leave it there. Let Francis do what he wanted with it.

No. He said, 'Give me your matches.'

For a moment he thought Francis was about to say something, but he dug silently in his pocket and held them out, holding the box carefully between his thumb and forefinger as if he wanted to make sure Michael didn't touch him by mistake.

Michael was thankful for the dark. It meant Francis couldn't see how much his hands were shaking as he got four or five matches out of the box and struck them all together. He let the flame trickle upwards towards his hand, until the matches were almost burning his fingers. Francis didn't move.

Michael held the matches poised above the bag of Evgard stuff for a long, absurd moment, like he was waiting for Francis to call his bluff. He thought madly, *Come on, Harris, don't let me do this, surely Evgard means something to you. Surely you don't want to watch it burn? Please don't let me do this. You didn't let me* –

The flames licked maliciously up over his fingers and he dropped the matches. The edge of the plastic bag folded down on itself, melting; for a second he thought the flame had gone out. He leant forward to stare. In the corner of his eye he saw Francis make a slight movement, as though he was doing the same. So he *did* care; maybe he was about to say, *Wait, Michael, don't . . .*

A tiny ripple of fire peeled upwards and then bloomed, suddenly confident, as though something in the bag had caught fire. Michael could smell burning plastic. It hit the back of his throat and made him cough. He drew back. Another tongue of flame licked up, stretching out mockingly into the air, then sank again and slid along one side of the bag. The whole thing had caught, now. The flames inched further down the bag, breathing out black smoke, making the edges of the bag tremble in the heat. The smoke was thick, blacker even than the dark, billowing out now like something haemorrhaging into the air. Michael hadn't expected it to be so acrid; it smelt bitter and plasticky.

Francis still didn't say anything. Michael could see the light from the fire playing on his face. God – was he *smiling*? Like he had a private joke. Like he knew something Michael didn't. He looked like he was enjoying himself.

Michael said, 'What's funny?'

Francis glanced up from the fire and looked straight at Michael. The light danced sideways across his face, turning the plane of his cheek gold, making his swollen lip glint evilly. He *was* smiling; smiling at Michael, as if the joke was something in Michael's expression, as if he was glad to see the look Michael knew must be on his face. 'I never knew you had such a penchant for the dramatic, Thompson.'

Michael heard himself choke. He closed his eyes, but he could still see the blazing mess of melting plastic and flame inside his eyelids. He could hear it and taste it too. What a way for Evgard to end. A stinking pyre in a back alley, and Francis laughing.

He turned and ran. He heard, or thought he heard, Francis say, 'Michael. Oh, shit . . . *Michael*! Wait, you tosser –' but he didn't turn back. The smoke was making his eyes stream already, making him cough and choke, wet-faced. The smell of it followed him, all the way home. He stopped and spat in the gutter, over and over again, but his mouth still tasted of burning grease and rubbish; when he wiped the spittle from his lower lip he heard Francis, the way he'd said, *I thought you wanted to be my friend again* . . . He rocked forward, felt his knees hit the pavement, and retched. He wanted to throw up but nothing came. For a while he stayed there, hanging his head. Then he got up and ran.

Even later that night he couldn't get rid of it. When he closed his eyes it was there on his skin. Like the whole cavity of his skull was full of smoke.

That's the smell of Evgard, he thought. *That's Evgard, burning.*

RHOPT

> ... in the lands of my birth, where the
> marshes are mirrors,
> We say to ourselves, you are all you can
> trust:
> Be true to yourself, be true, stay true.
> But now I am here, under colder stars,
> And old men and young men and children
> agree:
> Be enough for yourself. Be enough. Be all.
> (from Mydhen's Way, trans. MT)

The smell of smoke is everywhere. It sticks on your
skin like grease and wafts out of your clothes when
you move. It sits in the back of your throat so that
you can taste it on your own breath, as though you're
breathing fire, like a salamandron. It's as though it's
got into the walls of the castle itself, so that years
from now the stone will still smell of burning, secret-
ing the smell of ash like sweat. You can't get rid of it.

Most of Arcaster is burnt out, now. The School is
still there, and some of the Trade Streets, but the
warehouses, and the shops and marketplace where
the slave market was have gone. The South-West

215

Quarter, where the poorest people lived, has gone too. If you look in that direction from the castle walls all you can see is a dark grey wasteland. When it snows you can see steam rising from it. But most of the fires have died out. Now, instead of the sound of the flames – the rush of air, the crashes when buildings fell, the screams – there's a sort of deathly silence. The only noise comes from inside the castle. Even from the castle walls, or the dusty, freezing attic where I've been sleeping, you can hear the odd cry of jubilation, or the sound of a scuffle between men who are too weary to shout, or the smash of someone discovering a treasure too large to carry home. And after a while you stop noticing, except that your ears are always open for certain voices, for a particular inflection, a particular turn of phrase. Once or twice, in the last few days, I've heard someone speaking Evgard in a low, precise tone, and it made my heart jump. But it was never Columen. And after the first rush of disappointment, I was glad, because they didn't speak for long before they started screaming.

When we were little, Ryn and I played wars on the beach in the summer. We built whole countries of sand, towns and fortresses and waterways, and conquered them. I remember besieging London once – before we even knew where London was, or could imagine what it was like. For us it was a huge pile of sand, with hundreds of those knobbly turrets you can make by dribbling sandy water into little towers, and we besieged it for a whole afternoon, before it fell. And then we watched the tide wash over it and we went home for dinner.

No one but a fool would expect real wars – a real

rebellion, a real siege – to be anything like that. But when we read accounts of the Old Country wars at school there was nothing to tell us how *boring* they are. That first night, after I – after the Company got into the castle, there was fighting; all I can remember of that is a blur of blood and running, the smell of hot metal and sweat, and struggling to keep myself from throwing up. But now . . . Those days on the beach were more of an adventure than this is. I want to find Ryn. I want to search the castle until I find out what's happened to Columen and Iaspis. They might be alive – they *might* be . . . But the fear and guilt have worked their way into my bones, paralysing me. Whatever's happened here is my fault. I opened the gate. I killed that guard. And if Columen's dead . . .

So all I do is sit on the castle walls, huddled in the cloak he gave me, not daring to go looking for him, sickened by my own cowardice. It's been three days, now. All the servants and underlings have fled the castle, so there's no wood for the fires or food in the kitchens. The White Company are beginning to fight among themselves for bread and fresh water; the wine has long since been drunk or wasted. Sometimes I wonder if there's anything to wait for. But until I know about Columen, about Iaspis . . . I can't leave. Not until I *know* they're dead.

Until then, there's only the snow, blank, mercifully inhuman, and the smell of smoke.

'Argent!'

I turn to look; I'm aching and stiff with cold. If it weren't for my cloak I'd probably be dead, or at least deadsleeping. As it is, it hurts to move.

'*Argent*. I've been looking for you for *hours*.'

Ryn. But for a moment I don't recognise her, because I've never seen Ryn in anything but grimy wool and linen. I swallow, taking it in. She's wearing a tunic and trousers of silvery grey silk. The belt that holds her knife is made of shiny dark leather; it's slightly too big for her, so the hilt of the knife hangs outwards, where it'll be awkward for her to reach. Her hair is piled up on her head; there's a filet of silver net holding it in place.

She grins at my surprise, and gives me a mock Evgard bow. 'Do you like it?'

I turn back to look at the snow. I can't say, *Only barbarians loot and pillage*, and I'm not going to lie. I stare through the arrow-slit and hope she'll go away.

'Argent!' She grabs my elbow and pulls me back. 'What's the matter?' She wrinkles her nose. 'You look like someone chopped your balls off and pissed in the hole.' She sees my face, and adds, 'It's only a phrase, Argenshya. I just mean . . .'

'I know what you mean. Where did you get them? The clothes?'

'There's a whole room of them. Above the kitchens.' She squeezes on to the sill of the window next to me and peers over my shoulder at the snow. 'You should have a look. I bet most of it would fit you. There's loads of girls' stuff, too, all these fancy dresses in weird colours, but I like the boys' stuff better.'

'Of course. It's easier to fight in trousers.'

There must be something funny in my voice, because she turns and frowns at me. 'What's the matter?' She smoothes her hands over the tunic. 'You don't think I should have gone for a dress?'

'*No.*' She's still staring at me. 'What was wrong with your old clothes? Your own clothes?'

'Well, for a start, they're falling apart. And they don't keep the cold out.' She squints at me mulishly. 'Anyway, *you've* got Evgard clothes. Look at that cloak.'

'Columen *gave* me mine! I didn't steal them,' I say, before I can stop myself.

She sits back slowly. I can't hold her gaze. '*Columen* . . . ? As in, the Duke's son?'

I bite my lip. I shouldn't have told her. I promised myself – I was so careful not to tell her . . . But I can't, I won't take it back. 'Yes.'

'*Gave* you clothes? Personally?' When I don't answer she gives a harsh little whistle. 'What were you – his slave? His catamite?'

'His friend.' I can't help myself, but as soon as I've said it I know I should have lied. Her face freezes. She turns her head so that she's watching me sidelong. A moment ago she was looking at me the way she used to when we were kids and quarrelled about whose turn it was to carry the seaweed-basket to the beach; now she looks like someone different, older, someone who's killed people.

'*What?*'

'I mean –' *Go on, for* fargtt's *sake, Argent!* But that look in her eyes – calculating, suspicious. 'I only meant . . . He was kind to me.'

'*Kind* to you? You mean, he kept you alive?'

It's true, in a way. 'Yes . . .'

'He gave you a few of his old clothes.'

'Yes.'

'Is that all? Did he do anything else?'

Oh, *lyshe* . . . He stopped me jumping from the Ghist Tower. He saved me from his father. He treated me like I was human, like I was his equal – or almost . . . I look down, away from her eyes, which are silver, like mine, cold as a winter sea. 'No. Not really.'

'He treated you like a pet. That's all.'

'Yes.'

'*Varesh meither*, Argent, tell me you haven't said that to anyone else! That you were *friends* with the Duke's son –'

'No, I haven't.' Who would I say it to?

Ryn sighs out a long breath; it hangs in the air like smoke. She shakes her head. 'You shouldn't say things like that. People won't know which side you're on. It was hard enough before – after you opened the gate –'

'What? I let you *in*. If I hadn't –'

She puts her hands on mine, pressing them down. 'Yes, I know, I know. But not everyone understood what you'd done. They wanted to know how come you were wandering about the castle like that, when all the other Mereish slaves were in the dungeons. But if they heard you say . . .' She leans close to me, so close I could touch her lips with my tongue, if I wanted to. 'Promise me you won't ever say that again. That he was your *friend*. Promise me.'

'All right.'

'We're Mereish, Argent. We have to stick together. The Evgarders – they're different from us. They'll always treat us like shit. That won't ever change. We've got to *fight* –' She searches my face with her eyes.

'Yes.' I'm too tired to argue. I imagine my father,

leaning forward, shaking his head. He'd say, *Ryn, lass, that's not the way, that's not enough.* He'd say, *Whenever you fight there's someone who loses. And whoever loses fights harder the next time.* For a second I can see his face, every line of it, his eyes looking into mine; and I'm glad he's not here, that he can't see me like this, that he doesn't know what I did. Then suddenly I have to swallow again and again, pushing the misery back, because he *isn't* here. He didn't come for me. He didn't join the raid, hoping against hope that I was still alive; he's not here, leaving the others to loot and drink while he searches, not resting until he's found me, or my body. He thinks I'm dead . . . I say again, 'Yes.'

Ryn narrows her eyes. Then she relaxes. She's rubbing one hand absent-mindedly against her leg, over and over; she sees me looking and grimaces. 'I can't get clean. It's like it all gets under your skin – all the ash and mess and blood.' There's a track of rusty dark under each nail. She spreads her fingers and looks critically at her hand, the silvery nails, the skin so white it looks like quartz. 'I need some gloves, really.'

'Take mine.' I tug at the fingers of my gloves and offer them to her. They'll be too big for her, but they're black leather and sable. They were Columen's fourth-best pair.

She looks up with a little questioning smile. Then she tries them on and laughs with pleasure. 'Thank you.'

I don't say anything else. My own hands have already started to ache with cold. I don't know why I gave them to her. Not out of generosity, certainly; maybe something about those white, white hands, that set my teeth on edge. *Pisciculi albus* . . . I know what they meant, now.

'Anyway. Come on.' She stands up suddenly and

turns, pulling at my sleeve.

'What? Where?'

'Mathon wants to see you. Didn't I say? He wants someone who speaks Evgard.'

'Why?' They've been here for three days; why do they need to start talking Evgard *now*? I push away the jab of hope that says, *They're negotiating*. It's just as likely that they want someone to interrogate the prisoners, or just taunt them as they're being tortured. What if it's Columen –? I grit my teeth.

'How would I know? But you'd better come. Show everyone what side you're on.' She says it so casually.

'I opened the gate! I betrayed –' I hit at the stonework with my fist, feeling the cold jar right down to the bones. I killed that guard – with Columen's dagger . . . '*Varesh meither*, Ryn – what else do they need?'

She rolls her eyes. 'Yes, *I* know that, Argesha.' She hooks her gloved hands into her belt. 'But not everyone knows you as well as I do. Come on. Don't sulk. Please.' When I don't answer she shrugs and starts to walk along the wall, back towards the North Tower.

I follow her, dragging my feet in the icy, ashy sludge. I say to her back, 'Where are we going?'

'I told you. To Mathon –'

'No, *where*?'

'Oh.' She turns to look at me, brushing snow out of her eyes. 'The Square Gallery. Why?'

'Not this way. If we go down the Narrow Stairs, then there's a back way –' I shouldn't have said anything. Her face stiffens, suddenly hostile, and I know why: because there's a kind of ownership in my voice. I can't help it. In the last few weeks I've been every-

222

where in the castle, without let or hindrance, following at Columen's heels. He showed me all the secret
ways, too, the doors and levers and code-keys, the
walls that yield under the right pressure, the garderobe that's always kept locked, because it isn't really
a garderobe at all . . . I know Arcaster Castle as well
as any Evgard courtsnipe, and I'm proud of it.

She jerks her head; it's almost a nod. When I turn
towards the south again, and the Narrow Stairs, she's
there, at my shoulder, silently following me. It's only
because we grew up together – because we've been
friends all my life – that I can see the change in her,
the slowly hardening core of distrust when she looks
at me. But it's too late. There's nothing I can do about
it now.

The Square Gallery is dark, and crowded, and
smells of dirt and stale breath and blood. There's loot
all over the floor; people have used chests and bales of
cloth to block off areas of the room, so that it's hard
to get to the other side. Mathon has a makeshift desk
at one end, but he's hemmed in by odd pieces of fur-
niture and smoke hangs above his head like a pall. A
couple of people look up as we walk past, but no one
challenges us. I can't help thinking, *This is a shambles
. . .* and then, in spite of myself, *Columen would have
done better.*

Mathon sees us. He stands up and comes out from
behind his desk. A couple of the men slumped against
the wall follow his example, hauling themselves grace-
lessly to their feet. Ryn sketches a salute and pushes
me forward. 'Here he is, Captain. This is Argent. He
opened the gate for us.'

Mathon looks down at me. There's something

about him that makes my hackles rise. The way he stood up before we got to him, perhaps, as though he wanted to make a point of his huge bulk, the fact that I only come up to his shoulder. Or maybe it's that he looks like a parody of my father, except that where my father is wiry and weather-darkened, Mathon is heavy and ruddy from too much drink. He has very small eyes, as though poring over battle campaigns has made them retreat nervously back into his skull.

He looks me up and down. 'This is the Evgard boy?'

Ryn grabs my elbow in a quick protective clench. 'No, Captain, he's Mereish. He's one of ours. From Skyph. He got captured. Before the Sundark.'

'Argent . . . That's an Evgard name, isn't it?'

I stare back at him. As though it matters. It's only a name . . . 'My mother was from Petra Caeca.'

His nose twitches. There are tiny bristles on the end of it, growing out of the pores. 'So you're half Evgard?'

I start to say, 'I let you into the castle, didn't I?' but Ryn has already pulled me back and stepped in front of me.

'No, Captain – he's as Mereish as we are. He never knew her, his mother, I mean. She just went off when he was a baby. Selfish Evgard bitch.' She takes a step closer to Mathon. 'Honest, Captain, he hates Evgard more than any of us.'

I catch my breath. But the look Ryn shoots over her shoulder is so pleading, so apologetic, that I make myself bite my tongue. *Please, Argent*, it says. *Let me save your life.*

And Mathon nods, slowly. 'All right.' He looks down at me, chewing the side of his cheek. 'But one false move . . .' He stares at me, as though he's trying to read my mind. 'We know you're not above a little bit of treachery. So no funny business – or it'll be you begging for mercy on the Salamandron's Tail, and not your Evgard friends.'

I don't believe it. In a moment he'll relax, grin, slap me on the back, say, 'Ha! Thought I was serious, didn't you, sonny? Well . . . so it was you that let us through the gate? Well done, boy, well done. I'm glad to meet you.' But he doesn't. He clears his throat and spits into the rushes at my feet.

I gaze at him, incredulous. In my head the noise of the battering ram is surfacing again, the horrible sweaty stickiness of blood on my hands, the smell of rust hitting the back of my throat. All that, for this. *You're not above a little bit of treachery* . . . I blink, forcing it away. *Don't think about it.*

Mathon says, 'And if you think you're getting a share of the spoils you can think again. Keep your thieving little hands off, you understand?'

I want to say, *You bastard, I opened the gate for you. I killed that guard. I betrayed Columen, the only person I* . . . *You* shudfargtte, *you* meidburuchtts . . . but I can't speak.

'Hurry up, then, boy. Don't stand there like an idiot.' He glances at Ryn. 'He *isn't* an idiot, I take it?'

Ryn doesn't laugh or catch my eye. 'No, sir.'

'Hmm.' It's hard to tell from his tone whether he's pleased or disappointed. 'Come on, then.' He picks up his axe from the wall where it's been leaning and makes a few mock passes with it before slinging it over his shoulder. 'Chop chop.' He laughs, showing a rotten back tooth.

No one tells me where we're going, or why. After a while I begin to suspect we're taking a roundabout way to the Treasury. Everywhere we pass is deserted, with doors hanging off their hinges or kicked into piles of firewood. The reeds on the floor have been trodden into brown decaying wads. Most of the pictures have gone; a couple are still in place, defaced by obscene scrawls or crude drawings of skulls or phalluses. We go past the picture of the Lady Ilex that Columen showed me, and someone's written *WHORE* above her head. Mathon follows my gaze. 'Like it, do you, boy? Or don't you know what it means?' He makes a gurgling noise in his throat; it takes me a few seconds to realise he's laughing. 'Sounds like you ought to know. Sounds like your mother was –'

My dagger is in the small of my back. I know it's there. I don't need to think before my hand goes to it, and it slides up out of its sheath, fitting into my hand so neatly it's as if it's part of me. I don't even wonder what I'm about to do.

But Mathon has stopped dead, catching Ryn off guard, so she almost walks into him. 'Oh, *shudfargtt.*' He's not talking to me.

The corridor's been blocked. There's a long, massive table, set on its side, with pale splintered pockmarks where someone's reclaimed arrows, and bolsters slumped round the edges like dead children. There's even a huge pewter dinner-dish, with one edge curled up as though it bounced off the wall before it fell. A barricade. From the way it's been built –

strong, logical, the table too heavy to be moved without a team of men – I'd say it was Evgard soldiers, making a last-ditch stand. I'm glad we can't see the other side, where the bodies would be. Not that it's important, really, who built it; the only thing that matters now is whether we can get past it. And we can't.

'*Sbythageird meidburuchtts . . . varesh meither . . .* I told the stupid *ryglingim* not to fight face to face. The disobedient –' He uses a word that my grandmother would slap my face for using.

Ryn looks down, scuffs at the reeds with her foot. 'We can go another way . . . can't we?'

He turns on her. '*Which* way, you stupid little bitch? What do you know about it?'

My hand is still resting lightly on the hilt of my dagger. 'Where are we supposed to be going?'

He snorts and rolls his eyes at the ceiling. 'Oh, *min feirgtt'es lyshe*, the boy thinks he can help!' He kicks the barricade; the sound of it resonates in the stone and makes my teeth buzz.

I can help, you stupid, ignorant swine – if you'll let me . . . 'If you tell me where you want to go.'

He scowls down at me, arms crossed over his chest. Then he heaves a great breath. 'The octagonal room at the top of the high tower. Above the room that had all the coins in it.'

The High Treasury, above the Mint. I turn on my heel. 'This way.' I don't look to see if they're following me.

The quickest way to the Treasury goes through the dungeons, up a tiny secret staircase and through the Great Hall. But I don't take them that way. It's not that I don't trust them. I'm Mereish; they're Mereish; we're on the same side ... But weeks of knowing Columen, of playing shek or the traitor game every day, have left their mark. Knowing my way around, when they don't, is the only advantage I have. Something tells me to hang on to it.

So I take them back round to the north, up and down an unnecessary staircase, and through the baths. I can hear them trailing me – Ryn's light-footed sprint, Mathon's heavy panting lollop – but I don't give them time to catch up. At each doorway I wait until I can see one of them, then I start running again.

The baths are dry, mostly. The water-halls are blue and cold and silent, so that when my foot catches a broken tile and sends it spinning the sound echoes and echoes. The mosaics and statues and fountains have been torn down and smashed, and only a few lights are burning. As I pass one of the alcoves I catch a glimpse of a body, slumped on the slab as though he's still waiting for a slave to come and rub him with oil.

I run along the pavement next to the pool, down a few steps into the next water-hall, along, across ... As I run, there's a part of my mind trying to remember what order they come in (tepidarium? frigidarium?) as though this is all a game.

The last pool is the shallowest. There's a glass walkway just underneath the surface; I remember the first time I saw a slave cross it, carrying a tray of wine, and how Columen teased me. 'Of course he was walking on water. What's odd about that?' He stared at me, pretending to frown. 'You mean, Mereish people *can't* walk on water?' Then he started to laugh. I almost hit him. I remember that. I almost hit him.

The glass walkway is still intact – probably because there's still water in the pool, and none of the Mereish fighters have realised it's there. The water's icy, though. It gets through the seams of my boots, and in a vain attempt to keep my feet as dry as possible I run faster than I should.

And I slip.

I feel my feet slide out from underneath me; there's a long, horrible moment when I realise I've lost my footing, I'm irredeemably off-balance . . . I know I'm going to fall, but I flail at the air all the same, as though I can grab at the emptiness under my hands to save myself. No good. I'm falling, I'm falling – and desperately I throw myself sideways; I can imagine what that glass edge would do to a head, a face . . .

The water is so cold I hear myself cry out with the shock of it. It's like – well, it's like nothing else, water that's so cold it doesn't chill you gradually but bites right to the bone, as though it's sucked out your marrow, wiped you out and rewritten you. It's like another element: the twin and the opposite of fire. All the breath goes out of me. The pain, the shock – it's like *dying*.

But after the first jolt of it my instincts take over. My arms are scrabbling for the side, and my feet find the bottom of the pool, and I'm standing up, only waist-deep – shaking, my teeth chattering, but alive. I start to laugh weakly. I wade to the side of the pool where the steps are, underneath one flickering blue-shaded lamp. Freezing locks of hair cling to my face and I try to wipe them away with a wet hand. For some reason, I'm swearing in Evgard: *Oh, cunnus, cunnus, cunnus* . . . I walk right into the step and stumble forward, hitting the heels of my hands on the tiled pavement. Then slowly, still muttering to myself in Evgard, I drag myself out of the pool and sit huddled on the steps, listening to the water running out of my clothes, shivering in great convulsive jerks. There's no sound of Ryn or Mathon.

Slowly the iciness fades. I'm still bitterly, hideously cold, but it's an improvement. I stare at the blue light flickering on the water and try to make myself get up. But there's something hypnotic about the movement of it, the way azure and cobalt and black melt in and out of each other like oil. There's a tongue of pale blue that licks at a long column of darkness, tasting it, drawing back, reaching out again. I watch it, dreamily; raise my eyes to the statue that's making the shadow . . .

But it's not there. It's in pieces, scattered over the other side of the pool. The shadow – there's nothing to cast the shadow.

And with a horrible insinuating jerk, I realise. Another body. As I look, suddenly I can see the shape of it: a tall, slender man, an arm with a wide puffed-up sleeve that floats as if he's waving, a pale hand with an odd contour, as though someone broke the fingers trying to get the rings off. A shock of hair that floats like a weed on the water and glints dark purplish-red in the light from the lamp. The edge of a face, bloated now, pallid. An open eye that catches the light: blank, glazed, the colour of autumn leaves . . .

No. Oh, *lyshe*, no, please, *no* . . .

Not Columen; not like this, not bloated and unburied and forgotten. I'm back in the pool, fighting the water to get to him, hardly feeling the cold. My feet slide uselessly on the bottom, and my hands are too cold to get a proper grip on his sleeve. *Columen, please, I'm here, I'm sorry* . . . I try to drag him, but he's a dead weight. I'm gasping with the effort, with desperation, struggling to push him towards the steps. As I battle through the dark water his arms move in a parody of life. I can't help splashing and his sleeves start to fill with water, pulling him down. One more step – one more. *My lord*, I hear myself say. *My lord*. His skull hits the edge of the step with a tiny, tactless thud.

I clamber on to the steps and drag him up by his shoulders. His hands are flung out at an awkward angle but I don't care any more. I just want him out of the water. I just want him to start breathing again. I tug and tug at his clothes, trying to roll him over, as if I could bring him back to life. No, no, *no* . . . he can't be dead. Not like this. He can't be. Not Columen – anyone else, but not Columen. This can't be Columen. It can't be. Please, please . . . It must be someone else. I strain at his collar, desperately, and the body rolls over, reluctantly, like someone who doesn't want to wake up. His head lolls to the side; a trickle of water runs out of his mouth. One eye is open; the other one is a wet pale mess of . . . it looks like it's been chewed, then spat out again. His face is white and spongy and more obviously dead than anything I've ever seen.

But it *isn't* Columen. It's the Duke.

I pull back. All of a sudden I can feel air in my lungs, the cold waterlogged weight of my clothes, the sneaking tracks of drips down the back of my neck. It's not Columen. It's the Duke. The bloody, murdering, *meidburuchtts* Duke. I start to laugh, and then I can't help myself. I'm sobbing and yelping and gurgling with laughter, like a kid. I might even be crying, but my face is too wet for me to notice. I stand up, feeling the shaking in my wrists as I push against the pavement, still giggling.

'What the hell's going on?'

Mathon. And Ryn. I don't know where they sprang from. They weren't here a moment ago. I try to say, 'It's the Duke – I've found the Duke. Why don't you negotiate with him?' but the laughter wins halfway through the first word and I have to bend over, clutching my ribs.

For the first time Mathon doesn't sound hacked off; now he sounds worried. 'What's the matter with him?'

Ryn's staring at me. 'I don't know.'

'The Duke – the *Duke* –' I point one shaking hand at the Duke's mashed, swollen face. Even that's hard to do, I'm laughing so much.

Ryn looks down at the body and back at me, trying to make sense of it. 'What happened? We thought – we heard you scream, and fall into the water – was there an ambush? We waited –'

'No – I *fell* –' But that's funny, too; I fell into the water, and it was only up to my waist! I try to fight another wave of hilarity, but it's no use.

'Are you hurt?'

I manage to shake my head. Ryn takes a breath that's half relieved, half wary. She looks down at the body of the Duke, then back up at me. 'Argent – are you *crying*?'

It sets me off again. 'No, you silly shepperling, I'm

laughing –' but I can't speak clearly.

Ryn frowns. Then her face goes blank, as if she's made a conscious effort to clear it. 'We'd better go.' She turns to me. 'Which way?'

I point; it's easier than trying to say, 'Straight on.'

Mathon gives me a long, heavy look. Then he grabs Ryn's shoulder and spins her round. 'Let's go.' And he strides off, still with his hand clenched in her collar, as though he knows where he's going.

I don't want to go with them. I feel sick from laughing so much. I want to find somewhere to sit on my own, where I can get warm. But they need me to show them where to go, and they're Mereish, and *orders is orders*, as Columen would say, in a mock Flatlands accent. And they might kill me, if I leave them now. So I don't have a choice. I run after them and overtake them without a word.

The steps up to the Treasury are longer and steeper than I remembered. When I get to the top, finally, and the guard challenges me, it's as much as I can do to gasp, 'Mathon – s'coming in a minute.' The guard looks me up and down. I can see him wondering who I am, but I look Mereish, and everyone's wearing Evgard clothes. I slump against the wall, thankful that at least I'm warm now, and wait for Mathon and Ryn. I try not to look round too much, because I don't want the guard to get jumpy, but I stare at the wall opposite and let my peripheral vision do the work. This guard; another by the door; the sound of a third in the antechamber. All heavily armed. Two locks on the door; both bars in place. And the High Treasury itself is the securest place in the castle, except for the oubliettes: at the top of the tallest tower, with no windows, and walls that look like chain mail from the number of metal loops set into them.

Mathon reaches the top, sweating, and walks past me without waiting for Ryn. He glances at the guard and jerks his head towards the door. 'Let me in. I want to talk to them.' He gives me a hard, level stare. 'You – come with me. And no talking to the prisoners, all right? Not unless I tell you to.' Then he looks back at Ryn, who's just got to the top of the stairs. 'You – stay outside.'

The Ryn I know would bristle and say, 'What? I don't *want* to stay outside.' But she doesn't. She just nods. She looks exhausted: pale, breathing quickly, swaying. I watch her, willing her to meet my eyes; if I were nearer I'd take her hand. But when she does look up she looks away again quickly, as if I make her uneasy.

'Come on. Jump to it.' I thought Mathon was talking to me, but the guard leaps into action, fumbling hurriedly at the bars on the door. Suddenly I don't want to watch. If Columen and Iaspis are behind that door – or if they're not . . . I don't know which is worse.

The guard isn't efficient, or quick; he's nervous, and he keeps putting the wrong key in the lock, or trying to turn it the wrong way, or trying to pull the handle before he's taken the bars off. But all the same the door opens sooner than I'd like. And the third guard, the one in the antechamber, knows what he's doing, so the second door swings open before we've even got to it. Then it shuts behind us.

The air is dark, and bitter, and thick with smoke. At first I can hardly see anything – only shapes in the middle of the room and the dull gleam of torchlight on metal. Then, as my eyes get used to the flickering, unreliable light, I realise I'm staring straight into Columen's eyes.

Once, when my father was feverish, he called me by the wrong name. I'd brought him a bowl of water, sweetened with hartwort-root, and as I stood beside his bed he sat up and reached for me so eagerly I spilt half of it on my shirt. 'Evnyss,' he said croakily, but with a kind of absolute, disbelieving joy in his voice. '*Ev* . . .'

'No,' I said, 'it's me, *Thatha*. It's me, Argent.' For a moment he looked around, as if I'd stolen something and hidden it from him. Then he sank back on to his pillows. He wouldn't touch the water; just waited silently until I left. I remember the look on his face: disgusted, tired, haunted . . . as though I had *decided* not to be Evnyss, as though I'd decided not to be the brother he thought I was. I hoped never to see that expression on my father's face again, and I never have. But it's there on Columen's, so precisely the same that I can't bear it.

I force myself to look away. I notice the grime and stains on his shirt, the long rip across one shoulder. In the smoke his skin looks darker than I remember, and much, much darker than the drowned, bloated flesh of his father's face. There's a deep red slash across his forehead. One hand, purple at the wrist as though someone disarmed him by slamming it on the edge of something, is poised above a game of *trecho*. I even make myself glance down at the game, but it's not like shek, you can't tell who's winning.

I don't know how long we've been standing there

silently. It seems like an eternity. Columen raises an eyebrow. Then, with an insolence I can't help admiring, he turns to Iaspis. 'Your move.'

Iaspis is looking at us, with a look on her face that slides down the back of my throat like a splinter of ice, it's so pitifully, stubbornly proud. It's only when Columen taps the back of her hand that she looks down at the board. She moves a piece swiftly, then looks back at us.

Mathon clears his throat. 'Right, you lot.' Suddenly I realise there are more people in the room: Columen's cousins, the two older boys, Teres and Latus, the girl, and the little boy. They've got chairs, too, another table, even a few cushions. With a sick kind of shame I realise they're chained to the wall; and so are Columen and Iaspis.

Mathon turns to me. 'Translate, idiot!'

'What? All you said was –' He gives an impatient jerk of the head, so I swallow and say carefully to the wall, 'My lords and ladies . . .'

Columen freezes. Then he starts to tap his king on the *trecho* board.

Mathon says, 'Which one of you is the Duke?'

'The Duke? But the Duke's dead.' I say it more loudly than I mean to. 'I told you – the body I found –'

Mathon turns on me. 'I know that! But there must be an heir, right? And these are the castle kids. So one of these must be Duke now. Which one?'

The castle kids . . . perhaps he doesn't realise that Columen was his father's second-in-command. He must think of him as just an incompetent, arrogant child; the way I used to think of the Evgard children, before I saw what Columen could do.

'Go on. *Ask*. You're suppose to be translating, *shudfargtte*.'

Columen knows all the Mereish swear words now – I know he does, that was the only Mereish lesson I ever gave him – but he doesn't look up. And I don't want him to. I'm scared that, if he meets my eyes, I won't be able to speak at all. I clear my throat. 'He wants to know who the heir to the dukedom is.'

Columen doesn't respond; surprisingly, it's Teres that speaks. 'Why don't you tell him yourself, son-of-a-whore?'

Mathon says, 'Him, is it?' He jerks his head to one of the guards, who starts to move towards Teres.

Teres stares at the guard, as though he doesn't understand what's going on; then he looks at me defiantly. 'You scared to say anything, traitor-boy? Why don't you –'

Columen looks round sharply. 'Shut up.'

'But the little bastard *knows* –'

'I said *shut up*.' And Teres subsides, still glaring at me. Columen puts his king carefully back on the *trecho* board. 'Tell your captain it's me.'

I do what I'm told. 'It's him, Mathon. The tall one with red hair.'

'Right.' Mathon clicks his fingers impatiently at the guard. 'Not *him*,' he says, as though he knew it all along. 'The one who looks like a girl.' He stands in front of Columen and knocks over the *trecho* pieces with a casual, deliberate hand. 'Stand up.'

Columen's eyes are on the ruined game; he follows a piece with his gaze as it rolls gently to the edge of the table and falls on to the floor. Then, very slowly, he looks up at Mathon; then, very slowly, at me. There's an expression of distant enquiry in his eyes.

'He said, stand up. Please,' I add, but Columen isn't fooled. He stands up. He's almost as tall as Mathon.

Mathon beckons to the guards; they shepherd Columen out from behind the table, and stand either side of him, holding his arms. I see him flinch at their touch – out of distaste, I think, more than fear – then master himself.

'So. If you're the heir, who's next in line after you?' Mathon shoots a glance at me. 'Tell him to point at them.'

I start to speak, but halfway through the sentence I have to swallow and clear my throat. I stare at the wall behind Columen's head and start again. I can do it. If I don't meet his eyes, I can do it. 'He says, who's next in line after you?'

Columen blinks, once. 'No one. Not until I have a son.'

'He says, no one –'

Mathon slaps him, hard, across the face. I see Iaspis squeeze her eyes shut and clench her fists. When I look back at Columen he has a bead of scarlet swelling on his lower lip; as I watch, a drop of red slides down to his chin. '*Who?*' He takes Columen's jaw in his hand and leans towards him. 'It must be someone here. So who? The talkative one? The little tart in the low-cut dress? Or the brat? Which one?'

Columen doesn't wait for me to translate. He knows how this works; maybe he's done it himself, trying to get information out of a Mereish slave. He swallows and shakes his head. 'No one. Just me.'

This time he sees it coming. He has time to breathe

out, to force himself to relax, the way you're meant to, so that the blow doesn't meet as much resistance. But even so, he can't stop himself crying out. It takes him longer to straighten his head, this time.

'Ask him again.'

'Mathon – maybe he's telling the truth –'

Mathon turns to look at me, his brow creased in a look of incredulous disgust. 'Ask him again, clever boy.'

'But –'

'You want a taste of it too, do you? *Meidburuchtts lyshe*, whose side are you on, anyway? *Ask him again.*'

I swallow. 'Columen . . .'

Columen gives a quick spurt of laughter; a bubble of red spittle slides down his chin. 'Let me guess: who's next in line after me?' His words are slurred, as though something's broken in his mouth.

'Why don't you just tell him?' *Please. Then he won't hit you again.* Please.

He looks at me with such pitiless, inexorable contempt in his face that it takes my breath away. Then he turns his head away, so that he's looking straight at Mathon. 'There's no one. And he's a fool, a *foeda*, *copulatus* idiot, if he doesn't know that.' A pause. 'You'd better translate that for him.'

Mathon narrows his eyes. 'What did he say?'

'Just that – there's no one . . .'

There's a pause; I have time to think, *Maybe he won't hit him, maybe he won't* – before he does, slamming all the weight of his hand into Columen's face. This time there's an audible crunch as well as Columen's gasp, and he staggers and slips sideways so that the guard has to hold him up, cursing.

Mathon flexes his fingers one by one, like a *xixa* player limbering up. 'Tell the little *glydd* I can keep this up as long as he wants.'

There's no need to tell him that. He knows. Instead, I say, 'Please – Columen – just tell him. Please. What harm can it do?'

He opens his eyes. It takes him a second to focus on my face. 'Did you tell him what I said?'

'Not exactly. Columen, please –'

He braces himself against the guards and brings himself back up to standing. It makes me feel sick, watching him move so awkwardly, so painfully. He takes a deep breath. Then he tilts his head at an insolent angle. '*Du varesh meidburuchtts ryglyng shudfargtte.*' He can't move his mouth much; but the words are careful, and clear.

Mathon shakes his head, as though he can't believe what he's heard. 'Oh, so you speak Mereish, do you, you little bastard?' Then in one quick movement he puts his hands heavily on Columen's shoulders and jerks his knee up into his groin. Columen gives a little gentle sigh, as though he's just realised something. Then he drops silently to his knees and curls over. For a second he's absolutely still. Then, suddenly, he's retching and sobbing and moaning with pain. His hands scratch uselessly at the stone floor, as though he could dig his way out; his face is wet. I make myself look away. Some of the *trecho* pieces are on the floor near my feet, and I stare at them, trying to work out which ones are missing. The hand, the knot, the rose . . . but I feel as though Columen's gasps are coming from me, as though it's my knees that have given way, me that's pulling desperately at the stones. This is all my fault. I can't bear it.

Mathon says, 'So. Who's next in line?'

At first I don't think Columen's heard. He's still bent over, eyes blank and intent, as if he's looking for something on the floor. He scrubs at his face with the heels of his hands, wiping away the wetness. He's taking deep breaths; I can see him fight the impulse to vomit. But after a few seconds he looks up. For a moment, from the expression on his face, I think he's going to give in. He coughs, swallows, raises his eyes to Mathon. 'No one.' He says it very softly. Then he says it again. '*No one.*'

Mathon flicks a look to me, to check that it's still the same answer. Then he draws his foot back. He's going to kick Columen in the face.

'Wait – *wait –*'

Mathon sighs heavily. He pauses, his leg still poised to kick Columen, and turns his face to me. 'What?'

I lean forward, drop to my knees, so that I'm eye to eye with Columen. 'Columen, please, you're going to have to tell him. Just do it now. Please.'

Columen closes his eyes for a second. When he opens them he's looking me straight in the eye. There's no expression in his face at all. '*Cacas,*' he says. *Fuck you.*

I stand up again. I turn to Mathon. 'His sister, he says. The girl there, in the blue dress.'

'Good. We're making progress.' Mathon looks down at him, one side of his face screwed up into a thoughtful grimace. 'Now . . . I wonder if you're telling the truth?'

'No, *don't –*' but it's too late. Mathon's already

241

stamped on Columen's shoulder blade, grinding down with a quick twist of his heel.

Columen jerks, crying out wordlessly. Then he rests his face against the stone; a drop of water slides down towards his jaw. 'Oh, *mama meretrix* . . .' It sounds like a plea.

'What's he saying?'

'That he's telling the truth. He's had enough.'

'Hmmm.' Mathon looks down at him, rubbing the back of one hand against his beard. He turns to one of the guards. 'What do you think? You reckon she's his sister?'

The guard – the young one, who doesn't seem to know what he's doing – looks helplessly at Iaspis and back at Mathon. 'Well – they do look a bit the same, Captain.'

Mathon nods. 'You're right. They do.' He stares at Iaspis; she tries to meet his eyes, but in the end her gaze falters and she darts a glance at Columen. She's gone white as *yshwyt*, winter ice. Mathon clicks his fingers at me. 'Ask her if she's his sister.'

I clear my throat and try to catch her eye. 'He wants to know if you're Columen's sister.' She's still watching Columen in a kind of horrified trance. '*Iaspis*. He says are you Columen's sister?'

She looks up at me. 'You pathetic little traitor, you –' and there's a string of words I've never heard before, although I can guess what most of them mean. No one interrupts her. 'You *cunnus, copulatus cunnus, foeda catamite*, you *cacate serpens* . . .' Then her voice cracks and she starts to cry.

Mathon has a smile playing round his mouth. It makes me think suddenly of the jokes Evgard soldiers make about raping Mereish maidens. 'Was that a yes or a no?'

I don't look at him. 'Yes.'

He nods again, satisfied. 'Yes . . . that makes sense. Both pretty feisty, aren't they?' But he doesn't wait for an answer. 'Right. Get them down to the dungeons. The one with the *machinae* in it.' He doesn't seem to notice the irony of the Evgard word; or the way Columen looks up when he hears it. *Machinae*. For the first time it strikes me as odd, that the Mereish don't have a word for instruments of torture.

Mathon kicks Columen one more time, perfunctorily, as though it's just for the principle of the thing. Then he walks back towards the door. 'I want them there in two *shandeir*, all right? If not sooner.' He turns to me. 'Can you write? Mereish *and* Evgard?'

'Yes.'

'Good. Find something to write on and follow them to the dungeons. You can be the scribe.' He winks, mirthlessly, so that for a moment I think he's got something in his eye. 'The first Evgard-Marydd treaty. The Treaty of Arcaster, recorded by the Traitor of Arcaster. You'll be making history, boy.' He leaves, gurgling with laughter.

A Treaty of Arcaster. Columen would never sign it. He'd die first.

The guard, the young one, looks helplessly at his comrade. 'Where are we taking them?'

The older guard makes a scraping noise in the back of his throat and spits a gobbet of phlegm; not exactly *at* Columen, but not away from him, either. 'Didn't you hear him, you dozy get? The dungeons, he said. The one with the *machinae*.'

243

'Yeah, but where's that? *I* don't know where it is. How could I? I haven't *been* anywhere. I've been stuck in this horrible little room, ever since we got in. I haven't even had time to have a look round –'

'Oh, for *fargtt's* sake, stop whingeing!'

I force myself to look away from Columen, who's bent over with his forehead on the floor. I swallow and say casually, 'It's just to the north of the South-West Tower, underneath the kitchens – if you go down the stairs from here you take the first on the right, past three corridors on the left, take the next left, down one flight of stairs, along a bit, down another flight of stairs, along the gallery, there's a window on the right, you'll see it, then you go through the little chamber and –'

'*Varesh meither*, I can't remember all that!' The younger guard rubs the back of his neck with one hand. 'You'd better come with us. Show us the way.'

I take a long, steady breath. Then I frown. 'I don't know . . . I've got to find some parchment or something. For the treaty. That's what Mathon said.'

'Do that afterwards. Come on, mate. Do us a favour. We'll take care of the prisoners – you just show us where to go.'

'I suppose I *could*.' For a moment my heart is beating so hard my knees are too weak to hold me up. I squat down suddenly, leaning forward with my hands on the floor. I pick up a *trecho* piece and hold it in front of my eyes, as though I just wanted to look at it, and wait for my breath to come easily again.

'Great. Good man.' The guard turns to the older one. 'You've got the keys to the chains, right?'

The other guard nods without saying anything and

gets a bunch of keys out of the pouch at his side. I don't dare to watch him unlock Columen and Iaspis; I'm scared he might see the desperation, the hope in my eyes. Instead I look at Ryn.

She's bent over, her hands on her knees, breathing heavily. As I watch she shudders and coughs, then wipes her mouth with her hand.

'Ryn, are you all right?'

She straightens and shrugs. She's very pale; you can see all the veins in her face, a net of blue under translucent skin. 'I'm fine . . . just tired. I haven't slept for four days. And all this . . .' she looks at Columen. 'It's not much fun.'

'No.'

She coughs again. 'But I'm all right. And we have to do it.' For a second her eyes light up. 'Imagine it, Argent – a treaty between Evgard and Marydd. No more raids. No more slavery.'

'But if –' I bite my lip, just too late. *But if we tortured people to get it . . . if you put Columen on the Salamandron's Tail so that he'll sign it . . . if Columen dies, like that . . .*

She stares at me. 'But *what*?'

'Nothing.' I nod vehemently. 'Yes. It would be miraculous. Wonderful.'

'Yes. It would.' She looks at me and all of a sudden her face is so *sad*. I don't know why. 'Oh, Argent . . .' For a moment there's such tenderness in her voice, and it makes me sad, too, because if she'd looked at me like that two months ago I would have kissed her. Now I just stare back, wishing we were at home and none of this had ever happened.

The guard says, 'You coming, or what?'

'Yes. Yes, I'm coming.' I turn to Ryn, trying to keep my voice matter-of-fact. 'How about you? Are you coming, too? Or should you go back to the Square Gallery?'

'I –' Ryn coughs dryly, more violently than seems necessary. 'I'd better get back. You go ahead. I'll see you later.'

'Right.' My tone's as neutral as I can make it; I'm trying to hide my relief. I give her a casual, friendly smile, and turn back to watch the guards hauling Columen to his feet. The other prisoners are looking studiously away; Iaspis is already standing straight, one hand pressed flat on the bodice of her dress. Her shoulders are rising and falling with each breath.

'Right. Quick march,' the guard says, pushing Columen in front of him; I think he must be joking, because Columen can hardly walk. The other guard, the older one, takes Iaspis's arm without ceremony and pulls her after him. 'Lead on, then, clever boy.'

I turn away, spinning on one heel as though I'm completely at ease, and go down the stairs. Somewhere behind me I hear their footsteps following me – two sets of heavy footsteps, a light, elegant step that must be Iaspis's, and an unsteady, determined pace that makes my throat ache unbearably. Then there's the sound of the third guard locking the doors again. I keep my eyes on the stairs, in case anyone can see my face.

Down the stairs. First on the right, along the corridor to the end, and then left. A flight of stairs, which are narrow and dark and might be a good place for a fight, except that there's nowhere to escape to. Along a bit – no good, too much space, too much light –

246

another flight of stairs . . . Then the West Gallery, with the Sunset Window. There'll be a lot of light from the window, and it won't be cramped enough to favour the element of surprise. But at the end of the room there's a secret door and a passage that goes down to the Underlake. And from there you can row to the staircase that takes you right up into the Closed School.

The West Gallery, then.

I slow down at the bottom of the stairs and wait for the guards to catch up. I can feel my heartbeat in the roof of my mouth, racing, like wings beating against my palate. It's a few seconds before they come into view, round the last curve of the staircase: Iaspis first, treading lightly, head held high; then the older guard; then Columen, walking steadily now, ungainly and limping, but *walking*; then the younger guard.

I beckon. 'This way.'

'Right.' The older guard pushes Iaspis forward, dirty hands on her bare shoulders, and she walks past me. As she passes she shoots me a look of utter, utter disdain. But it's not like the looks she used to give me, after Columen won me from their father. Now there's an edge of fear in it, a deeper resentment. It's the difference between how you'd look at a worm and how you'd look at a traitor. I think I prefer it.

But Columen's face . . . it's empty. I always imagined that despair was something you could see in someone's eyes, or smell, like fear, but now I know it's not like that. His expression is neutral, blank, as though he's dead already. There's no hope, no choice. It's calm – serene, even. But it's the worst thing in the world.

And if I wasn't sure before, I am now. I'd do any-

247

thing to undo the damage. I swallow. I have to bite my lip, hard, to stop myself saying, *Don't worry, I'll get you out, I promise, I'll do anything it takes* . . . He doesn't even look at me as he goes past.

Across the passage, and down the second flight of steps. Into the West Gallery, and as we walk into the great blaze of coppery red light from the window my whole body tenses with fear and anticipation. I don't have much time; only a few seconds, the time it takes to walk the length of the gallery. Go *on* . . . but suddenly I know it's useless. I'll get us all killed, or worse. In my mind's eye I can see the *machinae* in the dungeon – choke-pears, the rack, the Salamandron's Tail, the Old Man of the Sea – and a tongue of bile rises in my throat. I can't. I can't. I'm not brave enough. I can't do it.

And anyway, why should I? I'm *Mereish*, for hell's sake, I'm on the other side. I'm from Skyph; I'm Mereish. And Ryn's right: they're not like us. You have to stick to your own kind. I don't owe them any allegiance, these bloody Evgarders, I don't owe them anything . . .

Columen stumbles. His shirt is dark and dank with sweat. Automatically, without thinking, I move to help him, holding out my hand. And automatically, without thinking, he takes it and pulls himself back to standing. There's a tiny, tiny silence. We look at each other. Then he turns away.

The guard says, 'Hey, what do you think you're –'

I whirl round, pointing at the window. '*Varesh meither* – look!'

He's distracted for a moment. 'What?'

'The light! There must be a fire somewhere – the

248

city must be burning!'

The guards swap a glance. Then the older one says, in the sort of loud, slow voice you'd use to talk to a child, 'It's the sun setting. We're facing west.'

I look from one to the other. 'But the sun set ages ago! At least a *shandeir* and a half ago. It can't be the sunset. Don't you know what time it is?' I think, *This is stupid. This can't work – it can't possibly work . . .*

But they swap another glance, uneasy now, half convinced already. The older one says, '*Shud* . . . It's true. I saw the sunset when I went out to take a leak, two *shandeirim* ago. It must be dark now.'

'But . . .' The younger one twists round to stare at the window, the lovely glaring unwavering red of the sunset. 'But – if another fire's broken out . . .' There's real dread in his voice; they've seen what fire can do, these two, they know what it's like.

'We have to tell Mathon! Otherwise, it could spread.' My voice cracks with urgency and hope. If the same trick can work twice . . .

The older one stares for a long moment at the window. I can see his mind working: if there's a fire, and Mathon doesn't find out about it until it's too late, there'll be hell to pay. He looks back at me, and the younger guard, weighing up the possibilities. But these men aren't as well trained as the Evgard soldiers; they don't stay at their posts come world-end or winter. He says, 'Right. You take them down to the dungeons. I'll go to the Square Gallery and tell Mathon there's a fire in the West Quarter.'

For a horrible moment I know he's going to tell me to go with him, to show him the way. When he strides off without a backward glance I have to drop my gaze to the floor to hide the look on my face. It's worked. *Levthe lyshe,* it's *worked*.

But the other guard is still holding Columen's arm, and Columen is in no state to fight anyone. What do I do? Attack the guard, so he'll let go of Columen? Kill him? I've done it before: it should be easier this time, as long as I don't think about it. I reach behind me for my dagger – for *Columen's* dagger – and it slips from its sheath into my hand. The hilt fits perfectly into my palm. I walk towards the guard. It's as if I've done this all before. I know how it's going to be: the scuffle, the stab, the noise, the blood and the sudden heat on my hands. And this time, seeing him yank brutally at Columen's sleeve, I don't have any qualms.

He watches me walk up to him; he starts to say, 'What –?'

And then he's trying to shake me off, desperately pushing at me with one hand while he hangs on valiantly to Columen with the other. He's shouting something, but I don't hear what he says; it's as if it's in another language. I pull down at his wrist, push him back towards the window, yelling to Columen to get free, to run for it, to go . . . Then he's let go of Columen and he's fighting me with both hands, one hand across my mouth pushing me back, the other fumbling for his own knife. I'm trying to stab upwards, but I can't get the angle to get underneath his jerkin, and the leather turns the blade aside. He's not as tough as the Evgard man was, but he's younger, and stronger. He's going to kill me. All I can do is shove him backwards with all my strength, towards the window, pushing the way we'd push the carts when we harvested the marsh-reeds in Skyph, putting all our weight into it. I hear something crack in one of my shoulders. *Backwards, you bastard, backwards –* and he glances behind him, just for an instant. But it's enough to catch him off balance; before I've even thought about it I've laced my leg between his ankles and he's staggering backwards. Then he falls. He clutches at me, but it's too late.

He goes straight through the window as though it's water. I hear the crack of his spine against the lead upright; he throws his hands out to try to break the momentum and I see them smash through the glass, splintering it into hundreds of gleaming ruby-red pieces. For a second he seems to hang there, against the black dark, while the breaking glass falls into dazzling splinters. Then he's gone. The crash resonates briefly in the stone gallery. After that there's nothing but the shining debris of the lightlead glass on the stone floor, burning with the sunset of half an hour ago. Outside there's darkness.

I hear myself breathing. I put the dagger back into its sheath; it's still clean. I hardly even touched him with it.

Iaspis says faintly, 'Do you have any idea how much lightlead glass *costs*?'

I walk to the other side of the room and pull the tapestry aside. I've never felt so tired in my life. It's dark, now that most of the window is gone. I can still see the man hanging against that background of light, the shape of him before he fell, and I try to blink him away. I find the lever to unlock the secret door. I pull it down, and it moves smoothly, hardly offering any resistance. Someone must keep it oiled.

251

I turn round and look at Columen. 'Come on. This way.'

He's sitting on the floor, head on his knees, as though he just collapsed when the guard let go of him. He raises his head stiffly. 'Where?'

'To the Underlake. Then we can get to the Closed School, and out of Arcaster.'

He rubs at his face, like a little boy. 'Why?'

'What do you mean, *why*? To get out. To escape.'

'Yes. Why?'

'To . . . don't you want to? Come *on*. We haven't got time for this. You can't stay here.'

He shakes his head. He's got one hand inside his mouth, checking his teeth with his fingers, so when he speaks it's hard to hear what he's saying. 'No. Why *you*? Why now?'

'Because . . .' I stare at him. At least now he's meeting my eyes. 'Because I don't want you to go to torture and certain death.' I can't stop myself from adding, 'Obviously.'

He doesn't smile. 'It didn't bother you before.'

'I'm Mereish, Columen, I had to help them . . . I couldn't betray my people. I *had* to let them in. You'd have done the same, if they'd been Evgarders. Wouldn't you?' Would he? I don't know any more. 'I didn't realise they'd – I thought – I don't know. I didn't mean . . .'

'But you're betraying them now.'

There's so much I could say to that, and all of it would be useless. 'Yes.'

He pushes himself slowly to his feet. 'Do *you* know where your loyalties lie, Argent?'

I want to laugh with relief. They're going to come

with me. And the look in his eyes – not friendly, but . . . human, again; recognisable. 'I don't know. I don't care, right now. Please, let's go. Before anyone –'

An arrow thumps into the tapestry behind me.

It hangs there for a moment, the tip scraping on stone, then slips slowly downwards, tearing the cloth. Columen and I both watch it, mesmerised. It seems to take hours before it hits the ground. Then we turn round.

'Don't move. Argent. Stand apart from the prisoners. First one to make a false move gets an arrow in their throat.'

Ryn.

It can't be. She can't have . . . but she's standing there, with five or ten men behind her, three with arrows already nocked to their bows. Her face is still white, but flaming white, the colour of sunlight on snow. She tilts her head to one side, still looking at us, and says, 'I want them alive. All three, but especially the two dark ones. If they get away, you'll regret it.' Then, in a softer, warmer voice, like a thaw, she says, 'Argent, wormhead, why did you have to . . . ?'

I don't answer.

She shakes her head. 'I knew something was up. I knew you were a traitor – but to kill one of ours, for *this* . . . how could you, Argeshya?'

I flick a look at Columen. He's very still. But the look on his face isn't despair, any more. He looks like a hunter waiting for his prey – or, at least, a man who's going to go down fighting. And Iaspis is the same, poised, like a hawk about to take off.

I say softly, in Evgard, 'Iaspis, the door's three paces to your left. Columen, it's directly behind you.'

Columen's still watching Ryn. He murmurs, 'But the lever to lock it shut is at the bottom of the steps. We wouldn't reach it in time.'

Ryn says, in Mereish, 'Step forward, slowly.' She glances swiftly to right and left, at the archers. 'Argent, tell them what to do.'

I bite my lip. 'You can lock it with the lever here, right? The one I used to unlock it?'

A ghost of a frown crosses Columen's face. 'Yes. But you'd be closing yourself out.'

'All right.' I turn my head and look at Columen, taking in the ruined face, the discoloured skin, the scars that he'll always bear, his amazing autumnal eyes. 'When I say *go* – run for it.'

He turns to look at me sharply, meeting my gaze straight on. 'What are you talking about, Argent?'

'Run for it. With Iaspis. Shut the door behind you.'

Ryn narrows her eyes. 'I said, step forward! Argent, tell them. Go on. Now.' She raises her finger to the archer on her left, as if she's warning him to be ready.

'Columen – *go*.' I don't look to see if he's moved; I'm already running, throwing myself towards the edge of the tapestry, falling sideways against the stone and pulling desperately at the folds of cloth to get to the lever behind. There's noise, suddenly, shouting, the sounds of feet scrabbling on stone, a door swinging open, a twanging like the strings of a harp. I grab at the lever, start to pull it upwards, desperate to feel the mechanism lock, but it won't move. The door hasn't closed properly. I can't lock it. I crane my head to look at the doorway.

Columen's there, his body braced against the door, not letting it shut completely. The door's shielding

254

him from the arrows – but he has to *go*. If he doesn't go *now* he won't have time to get to safety before someone pulls him back. I say, 'Go, for hell's sake, Columen, go, *go* . . .'

'I'm waiting for you, idiot.' I can't believe the exhilaration in his voice, as though it's all a joke or a game. 'I'm not leaving you behind, Argent. They'll kill you.'

'I don't care – please, go, just go –' I twist round, my back flat against the wall, one of my hands still on the lever. 'Go, go, *go!*'

An arrow slams into the door, just at the height of Columen's head. He pulls back, laughing, like a man who's almost been beaten at shek and seen the trap just in time. But it knocks the breath out of me. What if it had hit him? I can't breathe, suddenly. It's as if I can feel it in my own body: the impact of it, the sound, the slow nauseating warmth of blood spreading out from the wound . . .

Columen's face goes white.

I say, '*Hath er badh, min lyshe?*' because for some reason I can't think straight. I shake my head and try to concentrate. Say it in Evgard, you fool, he doesn't understand . . . but the words keep coming in Mereish. '*Eir du gweuthed, min lyshe? Min levthe, min heird . . .*' I hear myself say again, '*Min heird . . .*' as though it's someone else's voice. He's gone so pale, suddenly. What's wrong with him? Is he wounded? But there's nothing, no arrow, no blood. What's the matter? I try to speak, but my mouth's gone dry.

He says, 'Argent. *Argent.* Come here. Please. *Please . . .*'

Why is he . . . ? I don't understand. I shake my head; try to say, 'No, my lord, *you* go.' But somehow

I don't have enough breath. I push at the air, as though I could force him back through the doorway just by gesturing at him. Any moment now, the soldiers will capture him. He has to *go*. He has to. I take a step forward, keeping one hand on the lever, and try to shout, but my legs give way. I'm sitting on the floor, my chin on my chest.

There's an arrow in my shirt.

There's an arrow, sticking out, over my breastbone. Horizontally. Sticking out of my shirt. The feathered end. Almost as though the other end of it is –

And blood. Not much; just a bit of blood. Nothing serious. Just a little circle of blood, round my breastbone. Probably about where my heart is. But not much. Not as much as you'd expect, if you had an arrow sticking out of you.

Somewhere a long way away Ryn says, 'Oh, *meidburuchtts* – I said *alive*, you stupid *ryglyng*!' I give a little helpless giggle.

Columen's still there. I wish he'd go, but he says, 'Please – Argent – we can get you to the Closed School – you'll be fine –'

My hand won't stay on the lever for the door. It's too heavy. 'Columen, please . . . go . . .' I summon another breath from somewhere and say, 'Go, go, *go* . . .' Or at least, that's what I mean to say. But I hear my voice, and I'm saying something else.

Columen shakes his head frantically. A lock of hair falls over his face. 'No, Argent, no, it's all right, it's all right, I promise.'

'Then *go*. Please.'

He looks at me for a long moment, a moment that feels as long as the months since the Sundark, as long

256

as my life. Then the door shuts.

And I pull the lever upwards as hard as I can, and there's the sound of the lock engaging. They're safe.

My breathing is very loud. I let myself slip further down the wall and put my head on my knees, like I'm going to sleep. The arrow in my chest feels odd, as though I've grown an extra bone. It doesn't hurt much; I'm just tired. I close my eyes and think of Columen and Iaspis, running down the stairs now, to the Underlake, to the Closed School, to safety. I did that. I saved them.

There's a babble of Mereish cursing. Ryn: *Varesh meither, shudfargtte* . . . and someone else, replying, not sounding much happier. Not that it matters, any of it. The game's over, now. That's it. I take a deep breath and taste something metallic. No Evgard-Marydd treaty, then . . . no Treaty of Arcaster . . . and somewhere below me Columen and Iaspis are safe, they're safe . . . The darkness behind my eyelids billows and sucks me down. That's it, then. It's . . .

THIRTEEN

It was over. That was it. No Evgard, no Marydd. No Arcaster.

And in a way it was a relief. Michael kept telling himself that, anyway. At least now . . . well, there wasn't anyone, anything else he cared about. Not properly. It was like he'd been in prison or something, tunnelling out of his cell, and he'd finally come up against solid rock. You pushed for a bit, until you were exhausted and sweaty and defeated, and then all you could do was turn round and go back. And in a sort of way it was good for you, because you stopped thinking you could have something better. You just had to get on with it. You looked round at the dungeon and started thinking, *Well, maybe I could tame some vermin or something . . .*

He'd never noticed before how much St Anselm's looked like a prison. When he walked through the front gates the next day in the pouring rain it was like he was seeing it for the first time. Jesus. It really *was* like a prison. Like a really classy, red-brick, Victorian prison, with well-kept lawns and a music block and a cricket pavilion. Then he had to smile in spite of himself, because for a second it was like he'd said it aloud and he could actually hear Francis's voice, taking the piss: *Oh yes, one of those prisons . . .*

He turned left automatically, the way he always did, to go down past the music block to the trees. It was a rule: you had to have a cigarette before school, like you had to bunk off early on Friday afternoon . . . even if it was raining, and you ended up squelching for the rest of the day. It was programmed in; so Michael wasn't even thinking about it, not even wondering if he'd be able to light a cigarette at all in this weather, just walking. And he still had that smile on his face, like he'd left it there and forgotten about it. Or like he was still talking to Francis. *Yeah, yeah, Harris, you know what I mean . . . But it does, anyway, it does look like a prison. Oh, by the way, can I scab a cigarette?* He actually caught himself glancing to one side, as though Francis was there, like some kind of imaginary friend.

It brick-walled him.

It wasn't that he *remembered*, all of a sudden. It wasn't like that. It was just . . . just the flat, merciless, sickening impact of it all, slamming into him. It stopped him dead, half reeling, aching, with a sharp precise pain in his larynx as though someone was squeezing it between two fingers. It hurt to breathe in. He crossed his arms over his stomach and pressed, like he could hold himself together, like he'd been stabbed.

He was crying. He couldn't help it. He was fighting the tears, driving his fists into his gut as though he could stop them that way, thinking, *Stop it, stop it, you pathetic fuck* . . . but he couldn't help it. He had just enough presence of mind to stumble past the window and lean against the wall, out of sight. Then he was sobbing, gasping for breath, drowning.

He hadn't cried for years. Not since he told his mum about . . . not for years. He'd forgotten how scary it was, because once he started he couldn't stop. It was like it wasn't *him* any more. There was something else inside his body, digging handfuls out of him and spitting them out, punching at his diaphragm, trying to choke him. He didn't have any choice; he just had to wait for it to end. He pushed his face against his arm and pressed the sleeve of his blazer against his eyes. He drew his knees up, bracing himself against the wall, and let the misery take over. He thought, *Thank God it's raining, thank God no one will see*.

He had no idea how long he was there. There was the sound of his own ragged breathing, the sibilant white-noise rain, the dark wet green of his blazer in front of his face. After a while he managed to stop sobbing out loud. He took deep breaths; the tears were still coming, but at least now he was a bit more in control. He could feel the rain on his head, running down the back of his neck. His shirt was clinging to him, sodden, freezing cold. Jesus, he was soaked . . . He ran his hands over his face, wiping the drips away, and pressed his fingers into his eyes. In a second he'd get up.

Someone said, 'Are you OK?'

Someone . . . but Michael knew, even before he looked up. Of course. It would be. He said, 'Piss off, Francis,' and looked straight up into his face.

For a second their eyes met. Then Francis blinked, deliberately, as though he was trying to make Michael disappear. 'Oh.'

That was all he said. But Michael saw from the way he said it that he'd only just recognised Michael, hadn't realised . . . His face was still swollen, although it didn't look as bad as it had. His chin was dripping with rain. As Michael watched he took a step backwards and raised a hand uncertainly to brush the wet hair off his forehead.

Michael felt the blood rushing into his cheeks. Christ. Francis, of all people, to see him like this . . . for a second it seemed the worst thing in the world, worse than if Shitley's mates had seen him, worse than Shitley . . . He scrubbed frantically at his face with one hand and pushed himself up to standing with the other. He swung his bag on to his shoulder so quickly the momentum made him stagger.

'Wait. Michael. *Wait*.'

'Piss off –' Michael heard his voice go and hated himself. *You stupid useless loser, Thompson*. He meant to walk away, but he was so shaky it turned into a sort of stumbling undignified run.

'Michael, for God's sake! Will you *wait* –'

A hand on his arm, pulling him round. Michael tried to pull away, but Francis's grip was stronger than he expected. 'Leave me alone.'

'I need to talk to you. Please. Christ, Michael . . . You look like –' He stopped and bit his lip.

'Like what? Like I've been crying my eyes out?'

Francis took his hand off Michael's arm, but he met his gaze. 'Well, haven't you?'

'Fuck *off*, Harris. Leave me alone.'

'Oh, Jesus . . . come on. Michael. Just let me –'

'Let you what? What are you going to do, Francis? Hit me? Tell me what a loser I am? How I deserved to get battered at my old school?' A tiny silence. 'Or do you just want me to lick your shoes?'

Francis stood very still. Then he swallowed. 'I . . .'

'Is that what you're after?' Michael was shouting now. 'Because if you come near me I swear I'll deck you.' He thought, *At least I'm not crying any more.* 'I promise you, I'll kill you, you bastard, you stupid fucking *pansy* –'

Silence. Or rather, not silence, exactly; just the sound of the rain.

Michael turned round and started to walk. He blinked the water out of his eyes, wiped his forehead with the palm of his hand. He heard his own footsteps on the path, soft but distinct, and he knew Francis was still standing where he'd left him, motionless, not following.

Prayers. English. Break.

And the rain carried on, determined, reasonable, merciless, as though the sky had decided to fall and was making a point of taking a long time over it. Michael watched it all the way through double Biology, until the window steamed up. Then he stared at the condensation. It was like the world was rubbing itself out.

When he got back to the common room at lunch the whole corridor stank of soggy wool and wet socks. Michael's shirt was still damp and clinging to him; he'd left his blazer on the back of a chair to drip-dry but someone had knocked it into a sodden heap on the floor. He picked it up mechanically and looked round for somewhere to sit.

But he didn't want to sit anywhere. There was a weird kind of feeling in the air: too many people stuck inside when they wanted to be outside playing football. Some of Shitley's mates were half-heartedly kicking a ball of paper around next to the drinks machine, but you could tell they were spoiling for a fight, just waiting for someone to tell them to piss off out of the way. Even Dave Murray was staring morosely at the blank window, watching the drips roll down from where someone had written *IAN SWEENEY IS A BIG FAT GAYER* in the condensation. Michael didn't like it; it made him uneasy, like he had something caught at the back of his throat. Too many people. Too many whited-out windows. He saw Francis sitting at one of the carrels, clicking his pen over and over again. He turned round suddenly, as if he'd felt Michael's gaze, and looked straight back at him.

Michael turned round and left. You were supposed to stay in the common room to eat your lunch, but he didn't care. Even if someone caught him eating in a classroom, that would be quite funny, really: if he got away with hitting Luke and then got shafted by a cheese-and-salad sandwich . . . He ducked into the English storeroom, praying that no one else was in there already. His luck was in; it was empty.

He sat down on a pile of books. Some idiot had left the window open – probably because it was a good place to smoke a joint before school, if you weren't worried about getting chucked out – and the rain had blown in and soaked the carpet. The copies of *Middlemarch* he was sitting on were all creased and soggy where they'd got wet. He closed the window. The glass was almost clear, and you could see out to the lawn and the flower beds below. Then he sat down again. He put his head in his hands and closed his eyes.

The door opened behind him. Automatically he jumped to his feet and whirled round, which was stupid, because he wasn't doing anything wrong, he was only sitting there . . . It was Francis. He closed the door quietly behind him.

Michael turned back to the window and stared out at the grey sky. *Oh, for fuck's* sake! *Why don't you just piss off, Harris, I've had enough, I'm sick of all this, I'm sick of you* . . . But he didn't say it.

Francis cleared his throat. 'Before you ask – yes, I followed you. And no, I'm not coming on to you. Don't flatter yourself. I just need to talk to you.'

'I don't care.' Michael didn't meet his eyes. He picked up his stuff and walked towards the door. 'I don't want to hear it.'

'Tough.'

Christ . . . if he hadn't looked like he was *enjoying* himself suddenly, like it was a game . . . Michael clenched his teeth and took a deep breath. 'Get out of my way, Harris.'

Francis leant back against the door and sighed noisily through his teeth. 'Michael, for God's sake! *Listen* to me. I mean, yesterday it was *you* trying to explain to me. And now –'

'I said I'd deck you, and I will.'

Francis ignored him. 'I wanted to say – about yesterday, when I said –' He swallowed and dug his hands into his pockets. Suddenly he looked about

Luke's age. 'I behaved . . . Listen. I promise, I *promise* you, I never seriously . . . it never even occurred to me that you'd actually –'

'I'd *what*?' *Don't say it*, Michael thought. *You bastard, I wasn't even going to kneel down – I wasn't . . . you bastard. I swear, if you say it, I'll kill you . . .*

Francis frowned; started to say, 'Well, when I told you to –' He met Michael's eyes. Then he looked over Michael's shoulder, at the window, biting his lip. He said slowly, 'I was really angry. You'd screwed me over and I couldn't even work out *why*. And the stuff you said . . .' He took a step towards Michael and then stopped as Michael moved back. 'Look. Luke told me what happened. I got it out of him in the end. I knew – I thought there had to be *something* . . . But if you thought I'd told someone else about Evgard – why didn't you *ask* me?' He shook his head. 'I mean, God, why didn't you *say* something, you tosser?'

'I don't know.' *Because I couldn't. That's all . . . Because if I've learnt anything, it's that you should never, never trust anyone. Because I knew you'd fuck me over eventually, and I was right. Because I thought you –*

'You *don't know*? Christ . . . You stupid idiot, Thompson! If you'd just *said* –'

'Get out of my way!' He grabbed Francis's arms and tried to shove him away from the door. For a moment he thought he could move him bodily out of the way, but Francis put his hands on Michael's shoulders and pushed back like he was rooted to the spot. Michael made himself relax for a second, catching Francis off guard; then suddenly he threw all his weight forward and heard Francis's shoulder slam against the bookcase. He reached out with one arm, trying to pull him away from the door, scrabbling for the handle behind Francis's back. 'Will you just *move*!'

'Or what?' They were both breathless. Francis had wedged himself between the bookcase and the door handle, so Michael couldn't get past. 'What, Michael? You're going to *deck* me?'

Michael dragged roughly at his shoulder. He just wanted to get out. 'Yes! Yes, I will, if you don't move out of the way. I'll knock your teeth out.'

'Really?' Francis grabbed his wrist with both hands, so Michael couldn't get to the door handle. For a second Michael wanted to laugh. Christ, this was stupid, they were like little kids having a scrap . . . 'Go on, then. Hit me. Go on . . . Hit me, and I'll get out of your way.'

'I will, I fucking *will* –' Francis's hands tightened on his wrist, twisting, like a Chinese burn. 'Will you *get off* me –' He pulled away violently, stumbled backwards, raised his hand ready to throw a punch.

He didn't know why he stopped.

Francis just watched him. Then he looked away, turning his whole face, so Michael was looking at the bruise, the scab on his lip. 'Go for this side, I would . . . for maximum effect.' A pause. Then he looked back at Michael, steadily, with an odd, guarded expression on his face. 'Don't you want to?'

For a second Michael did. For a second, staring at that damaged face, he wanted to smash it completely. He wanted to make it unrecognisable.

'It's all right, Michael. I won't hit you back.'

He almost smacked him one, just for that. *You bastard, you snide, superior git* . . . But there was something in Francis's eyes; he wasn't *being* disdainful. He was just telling the truth. He wouldn't hit Michael. Not even if Michael hit him first.

They stood still, looking at each other, for a long moment; so long that Michael almost forgot who was threatening whom, so long it didn't matter any more. Then he turned away and walked unseeingly over to the window. 'OK. Whatever.' His voice sounded funny, hoarse and strained. He swallowed. 'Fine. What did you want to say?'

He heard Francis breathe out softly. 'Michael . . . This morning . . .' Then he stopped.

Michael waited.

'Listen . . . When you told Shitley . . . *was* it because of what Luke did? Did that just freak you out?' Francis swallowed and made a noise as if he was about to carry on speaking. But he didn't.

'Yeah.' *If you knew*, Michael thought. *If I could show you what it was like . . . if I could tell you . . .* 'Yeah. That's right. It freaked me out.'

'And that's why you told Shitley I'd come on to you. As a kind of revenge.'

'Yeah.'

'And when you said, yesterday, you said you could *explain* . . . ? You were just going to say, *Look, Luke wrote me these weird notes and I was a bit freaked out, I thought you'd told Luke about Evgard?*' His voice was cold, steady: just making sure he'd got it straight.

'Yeah.' *Now*, Michael thought. *Now he'll piss off and never speak to me again. Now he knows everything he needs to know* . . .

A pause. Michael thought, *In a moment I'll hear the door. I'll hear him leave.*

'What actually happened at your old school, Michael?'

'Nothing –' He'd spun round, without even thinking about it. Nothing nothing nothing. For a second he saw grinning faces, crowded round him, felt the press of tarmac on his knees, the smell of cold sweat. *Go on, then, Clever Boy, don't you want to* – the pain, the liquid spread of warmth across his body . . . He choked the memory back. *Please, please . . . Jesus, no, I can't, leave me alone –*

He took a deep breath, dug his fingernails into the palms of his hands. 'Lots of stuff. It doesn't matter.'

'Tell me.'

Tell him? Michael stared, waiting for a smile or a shrug or a movement, something to say, *Don't worry, I wasn't serious* . . . But the look on Francis's face was a challenge. 'No – I . . . Why?'

'Because . . .' Francis ran one hand slowly up and down the bookcase, like he was testing the edge of a blade. 'Because otherwise it doesn't make sense. I thought I had you sussed, I thought that we – but then you do something like telling Shitley that I'd . . . It's like . . .' He gestured in front of him, holding the space between his hands as though it was something solid. 'Like you're playing some kind of game, that no one else knows the rules to.'

For a moment Michael had a flash of pure, cold inspiration – God, what was it? an idea for Evgard, in the corner of his mind – but he didn't have time to think about it. He looked at Francis: not at his face, but at his hands, spread out in front of him like he was waiting to catch something. He said, 'I'm sorry I told Shitley you made a move on me. I *said* I'm sorry. I'm really sorry.'

Francis's hands clenched, then came together palm to palm, fingers pressed flat against each other. 'What did they *do* to you, Michael? What happened?'

Michael glanced at Francis's face, and wished he hadn't. He couldn't tell him. He just *couldn't*, whether he wanted to or not. 'Look, I can't – it's over – I don't want to –' He stopped, lost for words, despising himself.

Francis pushed his hair away from his forehead with both hands, then ran one hand down the side of his face and grimaced. 'It can't be worse than what Shitley's lot do.'

Michael shrugged, his shoulders and throat too tight to talk.

'Can it?'

'*I don't know!* I don't fucking know, all right? It doesn't matter, any of it, it doesn't matter, I can't tell you about it, just *please* stop asking, OK? It just happened, that's all, it's over, it's not part of me, it's not written on my forehead – please, just piss off, just leave me alone –'

He hadn't meant to say any of it aloud. It just came; the way the lump just came into his throat, gagging him. He turned away, shaking, and smacked his hands flat against the wall as hard as he could. What *was* it about people, always wanting you to talk about stuff? As if that could help anything. As if! Like his mum: *Don't bottle it up, darling, you can't just pretend it didn't happen . . .*

269

'Michael?'

He turned round slowly. Francis was there, at his back, one hand poised as though he was about to touch Michael's shoulder. Michael thought: *If I flinch, he'll move away. If I step back, if I do anything . . . If I don't want him to touch me, he won't.*

He stayed absolutely still. He might even have been holding his breath; just waiting. For a second he was frozen, quiet, almost prepared to let Francis touch him. Then he recoiled. He couldn't stop himself. He saw Francis register the movement and step back. Michael turned to look out of the window. He didn't want to meet Francis's eyes.

There was a split-second pause, then Francis looked round, following his gaze. He leant forward, peering, and immediately drew back, gesturing at Michael to get away from the window. 'Careful. Father Bennett.' He craned his neck cautiously to look. 'Bollocks. I think he's seen us.' He added, with a sort of strained casualness, 'What *is* he doing? Arsing around in the flower beds like a complete tit . . .'

Michael tried to echo his tone. 'Does it matter? That he's seen us?'

'Not really . . . except he'll be up here in a minute, trying to catch us flagrantly eating our lunch.' Francis grimaced, almost normally. 'We'd better scarper.'

'Yeah.' Why did he feel so – *ashamed*? He picked up his limp cling-filmed sandwiches. He could feel Francis watching him. 'Francis . . .'

'What?'

The door opened. Michael turned to look at the same time as Francis; he thought, *Wow, that was quick . . .* until he saw it wasn't Father Bennett. He heard Francis swear softly under his breath; he couldn't tell whether he'd said *shit* or *Shitley*.

Shitley glanced from Michael to Francis and back again, smiling, like he was about to bite someone. He had two black eyes; it made him look even more venomous than normal. Then he slid into the room like he didn't have enough bones.

'Not interrupting, am I, gents?' His gaze settled on Francis's flies. Then he looked theatrically round at the bookshelves. 'Not as private as a toilet cubicle, right, Harris?'

'Oh, for . . .' Francis bit his lip and shook his head. 'Get some new fucking material, Shitley.'

'Why? Are you getting bored with being a sad, disgusting little poofter? Or are you saying there's something else we should know?'

'Why don't you just piss off?'

'So you can carry on your little tryst with darling Michael here?' It was weird that Shitley even knew what *tryst* meant, let alone that he could say it with such skilful, lewd nastiness. Michael stared at the ground and thought, *If Francis can handle it, then so can I.*

Francis shifted his weight slightly. 'How's your face, Shitley?'

A beat, then Shitley smiled. 'We're going to batter you again, Harris. One of these days . . . And there's nothing you can do about it.' A pause, like he was waiting for Francis to disagree. 'Of course, you could always *tell a teacher*, like a good little boy.' He put on a strangled falsetto. 'Please, sir, they're going to kill me because I'm a homo!'

'I think *Please, sir, they're going to kill me* would be

271

enough, don't you?' But there was something in Francis's voice: the crack in a glass, the first thread snapping . . .

'I wonder what your parents would say. When you *explained*.' It was pure bluff; for all Shitley knew Francis had told his parents already. But Francis's look said it all. Michael stared at him and thought, *Oh God, I did that, that's my fault* . . . He felt cold. He looked back at Shitley's evil purple-eyed face, and knew with a weird sick certainty that nothing could ever be OK after this. It was his fault. Nothing would ever be all right.

He said, 'You bastard, Shitley.'

Shitley turned to look at him. 'Wow. It can *talk*.'

Only just, Michael thought, and took another breath. 'You *bastard*. You evil fucking shitty bastard.' Francis looked at him with a faint inscrutable frown.

Shitley curled his lips upwards. 'Hey, Thompson – what's the matter? I thought you were with me on this one. Or have you come out of the closet?'

Suddenly, from nowhere, Michael was too angry to be anything else: not scared, not guilty, not sorry. He was searingly, blindingly angry, like a strip of magnesium in a flame, too bright to look at. He said, 'Why do you bully kids like Benedick Townsend?'

Shitley blinked. 'What?'

He almost said, *You remember, the kid you stubbed a fag out on* . . . but instead he looked Shitley straight in the eye. 'Because you can't think of anything better to do? Or just because you're a pathetic, sadistic, perverted shit?' In his peripheral vision he saw Francis still looking at him, but he didn't take his eyes off Shitley.

'Benedick Townsend? Oh, *please* . . .'

'So what makes you do it? Does it turn you on?'

Another laugh, but not as long, not as easy. 'Whatever.'

'No, really, Shitley, I'd like to know.'

Shitley looked him up and down, with his smile fading off his face. He said again, 'What?'

Michael breathed out gently, steadily, like he was blowing on a flame. The anger blazed, eating him from inside, eating the fear. 'Tell me. Why do you do it? Does it help you sleep at night?'

'Getting all *protective* suddenly, Thompson?' Shitley slid a look at Francis. 'Funny . . . 'cause when Harris was getting thrashed you just stood and watched, didn't you?'

Michael didn't let himself feel the shock – the humiliation – that Shitley even knew he'd been there. 'You're such a loser, Shitley. Tormenting little kids because it makes you feel good. Following us around at lunchtime so you can call us gay. I mean, Christ, how do you get off on that?' He took a breath in. 'Why is it, that you call everyone bent? Kids like Townsend . . . it's because deep down you're as much of a pervert – you're as much of a faggot – not to mention a sadistic, pathetic –'

'Shut up, Thompson.' Shitley was scowling incredulously; it was like he couldn't believe that Michael had the guts to say what he was saying.

'People like you, Shitley – you go round fucking everyone else up, because you're so messed up yourselves. You don't dare to admit to yourself that you're *revolting* and *nauseating* and *repulsive*. And so you torture little boys and get off on it, and you stalk

273

Francis . . . It's like you're obsessed. It's all you can think about – you pretend you're disgusted by it, but actually you're just too cowardly to admit you're one of –'

'I said *shut* it, tosser!'

'You're not denying it, are you, Shitley?' Michael met his eyes squarely; he was thrumming with an odd sort of excitement. A part of his mind said, *This won't work. This is stupid* . . . but he wasn't sure if he cared. 'What do you do, after you've stubbed a cigarette out on someone? Lock yourself in the bog and toss off about it?'

Shitley took a step forward and pushed him, hard, smacking the heels of his hands into Michael's shoulders. 'So you want a fight, do you, loser-boy?' He raised his eyebrows. 'Sure you're up to it?'

Michael heard the rush of fear in his eardrums, but it seemed a long way away. He made himself shrug, although he *did* want a fight, sort of. 'Bet your mates have sussed you already, Shitley. I bet they can see through you. It's pretty obvious, when you think about it – I mean, why else would someone be so homophobic? It's like you just can't help thinking about it, all the time –'

Another push; harder. This time Michael stumbled backwards with the force of it. 'No one gives me shit, Thompson. Why don't you learn from Harris's mistakes?'

'It's all right, Shitley, I know what this is about. You just want to touch me, right? You can't keep your hands off me. You may hit me, but what you *really* want is to –'

Shitley's fists smashed into his breastbone. Michael

274

heard the breath go out of his lungs with the impact, like a sort of reverse gasp, and suddenly his legs weren't underneath him, where they should have been, but somewhere behind him, dragging him backwards. He fought to keep himself upright. It was all he could do to stay on his feet. Jesus, there was so much *force* in it; not hurting, exactly, just throwing him off balance, making his feet betray him and stagger back, out of control. He was moving too fast to stop himself; he saw his hands reaching out, clutching at the air like a clown. He fell back against something solid – the wall – and his back smacked squarely against it, his feet scrabbling ridiculously on the carpet.

Something cracked.

No – shit, *no* . . . Glass. Behind him. Not the wall. The window.

Somehow, suddenly, he was living in slow motion. Not his body, because he didn't have time to twist, or look over his shoulder, or grab for anything; but his mind was floating in a sea of clarity, amazed at how much it could comprehend. He felt the contact of his shoulder blades on the glass of the window first: and actually had time to think, *Oh Jesus, it's going to break*, before he felt the smash spreading out from his back. He had time to want to laugh. And he had time to feel the shards fall away behind him and the momentum still carry him backwards, as certainly as if he was obeying gravity. He even had time to see the door open behind Shitley and wonder if that was Father Bennett or just one of Shitley's mates – before he was falling properly, backwards and down, through the broken window.

Then all he had time to think was: *Oh*, bugger. *I bet this is going to hurt.*

FOURTEEN

It would have been a good way to go.

If Michael closed his eyes he could see himself from the outside, falling through the window in a splash of broken glass, his arms outstretched, shards dropping into the flower beds below him. He saw himself spread against the grey sky, hanging, just for a moment, before reality kicked in and he dropped, too quickly for the eye to follow. That was how he remembered it. That was all he had: that image of himself, poised impossibly in front of the window, defying gravity, while the glass rained down around him, reflecting the light. Even if it wasn't like that at all, really, even if it was just a flailing mess of limbs and torn school uniform and crushed rose bushes and smears of soil and blood and rain. Even if there wasn't anything clean about it at all, anything dramatic, anything to be proud of – he still had that memory of it, the moment when he'd thought, *Yes* . . . The moment of flying.

He didn't remember landing.

But he did. He must have done.

*   *   *

'I'm fine. Really. I'm fine. I'm fine.' He kept saying it, over and over again, because no one seemed to believe him. After a while he started to think, *Maybe I should just shut up and let them work it out for themselves*, but somehow he couldn't stop himself. He tried to stand up. 'Look. I'm fine. Watch. I'm perfectly *fine –*' but someone laid a restraining hand on his arm and pushed him firmly back into the smashed flower bed.

'Just stay still, Michael. You're going to be all right.'

'I *know*, that's what I said, I'm absolutely –' but Father Markham wasn't listening. Michael raised one arm and waved it around. '*Look*. Everything's fine. I'm fine. I'm really –' A drop of blood rolled back down his wrist and soaked into his shirt-cuff. He thought, *Oops. Mum'll go ballistic if I've torn this shirt.*

'All right, Michael. I heard you. Calm down. We're just waiting for the ambulance.'

'I don't need an ambulance. I'm fine . . .' but no one took any notice. Michael dropped his head back and stared up into the rain. A crowd had gathered; someone was trying to shoo them away. He thought, *This is stupid. I'm perfectly all right.*

He heard the paramedics before he saw them; conferring with Father Markham in low voices, 'Fell out of a window? That one there, on the first floor?' and Father Markham saying, 'The one that's broken, yes . . .'

But even the paramedics didn't take any notice of him. When they leant over him he tried to tell them he was fine, really, he was fine, and they swapped a look

278

that said, *Hmm, looks like this one's in shock, he can't stop talking* . . . He said, 'Look, I'm *fine*, I don't need an ambulance, I'm fine, I'm just a bit –'

'OK, mate, let's just take you to hospital, get you checked over.' It wasn't like he had a choice. In the end he just gave up and thought, *Stuff it, if they want to waste their time* . . . and parts of him were starting to hurt a bit, anyway. From the corner of his eye he could see flecks and smears of blood on his shirt, a long cut across the back of one hand. And he thought something might have happened to his wrist. He closed his eyes against the rain and felt the damp soak through his hair. He almost wanted to fall asleep, right here, surrounded by idiots. In a way it was sort of restful, not having to worry, not taking any responsibility. At least no one had asked what had actually happened.

He thought, *Oh, bollocks. Mum.*

As they were putting him in the ambulance he said, 'Have you, has someone called my mum?'

Father Markham was obviously coming with him to Casualty. He said, 'Yes, of course, Michael. There's no need to worry. I'll call her again from the hospital.'

'No – I didn't want you to . . .' But they'd all gone deaf again. Michael stared at the air in front of his face and thought, *Great. She'll kill me. Or she'll go to Father Murdoch and tell him I'm being bullied –*

It was like his mind stopped dead; then it started again, like a CD skipping.

Oh Lord. Oh, Jesus Christ . . . He'd called Shitley a twisted evil bastard. He'd said . . . oh God. He'd said all that stuff –

For a moment he felt the old panic, the old reflex of

dread. *Don't fight back*. And then, suddenly, he felt *relief*, burning down his spine like electricity, so strong it almost brought tears to his eyes. It was nearly the euphoria he'd felt as he went through the window: falling without fear, losing without *minding* that he'd lost. An excitement, like being high, like floating, like freedom . . . As though somehow he'd won – not against Shitley, maybe, but against himself. Against the terror. It was a weird, skewed victory: but it was still a victory.

He was still smiling when they got to the hospital.

He *was* fine. He kept saying he was fine, every time someone asked him, and by the time his mum came to pick him up they'd all agreed that except for the broken wrist and superficial cuts and grazes and bruises and bits of embedded glass and flower bed – apart from all that, well, yes, they supposed he *was* basically fine. But they wouldn't let him wait outside; he had to sit with Father Markham on the plastic hospital chairs, clutching the painkillers they'd given him in his free hand. If Father Markham hadn't been there he'd have walked home on his own; he didn't want to see his mum, much less have to explain what had happened. What was he going to say? *Shitley pushed me out of a window. Shitley was taking the piss out of Francis, so I . . . I was winding Shitley up, so he pushed me . . . I was in a fight . . .* And the worst thing was, he couldn't help being proud of it. *I called Shitley a pathetic sadistic shit. Me.*

As soon as he saw her come through the doors he stood up and started walking; behind him Father Markham struggled to his feet, putting his vending-

280

machine coffee down sloppily on the floor.

'Michael!' She half ran towards him, one hand clutching the strap of her handbag. 'Are you all right? What happened? Your teacher said –' She turned and saw Father Markham. 'Oh, Father, thank you for looking after him. What happened? I was so worried.'

For a horrible moment Michael thought she might burst into tears. *Jesus, no, please* . . . He felt his whole face – no, his whole *head* – start to go red.

Father Markham said, 'Apparently Michael fell out of a window. We haven't got to the bottom of it yet.' He gave Michael a sharp, but not uncharitable, look. 'I can assure you it will all be sorted out tomorrow.'

'Fell out of a window?' Her face was shocked, then suddenly guarded, deliberately blank. There was something unreadable in her gaze as she looked at Michael. It made him uneasy.

'I'm sure Michael will be able to enlighten you further.' Father Markham smiled at her briefly. 'He was very lucky to get away with only a broken wrist. Now, I'm afraid I should be getting back to school.'

She nodded; Michael saw her make an effort to smile. 'Can we give you a lift?'

'Thank you. That would be very kind.'

Michael sat in the back seat, listening to them making strained small talk, and was glad he didn't have to join in. But after his mum had dropped Father Markham at the school gates and done a three-point turn in the driveway, she didn't say anything at all. If she hadn't been driving he'd have wondered if she'd died. In the end he almost said, 'OK, Mum, why don't you just stop the car and have a go at me now?' The silence filled the car like snow, smothering, bitterly

281

cold. He could feel how furious she was; he tried not to care, but he did. The euphoria had gone.

When they got through the front door he started to count in his head. One, two, three, four, five . . . he walked up the stairs. Nine, ten, eleven, twelve –

'Michael. Come down here, please.'

He paused. Then, slowly, heavily, he stumped back down the stairs again. She was sitting at the kitchen table, hands flat in front of her. He sat down at the table and focused on her wedding ring; it was easier than looking at her face. He thought, *What can she do? She can't actually* do *anything. Ground me? Stop my allowance? Hate me?*

She swallowed; it sounded very loud. 'What happened, Michael? And I want the truth.'

But the truth was too big, too complicated, even if he'd wanted to try. The best he could do was not to lie. He said, 'It was kind of a fight.'

'Who with?'

He almost said, *No one.* 'Just someone in my year.'

She was staring at him; he could feel it, even though he wasn't looking at her. '*Kind of* a fight?'

'Yes.'

'Not a *proper* fight, then?' She was getting at something. There was an edge to her voice. Michael raised his eyes to her face, in spite of himself, but it didn't make it any clearer. She said, '*What* kind of a fight was it, Michael?'

He thought, *If I say,* Shitley pushed me, *she'll think I'm being bullied again. She won't listen, even if I try and explain.* He said, 'Just a – what do you mean, what kind of fight? It was just a fight. It wasn't anything serious –'

282

'Not *serious*? Michael, you could have been *killed*. You've got a broken wrist as it is! How *dare* you try to tell me it wasn't serious!' She had half risen to her feet; he saw her knuckles whiten as she sat down again, as though she was anchoring herself with her hands. 'Don't lie to me, Michael. I want to know. Whatever happened. I don't care how bad it was. You have to tell me.'

He met her eyes. It was that look: *I know you're being beaten up and I am going to your headmaster and I will make sure he Sorts This Out once and for all.* He looked away, tried to bite down on the anger. He didn't *have* to tell her anything. Why should he? So she could muscle in on his life and screw it up even more than he had already? He said, 'I'm not being bullied, if that's what you think.'

'Then *what*, Michael? Am I supposed to believe that you just *fell* out of a window?' She stopped, suddenly, oddly, as though she'd given something away.

He thought: *No. I didn't just* fall. *Shitley pushed me because I finally had the guts to tell him what I thought of him. And I'm glad I did. I'd be glad even if he'd killed me.* He muttered, 'It was a fight. I *said*.'

She stood up; for a weird horrible moment Michael was sure she was going to lean across the table and hit him. But she walked stiffly over to the kettle, picked it up, walked to the sink, filled it with water, took it back, turned it on . . . Everything was very deliberate. She turned round to face him. 'Michael. For God's sake, why won't you *talk* to me?' There was a kind of desperation in her voice that shamed him. He didn't know what to say. In the silence he heard her

283

heave a great unsteady breath. 'I wish – oh Lord, Michael . . . why don't you just tell me? I promise I won't judge you for it. I promise –' She swallowed. 'Please. Whatever you did, whatever you were trying to do . . .'

He looked up, met her eyes. God, her expression. Like she couldn't speak the right language, and knew it. Like there was something she couldn't say.

Whatever you were trying to do . . .

He said slowly, 'You think I *jumped*.'

She didn't answer. But then, she didn't need to. It was enough, just the way she looked down, away from him, and pushed her hair away from her temple.

'I didn't. Oh, Mum . . . I *didn't*.' Silence. 'Mum. Dominic Shipley pushed me because I called him a – because I was winding him up.' He tried to smile. 'Anyway, come on, Mum, if I was going to jump out of a window I'd at least *open* it first.' She snorted. 'And I wouldn't choose one on the first floor. I'd go up on the main-building roof and do it properly. I'm not an idiot. If I was really trying to kill myself I wouldn't end up in a flower bed with a broken wrist, like a tit.'

Then he realised she was crying. She brought her hands up to her face and turned to face the wall, sobbing, leaning forward as if she could hide between the bread-bin and the kettle. *Oh, bollocks . . .* He watched her shoulders shaking, heard the jagged wet noise of her breathing.

'Jesus, Mum . . .' He went up to her carefully, the way he would have approached a damaged animal. 'Mum, I *didn't*. It's OK, please, I'm sorry, Mum, please don't cry, I'm really sorry . . .' He was scared she'd push him away, but she let him put an awkward arm round her. His other hand was in the sling; he patted her shoulder and then pulled a bit of kitchen towel off the roll and offered it to her. 'Mum, please, I didn't, I promise I didn't, Shitley pushed me, that's all . . .' He carried on, not listening to what he was saying, until she took her hands away from her face and sniffed emphatically.

'Sorry, darling.' She took the square of kitchen towel and blew her nose. She had strands of hair clinging to her cheeks and her nose was red, so that for a second Michael felt older than her. Then suddenly she turned to hug him, holding him tightly like he was a little kid. 'I was just so worried that you might have –'

'No, I didn't, I really didn't . . .' And suddenly he felt a wave of relief, gratitude, almost, that it wasn't like before. This time she'd just got it wrong. 'It's OK. Really. Mum, it's fine.' He closed his eyes and let his chin rest on the top of her head. It was strange, the way he could feel the guilt dissolving, like ice melting. It wasn't his fault. It wasn't because he was a victim or a loser.

She said, 'Thank God,' and looked up at him. 'But you would tell me, wouldn't you? If things ever got so bad that you felt that you – that you wanted to do something to yourself? You'd tell me?'

Michael hugged her back with his free arm, as hard as he could. 'Yes. You know I would.' He wasn't sure it was true, but it didn't matter.

The doorbell rang. Michael didn't move. His mum gave him a final squeeze and then detached herself briskly. 'I'd better get it, darling.'

'Right.' He let her go and stood where he was, listening.

'Francis! Come in. Yes, he's fine, well, he's broken his wrist, silly boy, but he's all right apart from that, and cuts and grazes and so on . . . It's sweet of you to come round.'

Francis was a lot of things, but Michael wasn't sure he'd ever call him *sweet*. He felt a kind of approximation of a smile happen in his head somewhere. Then Francis said, 'Thanks, I just wanted to check he was OK,' and Michael really did smile, because of the voice, the politeness, the way he didn't say, *Wow, you think I'm sweet, gosh, thanks . . .*

'Do come in, have a cup of tea or something. I'm sure Michael'll be glad to see you. It'll take his mind off his wrist.'

'Um. Yeah, thanks.'

Michael didn't move. He was still standing there, in the middle of the kitchen, when Francis came in. He waited for his mum to follow him in, but she didn't. He cleared his throat. He didn't want to be the first to speak. 'Hi.'

'Hello.'

'*Do* you want a cup of tea? Or something?'

'No. Thanks.' Silence. Francis had his hands in his pockets. He hunched his shoulders. 'I just wanted to check you were still alive.'

'Well. I am.'

'Right. Good.'

'Yeah.' Another pause. Michael opened a cupboard and took out a packet of biscuits; he wasn't hungry, he just wanted something to fill the silence. Without looking back at Francis, he said,

'What happened about Shitley?'

'They're having an inquest tomorrow. Father Bennett walked in just when he pushed you – did you see that? Or were you too busy falling out of the window?'

'Yeah, I saw.'

'With any luck he'll get suspended. Or expelled, preferably. I've got to talk to them too, tell them what happened.' He smiled faintly. 'Don't worry, I won't tell them the truth. But –' He stopped, and swallowed.

Michael put the biscuits carefully down on the side. 'But what?' He made himself breathe. 'But – I shouldn't have stood up to him? I shouldn't have defended you?'

Francis laughed: a brief harsh huff of disbelief. 'Is that what you think you were doing? Defending me?'

'I –'

'Don't tell me. You thought telling Shitley he was as much of a pervert as I am would make me feel better about the whole thing?'

'I didn't *say* –'

'Yes, you did, Michael.' Francis really laughed, this time. 'You don't even remember?'

'I just wanted to get to him. I didn't mean – oh, for God's sake, Francis! I didn't mean it like that. I just wanted – look, if I'd said, *Hey, Shitley, you're gay, but don't worry, there's nothing wrong with that*, it wouldn't have wound him up, would it?' Silence. Jesus, why couldn't Francis *see* the only thing that mattered was standing up to Shitley . . . ? 'Yes. Actually you're right. I wasn't defending you. It was for me, for myself. I thought you'd be on my side – but it really doesn't matter. And it wasn't *true,* it's not what I actually think . . . but I don't *care* if it was out of order. I'm really glad I said it.'

'Right.'

'I just wanted him to –' Michael caught himself. *I just wanted him to hit me.* But it wasn't that, not exactly. *I wanted him to fight me. Even though I knew I'd lose. I wanted to – hate the right person . . .*

Silence again.

He said, 'It wasn't about you. Not really.'

Francis met his gaze, steadily, not giving anything away. 'Not about me. Right.' Then, slowly, he nodded, without smiling. 'You know, Michael, it's weird. If you'd been trying to fuck me up, I can't think of anything you could have done better. But . . .' He dug at the scab on his lip with two fingers, his eyes still on Michael's face. He said again, slowly, 'But – it wasn't even *about* me . . .'

'I didn't mean –'

'*What?*' For a second – a split second – he thought Francis was going to hit him. 'You didn't mean *what?* Fuck it, Michael! Stop telling me what you didn't mean. Why don't you say something you *do* mean?'

Michael swallowed. 'All right. Give me a second.'

Francis blinked. Then he stood very still, waiting, like if he made a sudden movement Michael might run away.

'I mean, I got it wrong. I thought you were laughing at me. About Evgard. I thought you always had been. That we'd never been mates at all . . .' It wasn't that his voice cracked; just that he stopped in case it was about to. 'Evgard – meant a lot to me.'

Francis screwed his mouth up on one side, like he was testing whether his scab still hurt. He said, 'And me.'

288

'Jesus, Harris, you let me burn it – for fuck's *sake* –'
He smacked his good hand down on the sideboard.
'You haven't got a clue. It wasn't just something to do
on Saturdays, it was . . . You think it was some childish crappy game. You think it was *disposable*. Well, it
wasn't. It mattered. It mattered more than anything
else. More than anything.'

'More than *anything*?' Francis turned back to look
at him. 'Do you still think that?'

No. More than nearly *anything* . . . But he couldn't
say it. Wasn't it a betrayal, to admit that Evgard
wasn't as important as something in the real world?

Francis frowned, watching him, as if he was trying
to work something out. Then, suddenly, there was a
kind of movement in his face, like he'd stumbled. 'Oh,
fuck, Michael. Oh, Christ, I'm sorry. You still think –'
He rubbed his forehead with one hand, half laughing,
half grimacing. 'Shit.' He breathed out through his
teeth. 'I let you think . . . oh, Thompson, I'm sorry. It
wasn't – you didn't – that bin-bag you set fire to. It
wasn't Evgard. It was just a bag of rubbish. I thought
you'd realise as soon as you got home. I didn't tell
you, because I was pissed off, and I thought it was
funny. Shit. I'm really sorry.' He gave a sort of peni-
tent half-smile.

'It wasn't the Evgard stuff.' It was hard for Michael
to breathe in; like he'd been hit.

'No.' Francis pushed his hair off his face and
squinted at Michael underneath his wrist. 'I'm sorry. I
wasn't thinking.'

'Right.' Michael turned away and closed his eyes.
He'd just grabbed the bag from next to the bin – just
assumed . . . Not Evgard.

For a moment all he felt was scalding embarrassment, like a wave of boiling water. *Oh, dear God, what an arse, what a tosser* . . . He could see himself now, staring at the burning bag as though it was a funeral pyre. No wonder it stank of rubbish. *Oh God, what a* prat.

'It was an easy mistake to make.' Francis's voice was soft, almost sympathetic.

Michael turned to look at him. Francis was looking determinedly at the ground, biting his lower lip. His face was very still.

'You think?'

'Of course.' Still that low, considerate tone of voice. 'Anyone could have thought . . .' Then he looked up.

For a second Michael thought he was going to finish his sentence. But as their eyes met Francis broke off. His mouth twitched.

Michael couldn't help it. He had time to see Francis start to hunch over, his shoulders shaking, struggling for breath, before he'd lost it too, giggling hysterically, clutching at the sideboard with his good hand for support. He heard himself saying, 'Oh, God, you fucker, Harris, you bastard –' before he was choking and too breathless with laughter to speak. His whole body was shuddering, jarring his wrist, but he didn't care.

Francis gasped, 'The look on your *face*, Michael –' and then he'd gone again, bending over with his hands on his knees like an athlete after a race, his whole ribcage heaving.

Michael nodded, swallowed, managed to say, 'What a tosser –' but he couldn't get any further either. He clung on to the sideboard and laughed and laughed.

After a while Francis glanced up and caught Michael's eye. Michael felt himself grin like an idiot and looked away before Francis set him off again. *Jesus, Thompson, pull yourself together. It's really not that funny.*

And then he thought: *Evgard. Evgard isn't burnt.*

He ran halfway up the stairs before he realised he wasn't thinking straight. He *had* put it with the rubbish – so . . . He turned round and sprinted downstairs again, to the cupboard under the stairs where they put the stuff for recycling. It was paper, wasn't it? *Please, God, let it be there, let it not have been put out yet. Please God . . .* He pulled the recycling box out with one hand, yanked at the bin-bags behind it, trying to open them and twisting the plastic the wrong way. *Come on, come on . . . Please.*

It was there. The papers were all crumpled, battered at the edges. A couple were ripped. And they looked different from how he'd remembered, more amateurish, less *real*. But Evgard was there, in a bin-bag, under the stairs. He dragged it out; the bag ripped, and everything slid out over the floor. He knelt down and looked at it, waiting for the rush of relief, the jubilation. Imagine thinking your home had been burnt, then finding it intact, ready for you to go back to. Imagine that. You could go home.

But he didn't feel anything.

There was a shadow on the floor. He glanced up and saw Francis standing in the doorway, looking down at him. He said, 'I've found it.'

'Good.'

He started to gather up the papers one-handed and shove them back into the bag. He thought, *Why do I feel so tired?* He looked up again; saw the same look on Francis's face that he knew was on his own. He swallowed. Then he said, 'It's over, isn't it?'

'Finished, maybe.' It was funny, the way Francis could say *finished* so you knew he meant *complete, accomplished*. Not just *defunct*.

'Yeah.' Michael walked past him and swung the bag on to the kitchen table. He stared at it and thought, *I don't live there any more*. He felt empty.

Francis was behind him, at his shoulder. 'Are you OK?'

'Fine.' Then he turned round, so they were face to face. 'I dunno. I'm not sure.'

Francis was the first one to move. He took a few steps to the table, reached out a hand and pulled the bin-bag open so he could see the pile of stuff. He tugged at the corner of a sheet of paper, laid it flat on the table. The great Judas floor at Calston. For a moment he gazed down at it. Then he reached into the bag again and again, spreading out the papers carefully in front of him. Arcaster Castle. One of the *Fabianus Letters*. A map of the Flatlands showing where the main battles were fought. The Duke Columen's account of the Glacies campaign. The Book.

'What are you doing?'

Francis didn't turn round; he carried on spreading papers out on the table. He said softly, 'Don't throw it away.'

Michael looked at the back of his head and wished he could see his face. 'Why?' He wanted to say, *What would we do with it? It's finished, you said so yourself. It can't ever be the same.*

'Please.' He still didn't turn round. 'Please don't

throw it away.'

Michael stared at his back. *Please*. As though he wasn't sure Michael would say yes. Michael stepped forward; not close enough to touch him. 'Do you want it?'

Francis rubbed a fingernail across the lines of Arcaster. 'Yes.'

Michael stood still. Suddenly he felt an uninvited pang of possessiveness; a memory of what Evgard meant. *No*. Better to throw it away than give it to someone else. He closed his eyes and took a deep breath. 'You can take it, if you want.'

'Are you sure?'

When he opened them again Francis had turned round. God, the look on his face: like he understood. Like it would be all right for Michael to say, *No, I'm not sure* . . . But all of a sudden, looking into Francis's eyes, he *was*. He *was* sure. He grinned, almost effortlessly. 'Yeah. Take it. You're welcome to it.'

Francis said quietly, 'Thank you.' He smiled back.

Michael held his gaze and then had to look away; he could feel himself blushing. He couldn't think of anything to say. He held his hand out like an idiot, like they'd just met, how-do-you-do . . . God, he was such a tosser. He could feel his face burning. He was about to turn the gesture into something else – as though he was about to scratch his nose or something – but suddenly it was too late, because Francis had taken his hand.

For a second they just stood there, still, looking at each other. Michael thought, *This is weird* . . . He felt the warmth of Francis's palm, the smooth bony fingers, and felt his cheeks flare red again. He thought,

I'm touching Francis's skin. But he didn't take his hand away.

He waited for Francis to move, or say something, but he didn't. He held Michael's gaze, his eyes steady, unreadable.

Michael cleared his throat; said, in a rush, 'Francis – you know, don't you, you know I'm not –' He stopped.

One of Francis's eyebrows lifted, very slightly. Jesus, that *look* – a smile, almost . . . 'Not what, Michael? Not attracted to me? Not gay? Not very bright? All of the above?' Then, unexpectedly, he grinned. '*Yes*, I do know. I'm not a bloody idiot, Thompson.'

Michael said, 'You mean, unlike some people you could mention.'

For a second – so briefly Michael thought he'd imagined it – Francis's grip on his hand tightened. Then he nodded, still grinning. 'Unlike some people I could mention.'

'I'm sorry.' It was funny, how easily Michael could say it. 'I'm really sorry. I mean, about –'

'Shut up.' Francis shook his head. 'Forget it, OK? Oh –' he gestured at the bin-bag. 'Could you keep hold of that, just for a bit? I don't want Luke going through it.' He didn't wait for Michael to answer. 'Look, I've got to go. See you tomorrow for Shitley's court martial, if you're up to it.'

'Yeah.'

'See you, then.'

Michael said, 'See you,' and watched him go. Francis paused when he got to the door, and looked back at Michael; then he left.

Michael picked up the papers on the table, put

them in the bin-bag and walked upstairs with it bumping against his leg. He was too tired to think; he knew he was smiling, but he wasn't sure why. His wrist hurt. He put the bag down beside his bed and stared at it, letting his eyes go out of focus. It was weird, not having Evgard any more, not *living* there . . . although he still had it. It was still *there*. It just wasn't – real. He was here, instead.

He lay back on the bed and closed his eyes. He was so sleepy. He drifted on the edge of being awake, letting his mind wander, letting the world rock him to sleep . . . *like a boat*, he thought, *like a boat in the dark, like Columen escaping across the Underlake* . . . and he smiled into the blackness behind his eyelids. Evgard was still there, still safe; not tugging at him, any more, not *demanding* . . . but still there. And Columen had got away.

And . . . distantly, like something starting to itch, he thought, *There was something I thought of, something I was proud of, that I wanted to remember. Not that it matters, but it was good; we could use it, maybe* . . . What was it? Something that . . . *like you're playing some kind of game, that no one else knows the rules to* . . . Damn, what *was* it? He dug for it, trying to get the thought out whole. Oh – *yes. Some kind of game* . . .

He was too tired to get up and write it down, but that didn't matter. He could tell Francis tomorrow.

ACKNOWLEDGEMENTS

I'd like to thank Rosemary Canter, Sarah Ballard and Jodie Marsh at United Agents; everyone at Bloomsbury, especially Emma Matthewson; Mara Bergman; Nick Manns; the Arvon Foundation; Philip Gross, for his past help and advice; Linda Newbery, for her generosity and encouragement; Emily Collins, for her wise feedback and suggestions, most of which I ignored; and my parents, for their (almost) unstinting support. Thank you.

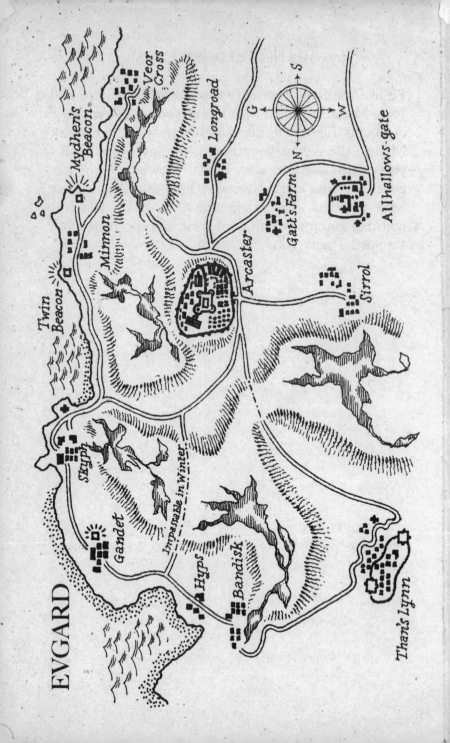

EVGARD